FATAL DEPTHS

A gripping crime thriller full of twists

PAULINE ROWSON

The Art Marvik Mysteries Book 4

Originally published as *Dead Sea*

JOFFE BOOKS

Revised edition 2023
Joffe Books, London
www.joffebooks.com

First published by Fathom in Great Britain
in 2021 as *Dead Sea*

This paperback edition was first published
in Great Britain in 2023

Cover art by Dee Dee Book Covers

ISBN: 978-1-80405-824-4

CHAPTER ONE

Wednesday 4 May

Marvik stared at the contents of his safe deposit box, puzzled. The small dark-blue notebook with a three-and-a-half-inch floppy disk attached to the inside back cover that he had placed there on 31 March had gone. But that was impossible because only he had access. Correction: he and his solicitor, Michael Colmead.

Marvik pressed the buzzer to summon one of the bank security guards, who appeared almost instantly.

'I need a large carrier bag,' Marvik said abruptly.

The guard looked at him as though he'd asked for a first-class flight to Barbados.

'Anything will do,' Marvik added.

While the security officer went to find one, Marvik began to stuff the contents of the four boxes into his ruck-sack. It wasn't big enough to take all the folders and paper-work, hence the request for the carrier bag.

'This is all I could find, sir,' the security officer said on his return a few minutes later.

Marvik took the supermarket plastic bag and placed the remaining files into it.

'Is there something wrong?' the officer asked anxiously.

Very wrong, thought Marvik, but he wasn't going to say what exactly. 'I'd like to see the signing-in log for my boxes for the last two months.'

The officer's concerned expression deepened, but without question he led the way to a counter opposite the lifts and, after locating the appropriate file on screen, swivelled it round to show Marvik. There were three entries: his own, on 31 March, when he had placed the notebook in the box; another half an hour ago when he had arrived; and one yesterday, on Tuesday 3 May. It was that one that interested him greatly, and concerned him.

His bewilderment increased. He had expected to see Colmead's name and signature. Instead he was staring at that of a man called James Dewell. Marvik had never heard of him — all he could assume was that he worked for Colmead.

He requested to see Dewell's letter of authorization, which was duly produced on screen and proved to be on Colmead's legal firm's headed notepaper. Marvik asked to see the original. Again this was produced and, as far as Marvik could tell, both the headed paper and Colmead's signature were genuine. The officer confirmed the latter had been scan-checked against the specimen provided and had been approved. Dewell had come with the unique authorization access code, which only Colmead had been given, and which Marvik had assumed was kept securely in his office safe in Southampton. The only thing Colmead wouldn't have had was Marvik's palm print, but the instructions Marvik had given to the bank was that the palm print was to be waived if Colmead came in his place with all the necessary requirements. Marvik hadn't left any instructions for Colmead to send a deputy. So what the devil was going on?

'Did Dewell show passport ID?'

'Yes, sir.'

'What did he look like?' Maybe he would recognize the description as someone from the solicitor's office, although that still didn't answer the question as to why Colmead had sent Dewell and why the man had stolen from him.

'He was dark-haired, clean-shaven, about six foot, and slender.'

Certainly not Michael Colmead, who was balding, about five feet nine inches, and portly.

'Age?'

'Late forties.'

Colmead was mid-fifties.

Marvik requested a copy of the letter, told the officer he would no longer require the bank's safe deposit service — which he would confirm in writing — and stepped into the busy London street, where he found the nearest shop selling briefcases. There he purchased a large, stout one with a shoulder strap and, ducking into a hotel, made for the gents. In one of the cubicles he transferred the contents of the plastic carrier bag into the briefcase.

Slinging it and his rucksack over his shoulders, he made for Waterloo Station, his mind running over his recent discovery. Of course that might not be the only thing missing but he was betting it was. Dewell had come for the computer disk because the notebook had contained only blank pages. On the front of the notebook, in his father's handwriting, had been one word, 'Vasa', but when Marvik had more closely examined the computer disk before depositing it, he had seen it was followed by 'II' very faintly — the name of his late parents' research vessel, *Vasa II*.

The departures board told him the train to Southampton hadn't yet arrived. Stepping away to a less crowded area, he pulled out one of the three mobile phones he carried — the one issued to him by his former Royal Marine colleague, Shaun Strathen, and a basic, pay-as-you-go model with no internet access and no tracking device. Strathen answered promptly.

'Someone has gained access to my boxes,' Marvik announced. 'The notebook with the disk attached to it is gone.'

'He got through the bank's security checks?' came Strathen's shocked reply.

'Yes.' Marvik told him how. 'I'm going to pay a visit to Colmead. I want to face him directly with this. I should be able to catch him before the office closes.'

'I'll see what I can get on a James Dewell, because I doubt he's an employee of Colmead's. If he had been then Colmead would have informed you, and that doesn't answer why Colmead would have needed access to your bank anyway, seeing as you are very much alive.'

'Maybe someone told him I was dead.'

The platform number flashed up on the screen. 'I've got to go. I'll call you later.'

Marvik made for the train. When seated he let his mind return to the notebook and disk. He'd discovered them in the belongings of a marine archaeologist called Sarah Redburn, whom he had met in March during an investigation for the UK police's National Intelligence Marine Squad, the unit that both he and Strathen worked for undercover. Marvik recalled his one and only meeting with Sarah in a steamy café on the seafront in Swanage. She had professed to be a great admirer of his late mother, Dr Eerika Marvik, a renowned marine archaeologist. Shortly after that Sarah's body had been found at the foot of the cliffs just outside the Dorset coastal town. She'd been strangled. Her killer had, so far, eluded the police.

Marvik's boss, Detective Chief Superintendent Crowder, had told him that he believed Sarah's murder was connected with the death of Marvik's parents, Professor Dan Coulter, a leading expert on ocean turbulence and the world's ocean seabed, and Dr Eerika Marvik. Both had been killed in an underwater explosion in the Straits of Malacca in 1997. Crowder wouldn't or couldn't tell him more. Perhaps because he had no more to tell, or perhaps he didn't know, but something had triggered that idea. Marvik didn't think that Crowder had seen the notebook or disk, nor was aware of them, though he could be wrong.

Whatever was on that computer disk was obviously of sufficient interest to one party for it to have been stolen by them. But what could it be? Marvik hadn't looked. He'd been called away by Crowder on a mission shortly after finding it. And perhaps part of him had put it off because it concerned his parents and he'd managed for many years to put them, and his childhood, behind him. How had the notebook and disk come to be in Sarah's possessions? Who knew of their existence? More importantly, who knew he had found them and placed them in his bank deposit box over a month ago? Not Crowder, because Marvik hadn't told him. And not Colmead either. Strathen was the only person and Marvik trusted him implicitly. Strathen also had the ancient hard drive able to open the disk, and the skill to retrieve and analyse its contents. Contents that, Marvik now thought, must be explosive, certainly to someone.

The train seemed to take an age to reach the south-coast town of Southampton, and it was close to five when Marvik finally alighted and hurried towards the solicitor's office. He was relieved to find it still open but disappointed and then suspicious to be greeted with the news that Michael Colmead was on holiday.

'When did he go?' he asked the receptionist.

'Yesterday,' she answered readily enough, but Marvik sensed and noted her unease. His suspicions deepened.

'When will he return?'

'I . . . er . . . I'm not sure.'

'Did he say where he was going?'

'No.' Her fair face flushed. 'Can anyone else help you?'

One man could but Marvik would be amazed if he was here. 'James Dewell.'

The receptionist blinked and eyed him askance. 'I'm sorry, Mr Marvik, we don't have anyone working here by that name.'

It had been worth a try. 'In that case I'd like to see Mr Merstead.' Donald Merstead was a senior partner of the firm Colmead had founded.

'I'll try him for you,' she said hesitantly, as though she had no hope of him being available.

Marvik crossed to one of the leather sofas and sat. At least Merstead was in the office, but whether he would know the whereabouts of his fellow partner and who Dewell was was another matter.

He picked up the newspaper from the coffee table but didn't read it. He heard the receptionist announce his arrival on the phone to Merstead. He also heard her say, 'No, I don't know what he wants. Yes, I told him Michael was on holiday.' She listened for a moment then replaced the phone. Still eyeing him nervously, she said, 'Mr Merstead will be with you in a moment.'

The moment stretched into ten minutes. Marvik silently speculated on what Merstead was doing during that time. Perhaps trying to contact his fellow partner. Marvik could try Colmead's mobile phone, and he planned to later, but he had a feeling that it wouldn't be answered.

The door to Marvik's right opened and a bulky man in his early sixties with greying hair and a false smile on his florid face apologized for keeping Marvik waiting. 'How can I help you, Mr Marvik?'

'Is there somewhere we can talk privately?'

'Of course. Come through to my office.'

Marvik followed him down a short corridor into a spacious room equipped with contemporary-styled furniture and paintings and a large desk on which rested a computer, telephone, a foolscap lined notepad and a slimline gold pen. Merstead gestured Marvik into one of the two leather chairs behind his desk and took his own opposite.

Marvik launched in, wanting to test Merstead's reaction. 'Do you have a man called James Dewell working for you?'

'No.' He looked bewildered.

'Has Mr Colmead recently mentioned him to you?'

'No. I don't—'

'An item I placed in one of my safe deposit boxes in London is missing. The bank informed me today that a man called James Dewell was authorized by Mr Colmead to access my boxes. I gave Mr Colmead no such instruction. And neither do I know anyone by that name. I have a copy of the letter signed by Colmead.' Marvik withdrew it from his jacket and handed it over. 'The signature is not a forgery.'

Reluctantly, as though the paper might be contaminated, Merstead took it. He looked up, baffled. 'It certainly appears to be Michael's signature. Michael must have believed Mr Dewell had come from you.'

'But he didn't check it with me.'

'Perhaps he didn't think he needed to. Maybe Mr Dewell came with authorization that meant there was no need to do so.'

'Such as?'

Merstead thought for a moment then shrugged his heavy shoulders.

But the lawyer had a point. Perhaps Dewell had manufactured some kind of evidence that had persuaded Colmead that a letter of authorization was in order. What could have made the solicitor believe that without the need to question it with him directly? Perhaps Dewell had claimed that Marvik was ill or incapacitated in some way — or dead, as Strathen had suggested. Could Dewell have posed as a doctor? But why wouldn't Colmead have checked? He would have done, surely? Unless he had been convinced by Dewell that he, Marvik, was beyond communication and that something belonging to his parents might stimulate him or, more exactly, his memory. Perhaps Dewell had claimed that he had amnesia or was in a coma.

Marvik said, 'I want to know if that authorization letter is on your records.' Someone had typed it out and printed it off, he reasoned.

Merstead looked as though he was about to protest but couldn't find a reason for doing so. He picked up his phone and after a moment was talking to someone called Julie. Colmead's secretary — Marvik had met her a few times. Merstead asked her about the letter and James Dewell. His expression grew more anxious as he listened to her replies and a thin layer of sweat appeared on his brow. After replacing the receiver, he cleared his throat. 'Julie says that Michael didn't dictate any such letter to her and there is no appointment with a James Dewell in Michael's diary.'

It was as Marvik had suspected. Colmead had typed the letter himself. Dewell didn't show up in Colmead's diary because he had either visited here after office hours by arrangement, or he had met Colmead off the premises. Marvik thought that there was little more he could extract from Merstead, except further lies about Colmead allegedly being on holiday, but he'd ask anyway.

'Where has Colmead gone?'

'France, I believe.'

A lie. 'When is he due back?'

'I'm not sure.' He shifted uneasily.

No, because there is no holiday.

'We left it open-ended,' Merstead tried to bluff.

'I'll call him on his mobile.' Marvik made to do so.

Merstead forestalled him. 'He's not taken it. He wants to be incommunicado.' The smile didn't quite come off.

Merstead was worried. Marvik thought he had the right to be. 'I'd like to see the file on the handling of my parents' estate after their deaths.'

Merstead looked perplexed. 'That's somewhat unorthodox. I'm not sure it can be arranged.'

'Would you rather I report this matter to the police?'

That got Merstead flummoxed. 'There's no need for that. I'm sure there's a simple explanation as to why that authorization was given.'

'But as we can't ask Colmead in person I'd like to see if there is anything in your files that relates to the item stolen from my safe deposit box.'

Merstead squirmed and only barely resisted the temptation to mop his brow. 'It's been archived.'

'Then retrieve it from the archives.'

'It's not in this office.'

'Then get it. I'll return when you have it.'

'But I can't see how it will help. We have nothing that belongs to your parents, everything was handed over to you.'

'You'll have a copy of the correspondence between my guardian, Mr Freestone, and Mr Colmead. You'll also have a list of my parents' personal belongings, which were catalogued by Nigel Bell.' Marvik was keen to check that against the lists he had retrieved from the files in the safe deposit box to see if anything else had been taken by Dewell. He rose and couldn't mistake the look of relief on Merstead's face.

The lawyer scrambled up. 'I'll get Julie to phone you when the file is here.'

Marvik wondered if he should wait for Julie to leave the office and ask her what she knew about Colmead's absence, but he'd speak to her soon enough when she called to say his parents' archived files were in the office.

He made his way back to his boat, moored at Ocean Village Marina, mulling over what he had just learned and putting it with the stolen notebook and computer disk. He didn't believe it was a coincidence that Colmead was missing, but was his absence intentional or had someone arranged it? If the former, and Colmead had deliberately gone on the run, was that from him or from Dewell, having coerced him into handing over the information? And if the latter, then Dewell, after he'd got what he wanted, could have eliminated Colmead.

Marvik retrieved his phone and rang the mobile phone number Colmead had given him. There was no answer, just a voicemail message. He didn't have Colmead's home telephone number or his address. Could the solicitor be lying dead inside his house? Had anyone checked? Maybe Merstead had gone there when his partner hadn't shown up for work on Tuesday and found it empty. Or perhaps Colmead *had* left a message with Merstead to say he needed a few days' break from the office.

At his boat, Marvik cast off and headed across the Solent to his remote cottage on the Isle of Wight. Much as he didn't want to, he decided to spend the evening trawling through his parents' papers, familiarizing himself with the contents and making a list of them, so that he could cross-reference certain items against those in the archived files to see if anything else was missing.

When he reached Cowes, he swung into the River Medina and motored slowly up to Newtown Harbour, where he moored up on the private pontoon close to his cottage. It was only when he silenced the engine that he caught the low throb of a motorboat heading out towards Cowes. Nothing unusual in that. The river was popular, particularly in the summer months, but it was early season and now fairly late in the day. He headed across the grass towards the house but as he drew nearer, he felt uneasy, as though someone was watching him.

Striding on he gave no outward sign of this while his gaze registered the scene around him and his brain rapidly assimilated what he saw, trying to pinpoint the reason for his discomfort. He strained his ears for any unusual sound, but only the wind rustling through the reeds disturbed the peace of the natural, isolated harbour. His old Land Rover Defender was exactly where he had left it. There were no other tyre tracks beside it.

Unlocking the back door, he stood just inside the kitchen, his eyes searching the room for any signs of a disturbance. There was none, and no sound nor sign of an intruder, and yet some instinct borne of years of training and operating in danger zones alerted him. Someone had been here. He could sense it.

He dropped the briefcase on the kitchen floor and his rucksack beside it. He didn't have anything of value in the cottage for the average thief to steal and the average one would simply have smashed a window or broken down the door, which wouldn't have taken much force. He didn't bother to set the alarm because there was no one within miles to hear it.

Swiftly, he went through the house, checking the five small rooms. Whoever had been here had been good, but not quite good enough. They also hadn't accounted for his photographic memory. There was a drawer left marginally open in the bedroom, a shoe at a slight angle in the bottom of the wardrobe, his shower gel and shaving cream fractionally out of place in the bathroom and a book at the wrong angle on the coffee table in the sitting room, as though it had been picked up, rifled through and placed down again. If nothing had been stolen — which he briskly and predictably discovered was the case — then either the intruder had left disappointed, or he'd come for another reason: destruction. Or perhaps for both purposes, to discover something and to kill.

With a quickening pulse, Marvik speedily considered the options. It would be an incendiary device triggered by movement or an electrical impulse. With careful haste Marvik began his search for such a device while his thoughts ran on auto. The fire alarms might have been disabled. But even if left intact, the fire brigade were too far away to arrive in time if someone happened to hear the alarm or see the smoke. Overcome by smoke, his burnt body would eventually be found. The blaze would probably be put down to an electrical fault.

It was possible that the device, if there was one, would be a remote one of the type he was well versed in handling. It would be in a small, concealed container primed to ignite the moment he switched on the toaster, kettle, his laptop, or even his electric toothbrush.

It took him only a few minutes to find it in the sitting room. It was behind a stack of books on the floor. With a grim smile of satisfaction, he scratched absentmindedly at the scars on the right hand side of his face, caused as a result of getting too close to such a device in a combat zone. He'd been correct in his assumption that it was of the type that would be triggered the moment he used an electrical item. Expertly he deactivated it and, returning to the kitchen, placed it in his rucksack. With the rucksack in his hand, he entered his bedroom and threw some additional clothes inside it. He had provisions and toiletries on board his boat and could buy anything he needed on his travels.

Slinging his briefcase across his shoulder, he closed the cottage door behind him and headed for his boat. Was someone watching him now? Had they rigged up outside surveillance? He wasn't going to stop to check.

He halted a few yards from the jetty and stood absolutely still. It was an hour off high water and the stiffening wind was sending the water slapping against his boat. It was a familiar sound. There was nothing untoward either in the harbour or on board. He cast off, leaped on deck, and set a course for Hamble Marina.

CHAPTER TWO

Marvik let himself in through the double-gated entrance of the whitewashed Georgian manor house, which backed on to Southampton Water. There he unlocked and entered apartment number one. Strathen looked up from one of the computer terminals in his operations room, showing no surprise at his arrival, but then Marvik knew he'd have seen him on his security monitors. The room was equipped with computers, plasma screens, whiteboards, telephones, a fax machine, typewriter, and the hard drive that could have opened the floppy disk.

'Colmead has gone AWOL,' Marvik announced, dumping his rucksack and briefcase on the floor and shrugging off his sailing jacket.

'Not surprising. Beer?' Strathen rose with an agility that belied the fact he had a prosthetic right leg, having lost it just below the knee while serving in the Royal Marines in Afghanistan when an improvised explosive device had gone off.

Marvik followed him into the kitchen. 'I need to check out his house to make sure he's not lying inside it dead. Can you get me his address?'

Strathen nodded.

'His partner says he's gone on holiday, but it's clearly a lie.' Marvik took his beer and followed Shaun back to his operations room. 'Especially in light of another development. Someone has entered my cottage. I found this.' Marvik reached into his rucksack and pulled out the incendiary device.

Strathen gave a low whistle.

Marvik threw himself on the seat opposite Strathen. 'Whatever is on that computer disk must be dynamite. I wish I'd asked you to open it for me instead of stuffing it away in the bank.'

'Someone thinks you might have done and discovered its contents, hence the need to eliminate you.'

'And they also thought they'd take a look around my house in case I had more of my father's disks stashed away. It was a very careful search. They left empty handed. And they're going to be very disappointed when they don't read of a body found in a fire in a remote cottage on the Isle of Wight.'

'They'll try again, especially when they learn you're asking more questions, which I take it you are obviously intent on doing.'

Marvik nodded and drank his beer.

'I'll give you some equipment you can use to check over your boat. If Dewell is clever enough to gain access to your bank, then he's bright enough to know you own a boat and spend a lot of time on board.'

'Thanks.' Marvik took another drink. 'What on earth were my parents up to in 1997 in the Straits of Malacca that warrants all this?'

'Did they mention anything about it to you, or did you hear anything of their expedition after their deaths?'

'No, on both accounts. I rarely saw them once I'd been packed off to school, and after their deaths I didn't ask.'

'Would they have confided in a relative?'

'There aren't any, hence the need to appoint a guardian, Hugh Freestone. He might still be around.' Marvik couldn't recall Freestone talking about the accident, or his parents come to that, but then he hadn't exactly been communicative during the two months before enlisting in the Marines. 'I suppose they could have corresponded with friends and colleagues, but I've no idea who they might be. After I enlisted, I gave Colmead instructions to field all enquiries about my parents and not to bother me with them, but Colmead might have logged them or corresponded with some of them. I might find some reference to them in these files, or the archived ones. I've asked Merstead to retrieve them.'

'Could Dewell be a past associate of one or both of your parents?' Strathen posed. 'Perhaps learning of the computer disk—'

'How?'

'Sarah told him before he killed her that she had it in her belongings in the house she was sharing with Bryony Darrow on Eel Pie Island. He went there but you had beaten him to it, not because you knew of the disk's existence — it was coincidence you discovered it there while working on a different mission for Crowder — but Dewell, seeing you there, thought it best to set fire to the house and eliminate you and the disk.'

That had been in March, and the assignment for Crowder's Squad had involved a search for the truth behind Sarah's father's disappearance.

Strathen said, 'Could Bryony Darrow have alerted Dewell, or been persuaded to tell him? After all, she saw you take the notebook.'

'She did, but she couldn't have known why or what was in it. I can't see her being involved in this.'

'Maybe she is, inadvertently.'

'She's been in Budapest since the middle of April filming for a new series of *Maigret*, her breakthrough role according to the media. I think Bryony is too intent on becoming famous to worry about someone else's past. She didn't even attend Sarah's funeral.' Sadly few people had, just a handful of past friends, the solicitor who had handled Sarah's estate, and her previous boss, Caroline Shaldon.

'Dewell could easily have located her and asked if you had taken something of Sarah's.'

Marvik still had Bryony's mobile phone number. She might have changed it of course, or, recognizing his number, she might not answer it. They hadn't parted on the best of terms. He said he'd try it and, failing that, Strathen said he'd either contact her directly through the same number or go through the production company.

'That doesn't answer how Dewell knew where you'd put the notebook or that Colmead was your solicitor and might know,' Strathen added. 'And there's the timing of Dewell showing up at your bank — yesterday — which indicates that he's only recently been alerted as to the disk's continuing existence and location.'

'No one knew that, except you. And I'll rule you out.'

'Thanks,' Strathen said with a grin. 'So who else have you been talking to about your parents' last expedition, besides Crowder, and I don't think he'd go to the trouble of sending an agent to get into your bank and steal the notebook, not when he could ask you for it or get a warrant to obtain it.'

Marvik had already been considering this. 'I phoned Colmead in April and asked him what had happened to my parents' research papers. He said everything had been handed over to the relevant experts, who had been tasked with sorting through them and giving them to the appropriate organizations. But when I asked about my parents' computers, Colmead said there hadn't been any on board *Vasa II* or at their home on the Isle of Wight. He gave me the name of the clerk who had catalogued their belongings, Nigel Bell. He's retired. I visited him on the twenty-fifth of April, and he said the same.'

'So either Colmead or Bell could have told someone you'd come nosing around.' Strathen sat back with a thoughtful expression on his craggy face.

'But why?' Marvik said with exasperation, knowing he wouldn't get the answer tonight, nor from Strathen. He'd only get it by finding out what had been on that disk and how it had come to be in Sarah's possession, and she was no longer around to ask. He said as much to Strathen.

'It's possible your parents backed up their research online.'

'In 1997!' Marvik said, surprised.

Strathen smiled. 'It wasn't quite the dark ages. There were online backup providers even then, but it's highly probable they've gone bust, while those that have survived have been gobbled up by other newcomers. If the latter, then there is a chance I can find the information. Accessing it, though, is another matter. For that I'd need the username and password. Could it be in your parents' papers?' Strathen indicated the briefcase.

Marvik shrugged and drained his beer. He knew if anyone could find backed-up material from twenty years ago, Strathen would be the one to do it. 'I'll go through the files tonight,' he said, not a task he was looking forward to. He'd avoided it for years, but then he'd had no need to rake over the past. It was different now. Murder had been committed and someone was very keen to add his to their list.

'Are you going to report this to Crowder?' Strathen asked.

Marvik had already considered it but he knew what the head of the National Intelligence Marine Squad's response would be. He would claim not to have any knowledge of what Marvik's parents had been doing in 1997 in the Straits of Malacca, which of course was most likely true, and yet something must have triggered Crowder's link between him and Sarah Redburn's death. Even if Crowder did know something he might not say, because Marvik's role, while working on a mission for the Squad, was to go in blind with little information, to ask questions, to probe, to stir up trouble and provoke a killer into the open. Only this wasn't a mission, this was personal. Or was it both? he wondered.

'I'll say nothing to him for now, but I would like to talk to my former guardian, Hugh Freestone. He must know more. *If* he's still alive. I last saw him when I was seventeen and we've not kept in touch. He was living in a cottage at South Stoke in West Sussex, two miles north of Arundel.'

'I'll check if he's still residing there.'

'What also puzzles me is the timing of the entry to my cottage. How did they know I wouldn't be there?'

'They saw you leave this morning.'

'Possibly.' But Marvik recalled the sound of that motorboat in the harbour. That could have been anyone though.

'Someone at the bank could have tipped them off,' Strathen added.

'Or at the solicitor's office.'

'Donald Merstead?'

'Or Julie, who knew I was there. But I can't see it being her, not unless she is in on it with her boss. And I can't see Merstead being involved either.' Marvik rose. 'I'll make us something to eat.'

'I'll get you Colmead's address.'

Half an hour later, Strathen reported that Colmead lived at Hythe. It was a small town just across the water from Southampton. Marvik knew it, and the marina based there, well. He'd put into Hythe several times crossing from his cottage on the Isle of Wight. He said he would take the boat round there in the morning and moor up on the visitors' berth.

Strathen had also discovered that Freestone was still listed as the resident of the cottage at South Stoke, in the opposite direction to Hythe, the east. He couldn't find a telephone number but Marvik said even if he had done, he wouldn't have called it. This needed a face-to-face meeting. Marvik wasn't sure how he'd feel seeing his guardian again. Their relationship had been transitory, though the circumstances and emotions surrounding it made it evocative.

After they'd eaten, Marvik called Bryony. He got her voicemail but decided not to leave a message. It was too complicated for that and he doubted she would return his call. Strathen said he would try it later. While Strathen began his search for online backup providers who had been around in the 1990s, Marvik settled down to go through the safe deposit boxes, steeling himself for a flood of emotions at seeing material concerning his parents, to whom he'd hardly given a thought for so long. He was surprised to find himself relatively detached, perhaps because it all seemed so clinical — birth, marriage and death certificates; medical records; educational certificates and awards; details of the sale of the house; stocks and shares; the closure of their bank accounts and the reinvestment of that capital into other accounts; shares and bonds in his name. He'd had no interest in money other than earning his salary from the Marines. When he had been certain that he was due to be medically discharged last year, he had cashed in most of his savings and instructed Colmead to sell his shares. He'd used the money to purchase his powerful and large motor cruiser. He still had a substantial amount left but he had no desire to put down roots and indeed no idea where to do so.

He found a copy of his parents' wills made in 1991, the year he had been despatched to England after having lived with them until then on board the boat.

'Colmead was appointed sole executor,' he said. 'There's nothing in the wills appointing Freestone as my guardian. There might be a letter in the correspondence files.'

There were two such files. One was headed 'Dr Eerika Marvik' and the other 'Professor Dan Coulter'. Some of the letters went back years and were related to projects, job offers, exchanges of ideas, along with some more personal letters from friends and former colleagues. Marvik didn't read them. He made to note the names, with the thought that he and Strathen might be able to trace them, when he noticed that the dates of the correspondence were all before 1991 and nothing after that. There was also no correspondence between Freestone and his parents and no letter detailing Freestone's guardianship in the event of their deaths.

'There might be something in the solicitor's archived file,' Strathen ventured, when Marvik relayed this. 'Or perhaps it was just a verbal arrangement.'

There were six small notebooks similar to the one he had discovered in Sarah's possession. They contained his father's scrawl but there were no computer disks taped to the back.

Seeing them, Strathen said, 'Anything?'

'Personal jottings dating back to when my father was at university, a kind of haphazard diary, which ends in 1990. Did he stop writing after that or were there others? If so, where are they?'

'There might be some indication of a password to a backup file in them.'

'Be my guest.' Marvik handed them over.

'Are there any diaries belonging to your mother?'

'No.' Marvik wondered if there should have been. He hadn't asked the bank security officer if Dewell had entered and left the vault carrying a briefcase for example, into which he could have stuffed a great deal of material. And no one would have searched Dewell because he'd had permission to be there.

'I don't think the answer is here.' Marvik rose and stretched himself. 'If it's with Colmead then it'll probably be impossible getting it as I don't expect to find him tomorrow, certainly not alive.'

Strathen agreed.

Marvik refused the offer of a bed and returned to his boat. After checking it over with the sonar equipment Strathen had given him and finding it clean, he showered and retired to his bunk, but his restless mind would not let him sleep. Instead, flashes of memories passed through it of his parents and of his childhood on board their research vessel as they explored various ocean depths around the world and the UK; of their trips to London and the time spent waiting in large architecturally impressive buildings; of wandering around the National Maritime Museum on his own and being intrigued by the displays while one parent or both had meetings; of university halls, marinas, wharfs, foreign cafés and restaurants. Then school.

He'd done well academically. His education on board *Vasa*, provided in turn by both his parents, had resulted in him being ahead of his peers. He'd also been a sporting success at school mainly because he had needed an outlet for his boredom, frustration and anger, the latter at being abandoned by his parents. He never felt he had fitted in at that school — he'd travelled too much and had seen so much of the world. When Freestone came to fetch him he'd felt glad, then guilty, because the reason had been his parents' deaths.

Marvik gave up further attempts at sleep. He made a coffee and took it on deck. Standing under the awning, he listened to the rain and the sounds of the wind through the masts. Flashbacks wouldn't get him the truth.

Did he want it? Yes, because as Langton, the psychiatrist who had treated him after his head wound had said, one day he would have to stop running from their deaths. He thought he had but clearly he'd been deluding himself. Wherever this took him, and whatever it revealed, he hoped he'd live long enough to find out.

CHAPTER THREE

Thursday

The red-bricked Victorian house at Hythe looked empty as Marvik surveyed it in the early morning sun. And no answer came when he rang the bell and knocked on the door. The house was screened from the road by a tall hedge. There was no car parked on the driveway to the left. The street was deserted and there didn't seem to be anyone watching him from behind neighbouring curtains or blinds. He didn't want to be reported to the police as a suspicious loitering person.

There was an alarm box above the door but no obvious surveillance device. That didn't mean there wasn't one — a small camera could easily be fixed under the alarm or above the porch. Would someone be watching Colmead's house to see who showed up? Only if Colmead had been pressurized into giving Dewell access to the safe deposit box, and that was probable. There was the chance that Colmead had been paid very highly for his services and had taken off, but surely it wouldn't have been enough money for him to chuck in his lucrative practice and his pension.

With a quick glance around to confirm he wasn't being watched by any neighbours, Marvik crossed to the driveway and pushed open the side gate into the small back garden, made smaller by a single-storey brick extension. There was a door on the side of it and swiftly, with the aid of a metal device on his penknife, Marvik easily opened it. He braced himself for an alarm, but none sounded.

He stepped inside and stood for a moment, getting a feel for the place. The smell of death was absent. But someone had been here and searched it. Cupboard doors and drawers stood open, utensils and papers were strewn on the floor and work surfaces. The fridge was open with mouldy milk and cheese inside. Colmead had clearly been gone for some days. And he hadn't left it like this to go on holiday!

There was no sign of a forced door or window, which could mean Colmead had let his intruder in, someone had got his house keys from him, or the intruder was an expert like him. Whichever it was this interloper wasn't the same person who had broken into his cottage, where he had left no sign of his invasion. Here there was total disarray. Then Marvik corrected his thinking, perhaps this time the intruder wasn't troubled about leaving his mark or had been in a hurry.

The living room displayed the same state of chaos as the kitchen. Sofa cushions had been upturned, and the contents of a sideboard were scattered over the floor. A similar scenario greeted him in the second room, which faced the front of the house on the other side of the hall, and was clearly Colmead's office. The contents of his desk, a cupboard and books littered the floor. There was no computer although Marvik noted a Wi-Fi router.

Inside one of the cupboards, on the far wall, Marvik found a safe. It was open. Had Colmead been pressurized into opening it or giving the safe code to whoever had come here wreaking this destruction? But as Marvik hurriedly sifted through the contents, he couldn't see that Colmead would have kept anything here relating to his parents. The authorization code to his safe deposit box would have been kept in the safe at the lawyer's office. There were the deeds to the house, a copy of Colmead's will, a few other papers pertaining to the law, Colmead's qualifications to practise it, and insurance for a motorboat, along with paperwork from Hythe Marina, where he moored it.

Marvik's eyes flicked to two photographs on the wall of a boat called *Curlew*. In one, Colmead was standing on the deck squinting into the sun. The other was of the boat anchored up in a wide bay against the backdrop of a sandy beach. Was *Curlew* still in the marina or had Colmead taken off on it? There were no boat keys so it was possible. And there was no passport, but that could be just window dressing to make anyone think that Colmead had done a bunk — though he'd hardly have wrecked his own house before doing so.

Marvik removed the picture with Colmead in it and pushed it into the pocket of his jacket. He checked the back of the other photograph just in case there was something secreted behind it. There wasn't.

The phone on Colmead's desk was flashing five. Taking a pen from his jacket, Marvik pressed 'Play'. Three messages were from Julie Pembroke growing increasingly worried with each call, asking her boss to ring her. Two were from Merstead, who sounded annoyed. His last call had been made yesterday evening after Marvik's visit to the office.

Marvik speedily checked the rest of the house, his ears attuned for the slightest sound. All he could hear was the traffic on the road and a blackbird squawking angrily, which seemed to set off a dog somewhere.

The bedrooms showed the same upheaval as the rooms downstairs. This had all the hallmarks of a rapid search, perhaps conducted after Colmead had been persuaded to open his safe and had been driven away in his own car by the intruder. Colmead's clothes were scattered over his bed and the floor. The mattress had been upturned, the bedclothes thrown in a heap. Two suitcases were in one of the cupboards.

He made to leave when his gaze alighted on the small grate and the blackened remains in it. There were radiators in the room, so why would Colmead want to light a fire? Taking his penknife from his pocket, Marvik raked over the ashes until he found a small fragment of paper burnt around the edges but with three letters on it. One looked like it might be a C or an O, the others were just as difficult to decipher, possibly a Y and then what looked like an S. He slipped it in to his wallet.

It might have no connection with Colmead's disappearance. On the other hand, why set light to paper unless it was to destroy confidential and perhaps incriminating evidence? Colmead could have taken it to his office and shredded it. Perhaps the solicitor hadn't burned the paper. Perhaps someone else had done so.

Marvik returned to the ground floor, stepped into the garden and crossed to the shed. The old and rusty padlock gave easily. The contents were of no interest to anyone, just a bicycle and gardening equipment.

He walked briskly back to the marina and located Colmead's boat. After checking no one was about, he climbed on board. He would have broken into it except the hatch was open and it was clear to Marvik that someone had also conducted a search here. The disarray was more limited on account of there being fewer items on board, but the contents of the lockers in the salon lay on the floor, and the same in the cabin. And, just as in the house, there was no sign of blood.

Marvik returned to his boat and cast off. If it had simply been the case of gaining access to his bank, then why the destructive search of the lawyer's property? Had Colmead kept evidence of Eerika Marvik and Dan Coulter's last exploration in 1997 at his home instead of at his office? Why would he do that? And what was going to greet him at Freestone's remote cottage, Marvik wondered, as he set a course for Littlehampton.

He called Strathen as he headed east and updated him on his findings including that of the charred remains of paper containing the letters C or an O and possibly a Y and then an S. Strathen said that when he had them, he'd scan them and enhance them on the computer. He also said he'd had no joy on finding any semblance of a password in his father's diaries or a backup provider, but it was early days yet. He'd spoken to Bryony Darrow, who had haughtily declared she hadn't spoken to anyone about Marvik's presence at her cottage the night of the fire, or that he'd taken something from Sarah's possessions. She'd put the whole incident behind her and moved on, and she was far too busy to even think about it. She'd asked him not to bother her again. Marvik thought they could rule Bryony out.

'I can't find anything on Dewell that matches the description you gave me,' Strathen added. 'But that's hardly surprising, there being so little to go on.'

Marvik decided not to phone Julie and relay what he had discovered at her boss's house. Not only did he not want to worry her, but he also wasn't very keen on anyone, let alone the police, knowing he had been there. They would start asking questions to which he didn't have the answers. He could report in to Crowder but again decided to hold back on that for a while.

It was early afternoon when he moored up at Littlehampton Marina, recalling memories of the time he'd last been here. He'd been working on his first case for Crowder in February, trying to find the killer of Helen Shannon's sister, Esther. He had succeeded with help from Strathen and from Helen. The thought of her forthright manner, courage and humour, along with her purple hair and Goth make-up made him smile. They'd again been thrown together in April on another mission and she now worked for Crowder, although Marvik had no idea what she did. Their friendship hadn't developed any further and he hadn't heard from her since the middle of April, which he regretted. Maybe he should phone her.

At the railway station he engaged a taxi, which, eight miles and twenty-five minutes later, deposited him in the deserted country lane some distance from Freestone's cottage. Something had made him baulk at being taken to the door. Maybe it was a reluctance to see the man who, for two months, had been his guardian, or perhaps it was his inbuilt training that warned him to be cautious. After all, if Colmead had been disposed of then Freestone too might have met the same fate if he had knowledge of Marvik's parents' last fateful expedition. If he did though, surely he'd have been silenced before now? But as Marvik's steps took him closer to the cottage, he reasoned that it was only recently that the notebook and disk had come to light, triggering this chain of events.

Despite his resolve not to let the past intrude on his thoughts, it did, along with the memories of the emotions he'd experienced on his arrival all those years ago — the anger at his parents for deserting him and dying, the confusion and resentment. He acknowledged the tightening in his gut. What he would feel on seeing Freestone, he didn't know. He remembered a tall man, lean and fit with the body of a runner, steady eyes behind steel-frame spectacles, a soft, gentle voice and easy manner. Quiet. How old had he been then? To a teenager he had seemed ancient, but he might have only been late forties, or fifty at the most, which meant he would now be in his seventies.

His footsteps slowed as he passed the small ancient church on his right and the derelict barns on his left. Nothing had changed since 1997. The grass in the tiny graveyard was overgrown. He didn't think a service had been held there in years. The church must once have served a wide community of farmworkers living in small cottages around here. They'd long gone, leaving only Freestone's brick-and-flint cottage at the end of the lane, which backed onto the River Arun.

Rounding the bend, it came into view. It was exactly as he remembered, standing in splendid isolation surrounded by small fields given over to scrub and pasture land and low hawthorn hedges. The road petered out just a few yards beyond it in a gated bridge that crossed the river and, from what he recalled, was only used by the farmer for moving his cattle from one side of the River Arun to the other. Marvik caught a glimpse of the sun on the water. It was high tide. He could have made it up here in the tender from his boat but hadn't thought that the correct manner in which to arrive to reacquaint himself with his former guardian.

The iron gate set in the low flint wall squeaked in the same way it had in 1997. The garden was well tended and the cottage well maintained. With a pounding heart, he pushed his finger on the brass bell and held it there for a few seconds. But even before it had ceased to chime, he knew that no one would come to answer it. This house, like Colmead's, appeared lifeless. And there was no sign of a car. Freestone must have one, living so far away from the nearest shop, which meant he must be out. At least, Marvik hoped he was, rather than having been abducted or attacked and killed.

He peered through the letterbox. The hall was narrow with the stairs on the right and a door ahead, which he recalled led into the kitchen. Straightening up, he walked around to the rear. The garden was mainly laid to lawn, which had been mown, and there was evidence of spring in the flowerbeds that bordered it. At the end of the garden was a wooden boatshed and the shimmering River Arun, which he remembered negotiating by canoe and a small dinghy with an outboard motor, both courtesy of Freestone. On one or the other of them, depending on the weather, and how energetic he had felt, he would travel to Arundel and on to Littlehampton, occasionally even out to sea. It was no wonder, he thought with a smile, he'd chosen a life in the Marines. He'd always been at home on the water, first with his parents and then briefly here.

He tried the back door. It was locked. Peering through the window he could see into a modern kitchen, which seemed to stretch the width of the house, a fact that was confirmed when he checked the window on the left of the door. When he had stayed here it had been two small rooms — the old, damp kitchen with a small boot room next to it. The whole house had smelled musty, as though it had been shut up for a long time. Now the kitchen was gleamingly modern and, on the island unit, he spotted a coffee mug and a plate with the remains of breakfast on it. Beside it was a newspaper, which meant that Freestone was around and wouldn't be away for long.

Marvik turned to face the river. It always looked better in full flow than when it was at sludgy low tide or an in-between half-hearted state. He made for the boathouse but had barely gone a few feet when a woman's voice startled him. 'Can I help you?'

Marvik spun round, annoyed with himself for not hearing the approach. Christ, he was losing his touch. That would never have happened a year ago. He cursed himself for being too immersed in the past. She was raven-haired, petite, early thirties with an anxious expression on her fine-boned, angular features. Her chocolate-brown eyes flicked to his rucksack and then to his scarred face, and he saw shock and annoyance in them before her hand plunged deep into her jacket pocket — probably, he thought, where her mobile phone lay, ready to summon the law. She obviously thought him a burglar with the loot stashed in his bag.

'I was hoping to see Mr Freestone,' Marvik quickly explained.

'He's not here. This is my house,' she answered, sharply.

Marvik hid his surprise. 'Did you buy it from Mr Freestone?'

'No. I don't know anyone called Freestone. You have the wrong address.'

This wasn't what Strathen had told him, and he knew who he believed. But why lie? He caught the sound of a car pulling up in the lane and saw her turn towards it.

'That's the estate agent,' she hurriedly added. 'I'm putting the house on the market. Now, if you don't mind.'

'Sorry to have been trespassing but I thought Mr Freestone might have been in the boathouse.'

'Well, he's not.'

Marvik looked beyond her to see a well-built, fair-haired man in his late thirties wearing a dark waterproof jacket, heading towards them with a wary look on his round, petulant face. The woman quickly addressed the man. 'Stuart Craven? I'm Amber Tunstone. I'll show you around the house. This man is just leaving.' She glared at Marvik.

'Of course,' he said politely and made for the front of the house. Amber Tunstone obviously didn't trust him as she followed him, keen to see him off the premises. There was only one car parked outside, the one he had heard arrive, a black Ford. He mentally registered the number before making in the direction of the church but, just before the bend in the lane, he paused and looked back. She was still there, watching him, her mobile phone in her hand.

He walked on. Reaching the church and the derelict barns, there wasn't a car in sight, so where was Amber Tunstone's vehicle? How had she got to the cottage? Judging by her heeled shoes she hadn't walked the four miles from Arundel. She, like him, could have asked a taxi to drop her off a short distance from the cottage, but if she lived there, as she claimed, then why not let the taxi take her right to the door? He hadn't heard another car approach and he was certain he would have. She seemed to have sprung from nowhere. Marvik didn't for one minute believe her story.

He waited two minutes before turning back. Amber Tunstone and her estate agent were nowhere to be seen. Soon he was at the gate that closed off the bridge and on his right was Freestone's boathouse and jetty. Alongside the latter was a small dinghy with an outboard engine. He turned and glanced up at the rear of the house. No one was visible.

Marvik vaulted over the low flint wall into the garden and dropped behind the cover of a shrub. He had a good view of the rear of the house. He saw Amber Tunstone enter one back bedroom and Stuart Craven the other. What were they doing? As Amber Tunstone didn't own the property he doubted Craven was an estate agent, and if that were the case they certainly weren't measuring up the rooms or taking photographs for it to go on sale. No, there was only one activity they were carrying out and that was a search. Why? Where had they got the keys to enter the house? And where was Freestone?

Thirty-five minutes later they both emerged and didn't look too happy. As they passed him on the way to the boathouse, he caught a snatch of their conversation.

'They won't be in there,' Craven said gloomily.

'Why not? It's as good a place as any.'

'Are you sure that man has gone?

'No, I'm not, so let's hurry up in case he returns,' Amber Tunstone said tartly.

He watched them enter, wondering what they were searching for. Was it connected with his parents? It seemed highly probable. Craven didn't match Dewell's description, but both he and Amber Tunstone could be working with or for Dewell. On the other hand, this search might have nothing to do with his parents. Marvik had no idea what Freestone had done for a living. He hadn't asked twenty years ago and Freestone hadn't volunteered the information or if he had, Marvik had taken no note of it. And he didn't know what Freestone now did. Perhaps he was into something crooked.

Their search didn't take them long. Within ten minutes they were hurrying past him. 'Waste of time,' Craven muttered.

'Oh, stop your moaning,' Amber snapped. 'I'll go back to him and see if he knows more. Let's get out of here.'

Go back to whom? Marvik wondered. Freestone? Was he being kept somewhere against his will?

He waited until he heard the car's engine fade into the distance then hastened to the front of the house. There was no sign of a forced entry. They had searched the house and found nothing, but he might have more success. For a start he was probably more expert than Amber Tunstone and Stuart Craven at searching, and for another, if it was something connected to his parents then perhaps he'd recognize what this treasure was, whereas they wouldn't. If it was notebooks and disks they would have found and seized them.

His thoughts took him around the house and to the back door, where, with expertise, he manipulated the lock and was inside. This was getting to be a habit, breaking and entering two houses in one day, he thought wryly.

His search of the kitchen drawers and cupboards yielded only the usual items. Crossing to the central unit, he glanced down at the newspaper. It was Saturday's *Daily Telegraph* and Freestone had filled in a couple of clues. Five days had elapsed. So where had Freestone been since then? It didn't bode well for the man. Captivity or death? Or perhaps he'd gone into hiding. But why? Perhaps he suspected someone was after him or, more precisely, after some vital information he held.

The evidence indicated that Freestone had left in a hurry. The half-completed crossword, the breakfast plate with bacon and a small piece of toast left on it. A half-drunk mug of coffee. Marvik sniffed at it. All he could smell was caffeine, not drugs or poison, but that didn't mean there wasn't any.

Keeping his ears attuned for any sound outside, he continued his search of the downstairs. Craven and Tunstone had been neat searchers. Everything was in place, including the books on the shelves. Marvik lifted them out one by one and flicked through the pages. Nothing. There was a telephone but no messages and the last call had been from a withheld number. In Freestone's study, he found bank statements with an extremely generous regular amount being paid into his bank from the Ministry of Defence. His pension, no doubt. There were the usual household bills, which confirmed the occupier was Hugh Freestone, and a letter from the hospital that stilled his hand. It was dated 26 April and gave details of a radiotherapy appointment, which could mean only one thing: Freestone had been having treatment for cancer.

Marvik found no deeds to the house or any other details of savings accounts. Perhaps Freestone didn't have the latter and the former was lodged with his solicitor. Was that Colmead? Marvik wondered, taking the stairs two at a time.

His gut twisted as he stepped into the back bedroom that had once been his, albeit briefly. Despite his best efforts to keep a check on his emotions the memories flooded back and with them the emotions of confusion and anger. He remembered how he'd lain on the bed counting how many stripes there were in the wallpaper, which had since been replaced by a small floral pattern — anything to stop him thinking of his parents' deaths.

The furniture, a chest of drawers and a bedside cabinet, were the same as when he had occupied the room. The single bed was unmade. He took a breath and hardened his resolve. The past couldn't be changed, only the future, and that depended on what he did next. There was nothing in the old room in any case. The cupboards were empty and no loose floorboards concealing anything.

In what was clearly Freestone's bedroom Marvik searched the pockets of his clothes hanging in the wardrobe without result. The same for his search of the chest of drawers. There were no photographs, no computer and no personal correspondence in the house apart from that letter from the hospital. He even checked the attic, wondering if Craven and Tunstone had done the same. Only dust and cobwebs.

Like the couple before him, Marvik made for the boathouse not expecting to find anything but boating paraphernalia. The wind was strengthening in fitful gusts, knocking the dinghy against the wooden jetty. The tide had turned and was beginning to go out.

The smell of damp wood he recalled from twenty years ago assailed him as he stepped inside. There was the canoe and paddles he'd used. In the corner was a heap of life jackets, alongside them lines in a muddle on the floor, and behind them a fishing rod. He didn't remember that. He might have tried the sport if the rod had been here then. But it looked new, and it was, he saw, when he picked it up. Freestone had taken up fishing. But something nudged at Marvik's memory. Freestone had once said how he despised fishing and couldn't see the slightest attraction in sitting for hours on end on a damp riverbank in drizzling rain waiting for a fish to bite and then to throw it back. Must have changed his mind.

Marvik went to put it back when something struck him. The fishing rod was in three sections, made of fibreglass and lightweight. There was no fishing tackle lying around, no lines, no net, no reels, baskets or flies and neither had there been in the house. With his heart beating a little faster, Marvik unscrewed the top. Shining his torch inside the hollow, he was astonished to find there was a piece of paper stuck in it. There was nothing in the other two sections. He eased out the paper, and unfurling it, was puzzled to find he was looking at a photograph of a classic motorboat. It couldn't mean a thing, he thought, stuffing it in the pocket of his jacket. He replaced the rod and decided he would use Freestone's small dinghy to return to Littlehampton Marina.

He started up the engine, but his hand stilled as he made to cast off from the jetty. There was something wedged under the wooden struts of the boathouse. The breath caught in his throat. From the shape of it, it was a body.

He silenced the engine, leaped out of the boat, ran to the boathouse and grabbed a paddle. Then, back inside the dinghy, he eased the paddle under the struts until it connected with the body.

Gradually he eased it out. The smell was nauseating. One he'd sadly come across many times in his career. It made his stomach heave but with expertise he controlled it and carefully and gradually drew the body towards him. It was face down, the head and arms hanging, and it had clearly been in the river for some days.

The back of the silver-haired head was caved in. The injury could have been caused by a fall but Marvik doubted it. Turning it over, he took in the bloated, yellowish-white skin, the protruding eyes, the sand and gravel around the mouth, and the marine life devouring the noxious flesh on the face and hands. Although he hadn't seen him for twenty years, Marvik knew without any doubt that he was looking into the dead face of his former guardian, Hugh Freestone.

CHAPTER FOUR

Friday

'There was ID on him,' Marvik said to Strathen early the next morning in the kitchen of his apartment. He'd used Freestone's small dinghy to motor back to his boat in the marina, had cast off, and then, when out in the English Channel, had set the dinghy loose. He'd sailed back to Hamble Marina overnight and grabbed a few hours' sleep after mooring up on the visitors' berths.

He'd searched Freestone's pockets and found credit and debit cards. Theft hadn't been the motive, but then Marvik hadn't considered that for one moment. There had also been a plastic driver's licence in the wallet but no house keys. It was possible that Amber Tunstone or Stuart Craven had taken them after killing him, although they'd waited a few days before using them. It would explain how they had accessed the cottage, and he guessed this could have been their second search, perhaps the first being too rushed for fear of being discovered after killing the man.

'What did you do with the body?' Strathen asked, cooking breakfast.

'Put it back in the water.' Marvik felt badly about that, but it would have taken some explaining to the police if he had reported it, and he wasn't sure they would have believed him. Crowder could have got him out of that but Marvik didn't want to waste time. He could have done it anonymously but he didn't wish them to investigate Freestone's murder yet. He needed to find out what this was all about, who had murdered Hugh Freestone and Sarah Redburn, and why.

He said as much to Strathen, adding that even if he had reported it anonymously his DNA and fingerprints were all over the house. Not that they would be able to trace him by that, and there was no reason for the police to connect Freestone with him when their association had terminated twenty years ago, but Marvik wasn't going to chance it. He was buying time, he told Strathen.

Strathen dished up the breakfast. 'OK, so we've got three questions.'

'Only three?' Marvik said.

Strathen smiled. 'One, why would someone want to kill Freestone? Two, why now? And three, who killed him? The answer to the first question must be linked to the second, and the answer to that has to be because it is only now that you've started asking questions about your father's research, which Freestone must have known something about.'

'Or the killer believes he did.'

'And that means that someone told the killer you were nosing around, and that you might get to Freestone.'

'We're back to Colmead again. He'd have had Freestone's address on file. But I can tell you now that Stuart Craven is not James Dewell, not unless he's dyed his hair blonde, put on weight since visiting my bank two days ago and shrunk a few inches.'

'*If* the security officer can be believed.'

'I can't see why he would lie.' Marvik tucked into his bacon. 'And what about Amber Tunstone and Stuart Craven? Are they working independently of Dewell or in league with him? What did they hope to find at Freestone's cottage?

When Craven said, "They won't be in there," he was referring to the boathouse. "They" indicates plural. More disks? Or notebooks belonging to my father? I told you there were more than three questions — there's an avalanche of them.'

'Yeah, I was being conservative.'

'Amber Tunstone said, "I'll go back to him and see if he knows more." Go back to who?'

'Colmead, who's being kept against his will?' suggested Strathen.

That seemed a good enough guess. 'His house was ransacked, unlike my cottage, so I think whoever turned over Colmead's place — and possibly abducted him — is a different person from the one who searched mine and left me the unwanted parcel. And we know who searched Freestone's house.'

'Could Craven have planted the incendiary device in your cottage?'

'Possibly. And Craven could have killed Freestone some days ago and returned with Amber Tunstone yesterday to search the cottage a second time because she thought Craven had done a sloppy job first time round. They must have had Freestone's keys to get in because they weren't on the body or in the house.' Marvik sipped his coffee, then reached into his pocket and retrieved his wallet. 'Here's the burnt offering I found in the grate in Colmead's bedroom.'

Strathen took the scrap of charred paper. After examining it he agreed that the letters appeared to be C or O, Y and S. 'I'll scan it into the computer and enhance it. I've managed to track down some online backup providers who were around in 1997. It's a case of following their trails either into bankruptcy or mergers and then seeing if I can find anything relating to your parents' files. I'll keep working on it. I'll also call the Arundel estate agents to see if they know or have heard of Stuart Craven, but I'd bet you now — if I was a betting man — that none of them will have.'

'Will you be able to trace the vehicle registration?' Marvik relayed it.

Strathen said he would. 'I'll also see what I can get on Amber Tunstone, who could have given you a false name.' He pushed away his empty plate and sat back easing his prosthetic leg. 'Were they expecting you to be there? Or was the timing of their arrival coincidental?'

'I've been thinking about that. Amber arrived at the cottage about eight minutes after I did. I don't know how she got there because there was no sound of a vehicle and none parked in the lane, but Craven showed up two minutes after her, so it's my guess that he dropped her off farther down the lane and she walked to the cottage, and it was their arrangement that he'd show a couple of minutes later.'

'But why the charade? Why not arrive together? Unless they knew that you, or someone, was in the grounds.'

'No one followed me there, and I didn't see Craven's car or any other vehicle parked on the approach road. It's possible it could have been behind the barns but again why wait there on the off chance that I, or someone, might come along. They might have rigged up a surveillance device first time there when they killed Freestone, which they removed before leaving the second time, but that still doesn't answer their prompt arrival. In order to be there so quickly — if they saw me mooching around the house and gardens — they must have been very close by, in the car. And if it was parked in Arundel then what were they doing there, and don't say working as an estate agent because, like you, I don't believe Craven is one.'

'Could Merstead have told someone you'd been to the office asking questions? Which alerted them to head out to Freestone's place to check it over again, in case you went there, only when they saw the taxi heading there, they decided to enact that pantomime for you.'

Marvik considered this. 'Merstead could have guessed I'd make for Freestone if he'd seen from the file he'd been appointed my guardian back in 1997, or Colmead had formerly told of him that, but it's a bit of a long shot. And how and why would he have told Craven and Amber Tunstone?'

'Or Dewell.'

'He denies knowing him. No — correction — I only asked if he had someone working for them called Dewell.' Marvik frowned and pushed away his empty plate. 'It's all speculation, Shaun, and it doesn't make any sense. I just can't see Merstead involved, but then I never thought Colmead would be. Perhaps it was just coincidence they arrived shortly after me and Amber Tunstone's role was to go ahead to make sure the coast was clear. She gave no sign of recognizing me, and neither did Craven, and I'm not completely forgettable with these.' He indicated his scars. 'Which means they're either both very good actors or no one has provided them with a description of me. I didn't give my name and Amber Tunstone didn't ask for it.'

'That could be because she knew it, and neither of them were surprised to see you because they'd been warned you might head there.'

'Well they didn't find anything. I did, although I'm not sure it's significant.' He stretched a hand into his trouser pocket and unfurled the photograph, turning it round to face Strathen.

'It's a boat!'

'What did you expect? A map with "X marks the spot of the buried treasure"?'

Strathen smiled and studied the picture keenly. 'It's not just any old boat. This is a classic. It's a Fairey Swordsman with an aft cockpit built at the Hamble by Fairey Marine, probably in the 1960s. Did Freestone own it?'

'He might have, although there was no paperwork relating to it in the house or any pictures of it. Even if it was his, why stuff a picture of it into a fishing rod?'

'A what?' Strathen's eyebrows shot up.

'You heard. Yes, it's unusual to say the least. I only looked inside it because it struck me as strange the rod being in the boathouse when there wasn't any fishing tackle. Freestone told me he hated fishing. And Amber Tunstone and Craven were searching for something. Probably not this—' he stabbed a finger at it — 'Nevertheless . . .'

'The picture could belong to whomever Freestone bought the rod from. Maybe he changed his mind about fishing and decided to take it up on retirement and he'd only got as far as buying the rod,' Strathen added thoughtfully. 'But the boat should be fairly easy to trace. The Fairey Owners Club will be able to help us. I'll get in touch with the commodore. We've even got the name of it, *Golden Fleece*. Reminds me of the film *Jason and the Argonauts*.'

'Well let's hope we don't meet any dancing skeletons.'

Strathen laughed before becoming more serious. 'But there are skeletons in someone's past.'

'I just hope it's not my parents'.' Marvik's mobile rang. He didn't recognize the number. Curious and slightly warily, he answered it. It was Julie Pembroke. She was calling early, well before office hours.

'I need to talk to you,' she launched, her voice anxious.

'I can be at your office within thirty minutes.'

'No, not there. Can you meet me in the Coriander Café in London Road, Southampton?'

He said he would. He rang off concerned and eager to hear what she had to tell him.

'Take my car,' Strathen offered.

'No, I'll go by boat. It'll be quicker by sea this time in the morning.' Although it was early, the traffic on the motorway would be building.

Forty minutes later, after mooring up at Ocean Village Marina, Marvik was pushing open the door of the Coriander Café to the north of the city. Julie was huddled in the far corner nursing a cup of coffee with an anxious expression on her drawn and narrow face. She looked up and her expression turned to one of relief before anxiety once again resurfaced. He asked if she'd like another drink, but she refused. There was no queue at the counter and within a couple of minutes Marvik was seated opposite her with a coffee in front of him.

'Donald lied to you on Wednesday,' she said in a rush, as though she'd been rehearsing her opening for minutes while she waited. In fact, she looked as though she'd been rehearsing what to say all night. Her light-brown eyes were bloodshot. 'Michael's not on holiday. He should have been in the office on Tuesday, the day after the Bank Holiday Monday, but he didn't show up. He has appointments in his diary all this week, and next, which I've had to cancel. Something's happened to him. I know it has but Donald won't call the police.'

Although Marvik knew Colmead's holiday was a fabrication he was excited to get confirmation of it from Julie and keen to discover why she had felt the need to contact *him*. He hoped it was because she knew more about Dewell.

'Tell me what happened,' he said calmly, his voice betraying none of his tension.

She dashed a glance around the café as though afraid someone might overhear them, but there was only a couple of people other than themselves seated.

'When he didn't arrive in the office on Tuesday, I rang his home number. I thought that perhaps he was ill. There was no answer, so I tried his mobile. Again, he didn't answer. It was on voicemail. I left a message on both his phones.'

Marvik had heard those she'd left on the landline.

'I tried again the following day, when he still didn't show in the office. Still no answer. I told Donald that I was very concerned and that someone should go round and make sure he was OK. Yesterday morning Donald told me he had called in at Michael's house the previous night but that there was no answer and his car wasn't there. He said to wait and see if Michael showed up for work today, but he won't, I just know it. I tried his mobile phone again this morning before I called you. The line is dead.'

Like Colmead? Marvik wondered. 'What car does he drive?'

'A black Mercedes.'

Marvik hadn't seen any such vehicle at the Hythe Marina car park. 'When did you last see him?'

'Friday, just after six o'clock. I asked him if there was anything he needed before I left the office but he said there wasn't. I don't know what time he left. I wished him a pleasant holiday weekend and he said the same to me and that was it.'

'Did he mention his plans for the weekend?'

'No. I assumed he'd be going out on his boat. I thought that maybe he'd had an accident. I rang the marina on Wednesday morning, but they said Michael's boat was still there. I told Donald yesterday that we should call the police. Michael could be lying inside the house, sick or worse.'

He wasn't but Marvik wasn't going to tell her that. 'That's unlikely if his car isn't there. Donald probably thought the same.'

'Then maybe he's had a road accident.'

'If he had the police would have notified you.'

'Not if he came off a country lane and no one has discovered the car.' She swallowed some coffee. 'Donald said I was fussing and that Michael has probably taken a few days off and he'd be in touch soon, but that's rubbish. Michael would never just go off like this without informing either me or Donald. I know what Donald's thinking, that it wouldn't look good for the firm, a missing solicitor. People will think the worst,' she said with bitterness.

And the worst, Marvik thought, was embezzling a client's account and taking off with the money. The fact that he had shown up on Wednesday claiming that Colmead had authorized someone to access his safe deposit box had put the fear of God into Merstead. He was probably desperately checking out Colmead's clients' accounts now, trying to discover if Colmead had been involved in helping himself to other clients' valuable belongings and siphoning off money.

Julie pushed a hand through her short, brown hair. 'I wondered if Michael had had a breakdown and booked himself into a clinic, too ashamed to admit it to anyone. Some people feel that way about mental health issues. There's still a stigma attached to it.'

Marvik knew that all too well. He considered what a practical, intelligent and concerned woman like Julie would do next. 'You contacted the clinics.'

'Yesterday afternoon. I tried the Priory Clinic at Marchwood before broadening my area of enquiry to take in other private clinics in Hampshire, Surrey and Sussex. I said I was a relative and was concerned about Michael but none of the clinics claimed to have admitted him as a patient. But maybe they thought doing so would be a breach of confidentiality. He still could be in a clinic, but I got the impression from all of them that he wasn't.'

'What about Michael's relatives?'

'There's an aunt in Poole, another in Durham and an uncle living just outside Maidstone. I contacted them all yesterday. I have their details on file so that I can remind Michael when their birthdays are and arrange flowers and birthday cards.'

The ever-dutiful secretary, thought Marvik.

'They haven't heard from Michael. I tried not to alarm them, so I made up a story about checking their availability for September, for a get-together for Michael's birthday, and asked if he'd mentioned it to them when he'd last seen or contacted them. They were only too glad to talk to me and none of them had seen Michael recently or indeed for some time. Michael is single with no dependants. I don't know who his friends are, or if he has any close ones. He's never spoken of anyone in particular. Donald is still insisting that Michael's OK and just needs a break. I'm not sure how long he can keep that up and I for one am not prepared to sit back and do nothing.'

'Why are you telling *me* this, Julie?'

She took a breath and studied him candidly. 'Because you went to see Nigel Bell and I heard Michael talking on the telephone about it.'

Marvik's pulse quickened. 'Before or after my visit to Bell?'

'After. The door to Michael's office was open. He thought I'd left for the day, and I had, but I'd forgotten something. I heard Michael say, "Nigel Bell didn't tell Marvik anything . . . Because I asked Bell . . . Everything's as it was."

Then he said, "I don't like this" and added something along the lines of "if I must", but he didn't seem too happy the next morning, or the next few days. Now there is no sign of him.'

It sounded as though what Marvik had discussed with Strathen was the case — Colmead had been reporting back to someone. Dewell? 'Do you know who he was talking to?'

'No.'

He believed her but he could see from her eyes and her demeanour there was more to come. He made no comment knowing she would continue when ready. After a few moments she did, lowering her voice even further so that Marvik almost had a job to hear her. 'After your visit to the office on Wednesday it kept going round and round in my head . . .'

'What did, Julie?' he said gently when she dried up.

'That perhaps this letter you mentioned Michael had written, which had given James Dewell authorization to your safe deposit box, could be connected with Michael's disappearance.' She looked down into her coffee cup before her red-rimmed eyes came up. 'Do you think it is?'

'Do you?' he asked, quietly.

He watched her skin pale. She hesitated for a moment but the need to confide, and her concern for her boss, was too great for her to contain what was troubling her deeply.

'Donald asked me to send for the archived file on your parents. Yesterday I telephoned the storage company to request them but I also asked when your parents' archived file was last accessed. It was a week ago, last Thursday, not by Michael but by James Dewell.' She looked distraught. 'But it can't have been him.'

'Why not?'

'Because he's dead.'

Marvik started. 'Dead?'

She shifted and looked miserable. 'James Dewell died on the second of February, very suddenly of a heart attack. He was a chartered surveyor and only forty-nine. Michael knew him both personally and professionally. Mr Dewell was divorced, no children and his parents were dead. Michael was his sole executor.'

So now Marvik began to see it. The real, and dead, James Dewell's papers might not be the only ones Colmead had used illegally. If the deceased had no dependants and Colmead was executor of the will then he had a free hand to stow away and sell the documentation for reuse. The death could have been registered but in this case it hadn't been because Strathen hadn't found it. And no one was going to check when a passport appears genuine and the details fit with the person carrying it, especially if it's backed up with other information, such as a letter of authorization and the code, as was the case at the bank.

'Why didn't Donald recognize the name Dewell when I mentioned it?'

'I don't know. Maybe he forgot it. Mr Dewell wasn't his client so perhaps he never really registered it.'

Perhaps he hadn't or perhaps he thought it advisable not to admit it, being already concerned that there had been a breach of a client's security.

'Does Donald know Dewell visited the storage company?' he asked.

'I haven't told him.'

'Did you ask them for a description of Dewell?'

'Yes. They said he was tall, dark-haired, well-built.'

The description fitted with the one the bank security guard had given him.

She looked at him despairingly. 'This just doesn't make sense.'

Not yet, but it would, he sincerely hoped. 'Have you heard Michael, or anyone in your office, speak of a Sarah Redburn?'

She thought for a moment. 'No. The name isn't familiar.'

Marvik hadn't expected it to be but it was worth a try. 'Can you find out if your firm handles the legal affairs for my former guardian, Hugh Freestone?'

'I can tell you the answer to that now. We do. Michael is Mr Freestone's solicitor and the executor of his will. Why?'

Marvik wasn't about to tell her. 'Do you know what Mr Freestone's occupation was? I believe he's retired.'

'He is. He worked for the Ministry of Defence, but I don't know what he did, or what his position was. I've never met him, only spoken to him briefly a couple of times on the telephone.'

'Have you heard of a woman called Amber Tunstone or a Stuart Craven?'

'No.' She looked distracted. 'Do you think I should call the police? Donald won't like it and I don't want to get Michael into trouble but I can't just do nothing.'

'Hold off for today at least. I'll see if I can find out anything more.'

'But how?'

'I'll talk to Nigel Bell.'

Was Bell safe or would he also have disappeared? What was behind the conversation Julie had overheard? Had Colmead taken off of his own volition? Perhaps his body would be found slumped over his steering wheel in an isolated spot, his death by suicide after being cajoled or threatened into assisting in a crime. Or perhaps it would be made to look that way.

Rising, she said, 'The archived file on your parents will be in later today. I'll call you when it comes in.'

He watched her walk towards the office. She was still deeply concerned but sharing her worries with him seemed to have helped her a little.

Marvik sprinted back to his boat. Nigel Bell lived in the coastal town of Lymington some twenty miles by road to the south-west. By sea it would be just as quick, if not quicker, than hailing a taxi, and he could moor up in Lymington Marina, which was a short distance from Nigel Bell's retirement apartment. He had Bell's telephone number but didn't want to alert him as to his arrival.

On the way, he rang Strathen and brought him up to speed. Strathen agreed it looked bleak for Colmead. 'No estate agent in Arundel, or the surrounding area, has ever heard of Stuart Craven. I can't find any trace of an Amber Tunstone either, which isn't surprising. But I'll keep looking. The Ford you saw outside Freestone's cottage was hired from a garage in Southampton. I called them but they won't say who hired it, quoted me the Data Protection Act and said that if I was a police officer then they would need to check it. I'll see if I can hack into their system.'

'Whoever hired it probably gave false details. It's possibly the phoney Dewell. Colmead could have handed over the dead man's driving licence as well as his passport. I'll see what I can get out of Bell.'

It was just after midday when Marvik pressed the buzzer to the former solicitor clerk's apartment. There was no answer. He could be out shopping, at the library, or a club. He could be away for a few days. After trying twice more, Marvik pressed the buzzer for the manager. Announcing himself in the intercom, he said he was a friend of Nigel Bell's and was concerned that he hadn't been able to get hold of him.

'He's visiting his daughter in America,' the manager, a woman in her mid-fifties, told him after letting him in. 'He left last Friday.'

Marvik didn't like the sound of that. He felt distinctly uneasy. It was the same day that Julie had told him she'd last seen Colmead.

'Was it a planned visit? Only he never mentioned it to me,' which was certainly the truth.

'No, a spur of the moment thing. He said he'd been invited and that he felt he needed a change of scenery.'

'He told you this in person?' Marvik asked.

'No. He dropped a note into the office. I have to check the apartments if I don't see the occupants around and Nigel obviously didn't want to worry me.'

Marvik felt even more perturbed. Had Bell really gone on holiday or had he been abducted and silenced as he believed Colmead had been? 'Did he say when he was returning?'

'No, just that he would let me know.'

Marvik stopped for some lunch before returning to his boat, mulling over this latest development. Troubled by it, he once again rang Strathen and gave him the latest update. Strathen said he had left a message with the Commodore of the Fairey Owners Club to call him. He hoped to have some information on the boat later that day.

Marvik's other mobile phone was ringing. He terminated his conversation with Strathen and answered it.

It was Julie. The archived file had arrived in the office.

CHAPTER FIVE

Julie ushered him into one of the meeting rooms on the second floor, where, on the table, was one large box file. Making sure the door was closed, she impatiently asked him what Mr Bell had said.

'Nothing,' he told her, 'on account of being on holiday.'

Her face crumpled with disappointment. 'Donald's called a partners' meeting for six o'clock to discuss Michael. They might decide to call the police and report him missing.'

That was to be expected but Marvik had a hunch that Merstead wouldn't mention anything to the police about his visit here, nor the breach of his safe deposit box, the letter from a dead client and the theft of a passport. It suited him if Merstead didn't because he needed time. He didn't want to get delayed by having to answer questions from the police. If that happened, he would have to call Crowder. And then he would have to tell him about Freestone and explain what he had done with his body. He hadn't heard that a corpse had been found in the River Arun, or off the beach at Littlehampton, but then he hadn't used his mobile phone to check the internet and he wasn't about to now. Strathen would be monitoring the news and alert him if that was the case.

Marvik was keen to crack on with examining the contents of the box. Julie told him to call her extension using the phone in the corner of the room if he needed anything further, and when he had finished. Left alone, Marvik applied himself to his task. As he lifted out the buff-coloured folders, each marked up in black felt pen in bold lettering and numbered, much like those in his safe deposit box, he mentally ticked them off the contents list and steadily ploughed his way through them.

Eerika and Dan's personal belongings from both from the house and the boat were listed and they matched with the items he had viewed in his own files. But again he noted there was no mention of their computers, or any disks, either in the house or boat contents. Something jarred at the back of his mind but he couldn't grasp what it was. Irritated that this vague thought refused to crystallize, he ploughed on, hoping that whatever it was that eluded him would come to him later.

There was a file on the sale of the house, including the valuation reports, correspondence with the estate agents, buyers and their legal representatives. Freestone had been copied in to all the documentation. He hadn't found any corresponding file in Freestone's cottage but that could have been destroyed years ago. There were files on handling the probate of the estate.

There was no letter appointing Freestone as his guardian and nothing on the sale of *Vasa II,* so who had handled that? Where had that money gone? Maybe his parents hadn't owned the boat as he had believed. Perhaps they had leased it from a specialist dive boat charter and diving vessel hire company. That would have been perfectly normal. But there was no correspondence to that effect. And if they had hired a research vessel for their project in the Straits of Malacca then he would have expected more crew than just one man to be on board with them. Frederick Davington was the man who had alerted the authorities when Eerika and Dan had failed to surface. Two days later their bodies had been recovered.

When Marvik had briefly spoken to Davington he'd maintained they hadn't been engaged on any research project and there was no submerged wreck or notes to contradict that. Davington had died shortly after that.

Marvik's fingers hovered over a file marked 'Correspondence with the undertakers.' He didn't need to look in it to know what it contained. He sat back, remembering that blustery late-August morning when his parents' ashes had been scattered at sea. To this day he could never sail around the Needles without it flashing into his mind. At least the dispersal of ashes, unlike the memorial service, had been a very private affair with just him, Hugh Freestone, Frederick Davington and Michael Colmead on board the vessel hired by the undertakers especially for the task. He'd got through the ordeal by imagining himself on the craft for another reason. It hadn't been too difficult because how could two urns of ashes be his parents? He couldn't even recall who had said a few words before the ashes had been sprinkled on the sea. Perhaps no one had. But someone had at his parents' memorial service. He couldn't remember their names. It had been an event he had long ago obliterated from his memory. The time for being sensitive was long past.

Casting his mind back, he recalled a lean man with eyes and a forehead that reminded him of an eagle, a smaller, stouter man with a voice like chocolate, who he had despised, and a fierce-looking, slight woman with darting movements that reminded him of a bird pecking at the ground. He also remembered thinking angrily, how did they know what his parents were like? Who were they to speak about them? He was the only one qualified to do that. He was their son and their only relative. But his anger wasn't at the feeling that imposters were talking about his parents, but that he didn't recognize the people they were speaking of. He'd felt dazed by the fact that he'd become so distant from them for the last six years of their lives.

Eagerly, he searched and found the relevant folder. There hadn't been copies of this in his safe deposit box, not even an order of service. Perhaps Freestone had kept hold of that and had subsequently destroyed it when Marvik hadn't expressed any desire to retain one. Maybe he'd even said so at the time. He couldn't remember. It had all been a bit of a blur.

The paperwork stated that the service had been held here in Southampton at the National Oceanography Centre. The speakers had been Dr Victor Lanbury, Professor Lawrence Ansler and Dr Letitia Galt. Where were they now? They would know of his parents' expeditions and hopefully more about the final one in 1997. Perhaps there was a contact number and address for each of them, although they all could have moved on since then, and probably had. Maybe the file on his parents' research papers would tell him more.

He located it and saw that there was a note beside each research project detailing which institution the papers had been passed on to and who had handled that distribution. He wondered why copies of this hadn't been passed on to him. His father's research had been distributed by Dr Lanbury and Professor Ansler to the National Maritime Museum in London, the Scottish Association for Marine Science on the west coast of Scotland, and the National Oceanography Centre at Southampton University, according to their subject matter. Dr Galt had handled his late mother's research, which had been allocated to the Maritime Archaeology Trust in Southampton and the Nautical Archaeology Society at Fort Cumberland in Portsmouth. He scrutinized the dates. There was nothing listed after 1991.

He replaced everything in the box and rang through to Julie, noting it was just before five. The day had raced away. He told her he had found nothing of significance and certainly nothing that could throw any light on where Michael Colmead was. He asked her to keep him informed if Michael contacted her or returned to his office, and to let her know of the partners' decision on whether or not to refer the matter to the police. Donald Merstead made no attempt to speak to him. Marvik didn't even know if he was in his office. Perhaps he was and was watching him leave the building. Could he be involved? Marvik would keep an open mind on that.

He didn't know what time the central library closed but he walked swiftly across the park to the grey-stone building to find it already shut. He could use his mobile phone to search the internet but he'd prefer a computer where his activities couldn't be traced.

He headed back to his boat in Ocean Village Marina but before reaching there, he turned into an internet café that he and Strathen had used not long ago while on a mission for Crowder and the National Intelligence Marine Squad. There he ordered a coffee and a sandwich and sat at one of the computer terminals. The café was busy with students, many of whom were using their own devices, but there were two men and a woman who, like him, either wanted to surf the net in privacy or didn't own a device with internet access.

He searched first for Dr Letitia Galt and was delighted when several results flashed up, including links to her website and to some social media accounts. Clicking on her website, he read that she was now Professor Galt and had been involved in marine explorations around the world, most specifically in the Mediterranean and the Indian Ocean. Marvik recalled what Sarah Redburn had said to him in that café in Swanage before her death. *I've worked in the Solent, the Mediterranean and the Indian Ocean.* Was there the possibility that she had worked with Professor Galt?

Avidly, he read on. Galt had made a name for herself while working on a major marine exploration in the Sargasso Sea funded jointly by American and British nautical institutions to find the wreck of the *Cessabit,* a 236-foot paddle steamer that was highly successful as a blockade runner during the American Civil War, making frequent trips between England, Bermuda and North Carolina. It was wrecked in November 1863 and Galt and her team successfully located it in 1996.

She'd since been involved in projects for private consultancies, government agencies and trusts. And she was currently project director for an exploration off Portland Harbour, Dorset, the SS *Carrick*, a cargo ship, shipwrecked in a storm in January 1920. Marvik knew that the coastline around Portland was treacherous, making it fruitful ground for the exploration of wrecks. The Royal Isle of Portland was less than fifty nautical miles west, which was good news — it wouldn't take him long to reach by boat. It was a small island, being only four and a half miles long by one and three-quarters of a mile wide, joined to the mainland by a narrow causeway from Chesil Beach and by a road to the seaside town of Weymouth. Marvik guessed Professor Galt was using Portland Marina as her base, either that or Weymouth. A phone call would quickly give him the answer.

He continued with his research, this time keying in Professor Lawrence Ansler. He read that Ansler had been an expert in undersea robotics with extensive experience in the Arctic, Marvik's father's field of expertise. He found references to Ansler's expeditions, some of which had been with Professor Dan Coulter. It came as something of a shock for Marvik to see his father's name on the screen. He had never searched the internet for information on his parents. Maybe he should, although he didn't think he would gain much from it, them being dead for so long. If he did find any references, they were certain to have been taken from the research papers donated to the various institutions. He discovered that Professor Lawrence Ansler had been attached to the Scottish Association for Marine Science and had died in 1999.

Next he looked up Dr Victor Lanbury. Again, he learned that Lanbury was also an expert in the Arctic and an oceanographer like Dan Coulter. Lanbury had been involved in deep-sea systems, climate change and polar science. But Marvik could find no recent reference to him; the last had been in 2003. He couldn't find an obituary or any notice of his death though, so he hoped that Lanbury was still in the land of the living.

His hand hovered over the keyboard. Then, taking a deep breath, he keyed in his father's name. He could no longer afford to be squeamish where his parents were concerned. There wasn't a great deal, just a few references to his work and his two publications, which were available online. They had been written in the 1980s and were about his Arctic explorations. Marvik also found references to his death along with that of Eerika's, stating that they had been killed in an underwater tremor while diving in the Straits of Malacca, offering no explanation or speculation of why they had been there. There was very little on his mother on the internet, just some mention of her expeditions and some background on her upbringing in Finland, where her mother had also been a marine archaeologist and her father a lecturer in Nordic Literature at the University of Helsinki.

Marvik rose and returned to his boat where, using his basic pay-as-you-go phone, he called Portland Marina and received confirmation that Professor Letitia Galt and her dive boat RV *Oyster* was indeed moored there. They were expected to be there for the next couple of days.

Good. He'd make for Portland and put in on the visitors' berths. But no sooner had he made the decision when Strathen called him.

'Thought you might like to know I've located the *Golden Fleece*.'

'Well, don't tell Jason.'

'Very droll. The Commodore of the Fairey Owners Club told me the boat has recently been sold by a Nigel Jellicoe, who had sold it to a semi-retired man who lives on the Isle of Wight. The Commodore doesn't know who, but he said he'd get Jellicoe to contact me. He wouldn't give me Jellicoe's number — irritating but the correct procedure — so I thought I'd ring round the marinas on the Isle of Wight, starting with those in East and West Cowes.'

Strathen had the advantage of knowing most of the marina staff, having put into both marinas several times on his powerful motor cruiser.

'She's moored at Shepards Wharf Marina, West Cowes. The owner is a Roland Culverham, who lives in Cowes. I thought a trip across the Solent to see the *Golden Fleece* might be in order. Do you want to come?'

Marvik hesitated. He wanted to find out what Professor Letitia Galt could remember about his mother but even if he headed to Portland tonight it would be too late to see her and one more night wasn't going to make much difference. And he was curious to know why the picture of the *Golden Fleece* had been inside Freestone's fishing rod.

He said, 'I'll pick you up at Hamble Marina in thirty minutes.'

CHAPTER SIX

The Solent crossing from Hamble to Cowes took twenty minutes and during that time Marvik updated Strathen on his research. Strathen agreed that talking to Professor Galt seemed to be the best way forward. She might also be able to give Marvik Dr Lanbury's whereabouts. If she couldn't, then Strathen said he would obtain them.

Julie Pembroke had called Marvik as he'd made for Hamble to tell him that the partners had decided to wait until Monday morning before reporting Colmead's disappearance to the police. 'Donald still thinks he's going to show up for work.'

Marvik doubted that was Donald's thought. In reality he and his partners would be spending the weekend carrying out an emergency audit of Colmead's client accounts trying to clean up any evidence of criminal activity on the part of their founding partner. He expected to hear from Donald Merstead at some stage with a request for him to say nothing to the police about a dead man's visit to his safe deposit box.

He told Strathen about the memorial service and the dispersal of the ashes, surprising himself by confiding his emotions, something he had never expressed to anyone. But then he'd never told anyone about those events, not even Langton, the army psychiatrist. He and Strathen went back a long way. They'd joined the Marines together, served together and faced danger, death and injury together.

He said, 'I never had the chance to say goodbye. I know many people don't but with them being away for so long before their deaths, I found it hard to believe they were dead. I didn't recognize the two people Galt, Lanbury and Ansler were talking about at the memorial service. I felt sure they must have got it wrong. And the scattering of the ashes was, I felt, disgusting. How could it be them? Again, common enough emotions, I know.'

'Doesn't make you feel any better or different though. It was very much the same for me, except I was much, much younger. When my father died, his body was flown home from China and buried in the family plot in the local churchyard, but at just five I was deemed too young to attend the committal. I remember feeling bewildered, as though there was some big secret attached to his death. For weeks and months I felt sure they had buried the wrong man. I was convinced he still lived. Even though I barely saw him because of how often he was away on diplomatic service, they should have let me say goodbye.' He shrugged. 'That's the way it was. And you'd never met or heard of Freestone, so it must have been bewildering for a stranger to show up and say you were now in his care. In my case, it was an aunt, my mother having died two years before my father. She did her best, albeit grudgingly I felt, though that could be my child's view, but I spent more time at school than I did at home. You grow up, you tell yourself it's the past. Nothing about it can affect you again. Christ, Art, we've handled far, far worse, since then, but it only takes one thing to crawl out of the woodwork and it all smacks you in the face as if you were back there, reliving all the memories and experiencing the same pain. My rude awakening was this.'

Strathen indicated his prosthetic leg. Marvik knew what torment Shaun had endured, both physical and mental. He'd seen it and been with him at the time and afterwards. But knowing wasn't enough. He couldn't *feel* it.

Strathen continued, 'It's not about being wounded, or losing a limb. I've come to terms with that. And it's not so bad. There's many far worse off than me.'

Marvik knew that.

'It was those faces around me, of my relatives, with that same pitying expression which I remembered seeing all those years ago as an orphaned child. Except this time I didn't feel so much bewildered as hateful towards them. Then there were the snatches of conversation in the hospital when they visited me — "Well at least you're financially secure." "It's not as though you need to find a job." "You don't need to work." "You can put the Marines behind you and move on." "You can have the best adaptations, the best prosthetic limbs, the staff to assist you." I felt like swearing at them. I expect I did.'

'Couldn't blame you if you had.'

'You see, I remembered the relatives at the house after father's funeral, and the same conversation. "Well, at least he'll be all right, his father has left him very well off." "He's too young to remember him much." "He'll want for nothing." No, only a father and mother.' Strathen shook his head in amazement. 'I guess they meant well back then and more recently, but I couldn't stomach it. I banned all visitors from the hospital, except you and some of our fellow commandos. I've never replied to cards, letters or calls. They probably think I'm bitter and taking being disabled badly. Let them. It's not their fault. It's mine. Maybe one day I'll return to the family seat and invite them all round for a big do. Perhaps when I get married.'

'Anyone in mind?'

'No, but I'll let you know when there is.'

Marvik wondered if it was Helen. He was surprised to find he hoped not. Not because he thought Helen unsuitable for Strathen, or the reverse, but because of the stab of regret that told him Helen might just mean more to him than he'd thought.

He was glad they'd reached Cowes and action beckoned. He was curious to see the *Golden Fleece* but not optimistic that it might tell them anything about the missing computer disk, his parents' last voyage or Freestone's murder.

Marvik swung the boat into the River Medina behind the Red Funnel car ferry from Southampton. The river split the town of Cowes in half, east and west. There was a marina on both sides. Marvik made to the west and the visitors' berths of Shepards Wharf.

Strathen alighted nimbly and tied off as Marvik silenced the engine. They made their way to the marina office and, after exchanging a few pleasantries with the staff, Strathen said they'd come to see Culverham's Fairey Swordsman but had got delayed. Strathen said he'd been unable to get in touch with Culverham to let him know. 'I tried his telephone number without joy,' he lied. 'I must have entered it incorrectly.'

Within minutes, with a skill that Marvik admired, Strathen had Culverham's mobile number, his address — an apartment on the exclusive Parade on the waterfront of the small town — the berth number of the boat, and more. It transpired that Culverham was a consultant in the petro-chemical industry and very much in demand by his company, often having to travel to Europe, India and Russia to assist on projects. He was a bachelor, no kids and had kept a boat in the marina for some years but in early April had sold his modern one for a classic.

'It amazed us because he'd said nothing about it and we didn't think the Fairey Swordsman was his type of boat,' the staff member told them. 'Don't get me wrong,' he hastily added, 'they're beautiful boats, but Roland's previous boat was modern, fast and sleek.'

Perhaps he just fancied a change, thought Marvik, as they made their way by the lights of the pontoon to the *Golden Fleece*. 'Culverham doesn't sound much of a fishing rod sort of man to me.'

'It takes all sorts,' was Strathen's reply. 'Culverham might be a friend of Freestone's and bought the rod for him as a present, or loaned it to him and had forgotten he'd stuffed a picture of his new boat inside it.'

Marvik looked at him sceptically.

'Or Freestone could have been given the rod at some point by the boat's previous owner, Nigel Jellicoe. Yes, I know that also sounds doubtful, but I'll check with him when he phones me back, and if he doesn't contact me, I'll get his number and address somehow.'

Marvik never doubted that. He did wonder though if this wasn't a wild goose chase.

'There's the boat.'

A new blue canvas awning stretched across the sleek classic motor cruiser and over the helm. The teak deck had been recently renewed and there were new cleats and deck fittings. Navy blue curtains were pulled across what looked like recently restored hardwood window surrounds, but it was the stern of the boat that drew Marvik's sharp attention and surprise.

'The name's been changed!' They weren't looking at the *Golden Fleece* written boldly on the transom but at the *Phorcys*. 'It is the right boat, isn't it?'

'I'm certain it is,' Strathen replied with conviction. 'There aren't two of this kind in the marina.'

'But to change the name of a classic boat like this doesn't make sense — its history is a huge part of its value,' Marvik said.

'Maybe Culverham isn't sentimental.'

'Then he wouldn't have purchased this boat.'

'Perhaps he despises the film *Jason and the Argonauts*.'

Marvik smiled. 'Why hasn't he told the marina staff of the name change?'

'Maybe he hasn't had the time.'

'It's bad luck to change a boat's name.'

'Depends how superstitious you are.'

'I remember the legend being told to me by my mother.' Marvik paused, realizing it was the first time he'd spoken about his childhood memories with her. The fact that he had seemed a natural extension of his earlier conversation with Strathen. 'She told me that every vessel is recorded by name in the "Ledger of the Deep", and is known personally to Poseidon, the god of the sea. To change the name of a boat without consulting him is said to invoke his wrath. There's an elaborate ceremony involved. I've never been to one but I'm told it involves a lot of champagne.'

'It does, good stuff too. The ruler of the deep won't be fobbed off by cheap plonk, and much of it gets poured into the sea, which to my mind is a terrible waste.' Strathen straightened up from examining the hull. 'There has to be a name purging ceremony. I went to one years ago. You offer at least half the champagne to Poseidon by pouring it in the sea, then more champagne is needed for the renaming ceremony immediately after the purge. Not to mention even more to appease the gods of the winds, assuring you of fair winds and smooth seas. And everyone ends up well and truly sozzled.'

'I'm sure the marina staff would have remembered such an occasion, and Culverham couldn't have conducted the ceremony elsewhere because the boat is registered in the marina as the *Golden Fleece*.'

'Which means he hasn't gone through the ritual, and he's forgotten to tell them the new name. Maybe he's been called away on business.'

But Marvik's mind was racing because as he recalled more of the ceremony, the thought that had been nagging at the back of his mind when reviewing the papers from his safe deposit box and at the solicitor's office crystallized. 'All trace of the old name needs to be wiped out, including that on the engine and the logbook, and that's what's missing from my parents' papers. There's no mention of a logbook for *Vasa II* in any of the paperwork I've seen. So what's happened to it?'

'Could it have been overlooked?'

'And ended up where?'

'Perhaps your parents didn't keep a log.' But Strathen hastily continued, 'Yeah, I know, impossible, they would have done. Sounds as though someone went to a great deal of trouble in 1997 to keep whatever it was they were doing secret.'

'And they're still doing it.' Marvik thought of Sarah Redburn's and Hugh Freestone's deaths. 'I'm not sure

Culverham will give us any answers but it's worth talking to him.'

'I'll try his number.'

Strathen did but shook his head. 'He might be working abroad. We could take a chance he's in and just not answering his phone, and call on him.'

It could give them a great deal more information. 'Let's look at his boat first,' Marvik said. 'There might be some paperwork on board that might tell us more about him, and why he gave Freestone a fishing rod with a picture of his boat in it.'

'If he did.'

'We might be lucky and find Jellicoe's contact details, which would save you time searching for it. Which means we have to—'

'Break in, I know. Seems sacrilegious on such a beautiful old boat but if needs must.'

Marvik, after checking no one was about, and there was no CCTV camera over them, unzipped the canvas awning and climbed on board. Strathen followed. Marvik reached out to the hatch. Surprisingly he found it open, just as Colmead's boat had been.

'Careless or forgetful?' posed Strathen.

'Perhaps Culverham thinks the boat is too easily traced for thieves to steal so is casual about locking it.'

'Someone somewhere will have an illegal market for this kind of classic boat.'

Strathen descended into the salon while Marvik checked out the on-board navigational equipment. It, unlike the boat's vintage, was bang up to date and included speed, depth and wind indicators, compass, autopilot, radar, navigational and electronic chart system. With some manipulation, using a device Marvik had fitted on his penknife, he switched on the ignition and saw that the last journey undertaken had been from Chichester Marina to here on 25 April.

'Beautiful craft,' Strathen said, as Marvik joined him in the main cabin.

It was and it had been lovingly restored and well cared for. The salon, where they stood, had a U-shaped dinette, with the heads opposite and a galley with a gas oven, grill, two-burner gas hob, twin sinks, worktop, crockery cupboard, cutlery drawer and fridge. The latter was empty. Beyond was the forward cabin with its V-shaped berth and shelving above, which, like the fridge, was empty, and there was no bedding on the berths.

Marvik stepped into the master cabin, aft, where there was a large double berth to starboard, again with no bedding. He searched the drawers underneath, the single wardrobe and drawers, and the heads compartment.

'No clothes or bedding on board,' he announced.

'And no paperwork,' said Strathen, completing his search. 'No logbook either. He might have taken it to his apartment.'

Alighting, Strathen once again examined the name. 'It looks to me as though it's been stuck on.' He manipulated a finger around the name. 'Short of using a knife on it, which would be vandalism, if it has been stuck on it's not going to be easily removable.' He straightened up. 'Want to try Culverham's apartment?'

'Might as well now that we're here.'

They made their way through the narrow streets of Cowes. Marvik usually avoided the town like the plague in August as it became a mecca for the sailing fraternity during the international sailing regatta of Cowes Week. But tonight, early in the season, it was eerily deserted, perhaps because of the damp drizzling rain. 'Seeing as you're such an expert on the origination of the name *Golden Fleece*, any idea what *Phorcys* means, or where it originates? Sounds Greek to me.'

'It is, if my classical education serves me right. In Greek mythology, Phorcys was the ancient sea god of the hidden dangers of the deep.'

'That being a reasonably apt explanation of my parents' deaths,' Marvik said thoughtfully.

'Seems so. Interesting, eh? Phorcys was the personification of the dangers of the sea's depths and the creatures that dwelt within it. He and his wife, Ceto, were also gods of the largest of sea creatures. "Ceto" means whale, or sea monster. Their children were dangerous sea monsters.'

'Not me then.'

'Some of the scum we've fought against and prevented from inflicting atrocities on innocent people might not agree.'

No. Flashes of those missions sped through Marvik's mind, some causing him to recoil, others to tense. There had been victories though. It had been an adrenaline-fuelled life that seemed a million years ago. Another era, another planet.

Strathen continued. 'Among their sea monster children were Scylla the crab, who devoured passing sailors, and the three Gorgons — "terrible ones" — Stheno, Euryale and Medusa, whose petrifying gaze is thought to have created the dangerous underwater rocks and reefs of the sea that catch unwary sailors. The dangers beneath the waves were important for mariners in Ancient Greece to know and avoid.'

'And for current ones,' Marvik replied, emerging from a narrow alleyway on to the promenade. Across the Solent, the mainland was obliterated by the sweeping, misty drizzle. He turned to view Culverham's apartment block, a modern building of seven storeys. Many were holiday lets and would be vacant at present. Strathen, locating the number of Culverham's flat, pressed his finger on the buzzer.

There was no reply.

'I'll try his phone again in the morning.'

Back on board Marvik's boat, Strathen cast off. Marvik headed across the Solent to Hamble, his mind full of thoughts of his parents and their fate. '*Phorcys* is a strange name for Culverham to choose,' he said, breaking the silence.

'Maybe he just liked the sound of it.'

'Do you really believe that?' Marvik turned from the helm to study Strathen.

'I would have done if it hadn't been for the photograph of the boat stuffed in Freestone's fishing rod when you say he never fished in his life, and now he won't be able to. Somehow Culverham is involved with Freestone and with what happened to your parents in 1997, hence the name change meaning "hidden dangers of the deep". But what hidden dangers? Apart from the underwater tremor that killed them. No one would have known of that. Not unless . . .'

'Unless it wasn't a natural phenomenon but an explosive device deliberately planted to kill them, much like that incendiary device in my cottage. The name Culverham doesn't feature in any of my parents' papers. Did he know them? How? When? Is he in danger?'

'He could be dead like Freestone and possibly Colmead.'

'Perhaps we should have checked his apartment.'

'If he is dead then it makes no difference.'

'But it might have told us more about him.'

'I'll see if I can find out more through my searches and from Jellicoe when I finally get to speak to him.'

And Marvik thought Culverham was another name he'd like to check out with Professor Galt.

'Are you coming back to the apartment?'

'No. I'll head for Portland Marina. I want to catch Professor Galt early in the morning before she leaves for her dive.'

Marvik left the engine running as Strathen gathered up his rucksack and alighted. With a wave and a 'Good luck' he was gone. Marvik swung the boat round and headed west for Portland in the strengthening wind. The visibility was poor and grew steadily worse as the drizzle turned to a more persistent downpour.

He considered the fact that there was no record of *Vasa II*'s logbook. Had it been lost or stolen? If the latter, why? There had also been no paperwork on the sale of *Vasa II*. He again wondered if that was because the boat had been leased and had been returned to the boat hire company. Perhaps the logbook had inadvertently been left on board. That was possible but Marvik didn't see how his parents' computers could have been overlooked. And even if *Vasa II* had been leased, there should have been some record showing that. Someone must surely know more about the boat and about his parents' movements around the time of their deaths.

No one had contacted him over the years, but that wasn't surprising because as soon as he was eighteen and no longer under the jurisdiction of his guardian, he'd given Colmead instructions to handle all enquiries. He'd had no interest in being notified of them, so he had no idea how many there had been, if any. Freestone had never approached him either, and Marvik hadn't kept in touch. *Now it's too late*, he thought sadly with a twinge of guilt at the memory of Freestone's body in the river.

It took him longer than he had anticipated to reach Portland Marina because of the weather, and he was thankful when he entered the more sheltered waters of the harbour in the early hours of the morning. He moored up on the visitors' berths and hit his bunk. His thoughts returned to Sarah Redburn and the sad, small gathering of mourners at her funeral in early April. It had angered him that there hadn't been more, and Sarah's executor had annoyed him even further when he had tackled him about it. The thin acid-faced solicitor called Brookfield had retorted that he'd placed advertisements in all the pertinent newspapers and the marine archaeological press so it was hardly his fault that few had seen fit to attend. It was clear to Marvik that Brookfield had discharged his duty regarding Sarah's meagre estate without going the extra mile.

Sarah's previous boss had been there — Caroline Shaldon, owner of the marine consultancy Sarah had just finished working for at the time of her death. Marvik recalled her, a dark-haired woman with a good figure, wide mouth and deep-brown eyes, in her early forties. She'd been on the curt side when Marvik had managed a few words with her before she'd hurried off to answer a call. She and the others Marvik had managed to speak to after the funeral, including Sarah's former boyfriend, didn't recall Sarah talking about Dr Eerika Marvik.

He mentally switched off all thoughts of the recent events and let the wind and the movement of the sea send him to sleep. Later that morning he hoped Professor Galt would be able to throw some light on his parents' last days, but perhaps that was just wishful thinking on his part.

CHAPTER SEVEN

Saturday

After a shower, shave and quick breakfast Marvik made his way to the marina office, paid his visitor's mooring fee and asked for the location of RV *Oyster*. He had heard a boat go out very early and hoped it hadn't been Professor Galt's. He was informed it was on L pontoon, which was on the opposite side of the marina to the visitors' berths and that Professor Galt was staying on board with her skipper, Guy Kranton, while the other members of the dive team were staying at a hotel on the Island. Marvik made for the *Oyster*.

It was a fresh, crisp morning with a cloudless sky. There was only a gentle breeze coming off the sea. Across the bay, behind the two giant stone breakwaters, built by convict labour in 1845, was the seaside resort of Weymouth. Stretching out eastwards from it were the white cliffs of the Purbeck coast, where in March he'd met Sarah Redburn in Swanage.

He'd slept well and felt refreshed but was steeling himself for disappointment from his forthcoming meeting. He speculated on what Professor Galt would be like and what she might tell him. He didn't want gushing praise and reminiscence, he wanted facts. *If* there were any to provide.

He was pleased to find RV *Oyster* on its berth. It was smaller than he had expected but was nevertheless very impressive with a crane and winch and other diving equipment on deck. He was about to hail the boat when a wiry woman in her sixties appeared from the main cabin. He knew her at once, not just from the photographs on her website, but from all those years ago at the memorial service. She had aged, obviously, but there was still that sparrow-like appearance about her.

'Professor Galt?'

Her small head shot up and her keen grey eyes seemed to bore into him. 'Yes.'

'I wonder if I could have a word with you.'

Impatiently she dashed a glance at her watch. 'I am very busy. What's it about?'

'My parents.'

Her eyes narrowed as she clearly tried to place him.

He put her out of her misery. 'I'm Art Marvik.'

'My God, Eerika's boy!'

He smiled. 'Yes, but no longer a boy.'

'You are to a woman of sixty-four. Come on board,' she said warmly, waving her thin, suntanned arms at him.

'I don't want to hold you up,' he said, climbing on to the boat. But he did want to speak to her urgently.

'Why not join us?'

He knew she meant on the dive. 'I don't follow in my parents' footsteps. Well, not in that respect. But I do have a boat. I'm moored up on the visitors' berths. And I have pursued a career at sea. The Royal Marines.'

'Is that where you got those?' She pointed to his scars and, not bothering to wait for an answer, continued, 'Makes you look interesting. Don't want to talk about it, I expect. Don't blame you.'

'Not much point is there?'

'No. I remember your guardian told me you'd joined up.'

'When was that?' he enquired casually, disguising his interest. There was no sign of her skipper, Kranton. They were alone and he was glad of that. He hoped it would stay that way until he could get some information from her.

'Oh, yonks ago. Coffee? We've got half an hour before the rest of the crew show up. Guy, my skipper has joined them for coffee and breakfast in the hotel. He hates my brew and I never eat breakfast.'

Marvik accepted the offer and hoped Kranton and the others would take their time.

'It must be twenty years since their deaths. Such a bloody waste.' She heaped two gigantic spoons of instant coffee into two large mugs. 'Milk?'

'Please.' It would taste like sludge otherwise. Now he understood Kranton's need to take coffee elsewhere. She sloshed in some milk and, as the kettle boiled, poured in the water and swished a spoon around. 'Help yourself to sugar and biscuits.' She jerked her narrow head at the table. 'Sit.'

Maybe he should bark and wag his tail, but he sat and suppressed a smile. He warmed to her forthright nature and her seemingly unbounded enthusiasm.

Crisply, but not in an unfriendly manner, she said, 'OK, so what do you want to know? I take it this isn't a social visit.'

'You spoke at my parents' memorial service.'

'Yes. I arranged it.'

Marvik hadn't known that. But then there was no reason why he should have done. No one had asked his permission to speak at it, and neither had they requested additional information from him. Perhaps Freestone had protected him from such requests.

Professor Galt continued. 'I had to liaise with your guardian. What was his name, Freeman?'

'Freestone, Hugh.'

'That's it. And the solicitor, Colmead. And of course, I had to liaise with him over the distribution of your parents' research material. I dealt with Eerika's papers, while Victor Lanbury and Lawrence Ansler dealt with your father's. They were both colleagues of his. Lanbury is an expert on climate change and the Arctic, and Ansler was a robotics specialist. He's since died.'

Marvik had discovered that from the archived files. He said, 'I'd like to know what my parents were working on when they died.'

'Wouldn't we all.'

He eyed her steadily. 'You didn't find any material outlining the project in the Straits of Malacca?'

'Not a thing. But you should have a list of all their projects and who received what.'

'I have, but there's nothing listed for 1997.'

'No, and not for the six years before that either.'

'Nothing at all?' he asked, her words confirming what he had discovered in the files, and yet hadn't really wondered at — until now.

'Not a single word. Maybe they thought they'd take a break from research, although I would have said that was highly unlikely, especially for six years. They were both passionate about their subjects, and they were both workaholics. It was as if they were on another planet during that time, as far as research went. Although they must have written to you and you must have seen them.'

'I did.'

'And did they say what they were engaged on?'

'No.'

She looked slightly disbelievingly at him. He'd been despatched to England and school in 1991. His pulse picked up a beat or two. Was that a coincidence? He was beginning to think not. But why would they have wanted him out of the way?

'Could they have been writing a book either individually or jointly during that time?' he asked, although that hardly warranted sending their only child away.

'I found no record of it and I would have done, or rather that clerk, Bell, would have done. Unless the idiot thought it was rubbish and destroyed it, as he might have done with other research papers. I wrote to Colmead telling him I thought it odd that there was nothing for the period 1991 to 1997.'

He hadn't seen any letter about this. Had it been destroyed or stolen by Dewell? Was it possibly the burnt fragments of paper in Colmead's fireplace? Had Colmead or his confederate or abductor burned that letter? But why would they? Perhaps because, until now, no one had enquired about that missing period. Neither had he, only 1997.

She continued. 'Colmead told me that Bell had catalogued all the research material from the house and that found on *Vasa II*. He insisted that we had everything and no one had been given access to Eerika and Dan's material before then, except, of course, Davington, their assistant.'

'Did you ask Davington about the research material?'

'Yes.' She took a gulp of coffee, impervious to its scalding heat. She was drinking it black. *She must have a mouth like asbestos*, Marvik thought.

'He said there wasn't anything other than what was on the boat and in the house, but he was very evasive and edgy,' Galt went on. 'I thought he might have passed some papers on to someone else who was hoping to capitalize on your parents' research at a later date. I was very suspicious of his motives, especially if your parents *had* been on the trail of the *Flor de la Mar*, a 400-ton Portuguese frigate built in Lisbon during 1502.'

'Why do you think that?' Marvik asked. It was the first he'd heard about a Portuguese wreck although Sarah had thought they were wreck-diving but hadn't said for what.

'Because the *Flor de la Mar* was carrying the largest treasure ever assembled in the history of the Portuguese navy, when she and four other ships went down in a violent storm on 20 November 1511. Any marine archaeologist or wreck hunter in the Straits of Malacca would be searching for it. Its exact location is unknown, because of the crap maps at the time. I don't think they could have located her because no one's stepped up to the plate to say they've found it, and Davington died before I could pursue it with him and before I could ask him where Eerika and Dan's backup disks were.'

'They both used computers then?' Marvik said keenly.

She eyed him as though he was an imbecile. 'Of course they did, Marvik,' she answered curtly. Then she relented a little. 'But they would also have recorded their work in note form because computers weren't as reliable then as they are now. Back then computers had a nasty habit of failing in the middle of your work, and they didn't automatically save everything as you went along, which meant you could inadvertently lose hours of typing if you didn't remember to physically hit "save" every so often. You could also be working in a very harsh environment, without access to electricity, so pen and paper were always your backup. And that was another question I asked Colmead — where the devil were their computers?'

Precisely, thought Marvik. But why had this matter not been pursued? Or had it, and Freestone or Colmead had not informed him about the outcome. Was it something they felt he needed protecting from? But he couldn't fathom why. Could the written notes, the details of that fateful last expedition, have been in that dark-blue notebook that had the pages torn out of it and the computer disk taped to the back of it? But where were the other notes from 1991 onwards? Eagerly, he put his full attention back on the birdlike creature across the table from him.

'Lanbury, Ansler and I should have been given access to everything. But we only got the written material and that, as I've said, was pre-1991.'

Marvik's mind raced with thoughts. 'What was Colmead's answer?'

She took another gulp of coffee. 'He said there had been some considerable confusion after the underwater tremor had killed your parents, and it was believed their computers and disks had been seized by the Indonesian police and either lost or inadvertently destroyed by them.'

'Why?'

She shrugged her bony shoulders. 'Perhaps they thought your parents were international terrorists or spies. Yes, unlikely, but people can get paranoid. But it's possible the

Indonesian government thought your parents might have found the *Flor de la Mar* and they wanted to make sure they got a percentage of the treasure. When they discovered that wasn't the case, and after having taken all the stuff off the boat, they didn't want to admit to the British Consulate that they'd seized it, so they simply lost it.'

And that to Marvik looked to be the official line but not the truth. Maybe Galt really believed that. Maybe not.

She said, 'We weren't permitted to enter your parents' house to go through the paperwork and files. We had to be content to look at the boxes of material the clerk brought back to the solicitor's office in Southampton and go through them there. I also wrote to your guardian, Freestone, although I had to address the letter via Colmead, to ask if you knew anything about the whereabouts of your parents' computers, disks and research papers for that period, and Colmead wrote back to say you didn't, which sounds about right from what you're saying.'

Freestone hadn't asked him, Marvik was certain. Maybe he hadn't wanted to bother or upset him. Or perhaps Colmead had never made that enquiry of Freestone. He drank his coffee with questions swirling round his head. Before he could speak again, Galt ploughed on.

'I asked my contacts and colleagues in the profession if anyone knew what they had been working on since 1991 and where the rest of their research material might be, but no one claimed to know a thing. I was in the Sargasso Sea for much of that time on the trail of the *Cessabit* so had lost touch with Eerika. I returned to the UK late in 1996 after locating the wreck. I wondered who might have been funding your parents' exploration but no one came forward at the memorial service to say they'd had a connection with your parents from 1991 to 1997, and I've never come across any colleagues since then who have claimed to know where they were or what they were doing.'

'Did you keep a copy of your correspondence with Colmead?'

'Might have done somewhere in the tip of my house. It might take an age for me to find it. Colmead should have it though — ask him.'

Marvik simply nodded. He wasn't going to say that Colmead had gone missing. He asked her if she knew a man called Culverham or had come across him in relation to his parents. Her blank look provided the answer.

Voices sounded from the quayside. Professor Galt, also hearing them and obviously recognizing them, rose. Marvik followed suit. A large, muscular man in his early sixties stepped down into the cabin, filling the space even though the boat wasn't small. His light-brown eyes beneath a prominent forehead flicked between them, the fine lines at the corner of his eyes on his rugged, strong-featured, weathered and bearded face creased up.

'This is Art Marvik,' Professor Galt introduced. 'Marvik, this is my colleague, Guy Kranton.'

Marvik stretched out his hand. Kranton took it in a fierce vice-like grip with a puzzled air, then his expression registered surprise. 'You're related to Dr Eerika Marvik and Professor Dan Coulter?'

'My parents,' Marvik answered, returning the pressure of Kranton's handshake. The boat rocked again as more people boarded and the sounds of their conversation filtered into the cabin.

'I never met your parents, but I've heard so much about them and read their work. Are you joining us?'

Marvik supposed that was a natural assumption. 'No, I just needed a word with Professor Galt.' He turned to her. 'Do you know a woman called Sarah Redburn?' He deliberately used the present tense to see what reaction he got.

Only a gaze of bewilderment. 'No.' She emptied the remainder of Marvik's coffee into the sink and put the mugs there.

Kranton said, 'I'll check over the equipment and get the rest of the team organized. Nice to meet you, Mr Marvik.'

'It's Art.'

Kranton smiled and his bulky, bearded figure retreated to the deck.

Marvik turned to Galt. 'Sarah Redburn was a marine archaeologist who was working on a project at Eastbourne and was due to go to a new one in Gibraltar but she was killed in Dorset before she could.'

'An accident?'

Marvik could see Galt's mind was already on the dive and she was itching to get away. 'No. She was strangled.'

Galt frowned.

Marvik continued. 'I thought you might have come across her or worked with her on an exploration.'

'I meet so many young marine archaeologists. I take it she was young?'

'In her thirties. She worked for various consultancies, universities and charitable organisations. She was engaged by Nautilus for her last project.'

'Then Caroline Shaldon should be able to help you.'

Marvik didn't say he'd already had a brief word with her at Sarah's funeral.

'Caroline will be here some time over the next couple of days,' Galt said vaguely.

'Here? Why?' Marvik asked surprised.

'This research vessel belongs to her, or, I should say, to her company. We've hired it for the project. I've got to get a move on.' She didn't ask why he was interested in Sarah. Her mind was already on the day's task.

He followed her on deck. There were now four people on board including Kranton. The other man with him was in his mid-forties with dark hair and deep-brown, almost black eyes and a broad mouth. With them was a woman of about the same age as Sarah Redburn, mid-thirties, and a younger woman in her mid-twenties.

He said, 'Did you get to see the logbook for their boat *Vasa II*?'

'No, and that's another thing I queried with Colmead. The logbook could have given us an insight into why they were there and what they might have discovered, but he just came back with the same old twaddle, that the Indonesian authorities must have taken it. Maybe they did,' she sniffed.

Before alighting, he asked her if she had known Hugh Freestone before he had been appointed his guardian.

'No. Eerika never mentioned him. I suppose he could have been a friend or colleague of your father's.'

Possibly, but that still didn't explain why there was no official letter appointing him guardian. Perhaps Freestone had just assumed the role for his late friend. Marvik asked if she had a contact number for Dr Lanbury. She did, a mobile number. Marvik punched it into his phone.

She said, 'I don't think he'll have anything to tell you about your parents' research after 1991 or what they were doing in the Straits of Malacca when they died because he was as mystified as I was over the lack of material for that period, and he's never come across anything connected with it over the intervening years because if he had, he would have told me. If you find anything will you let me know?'

Marvik promised he would. He took her mobile number and made his farewells but instead of making for his boat, he headed for the nearest public telephone and called Dr Lanbury, hoping he wasn't in the Arctic. How old would he be now? About the same age as Professor Galt, mid to late sixties? Possibly older.

The phone was answered a little warily probably because Lanbury didn't recognize the number. Marvik quickly said that Professor Galt had given him his contact details and he introduced himself, but before he could go into explanations Lanbury leaped on the name and interrupted him, all trace of wariness gone, leaving only enthusiasm, excitement and warmth in his voice.

'Dan's son! My God, I've been wondering about you for years. I've been trying to find you.'

'Why?' Marvik asked, his heart beating a little faster.

'Where are you?'

'Portland, Dorset.'

'I'm in London. Can you get up here?'

'Today?'

'Yes. I can meet you in the members' lounge on the first floor of National Maritime Museum. How soon can you get here?'

There seemed no alternative and Marvik was as keen to speak to Lanbury as he was to speak to him, possibly about different subjects, but he'd soon establish whether or not that was the case. Marvik didn't know the times of the trains but he did know it took over three hours to reach London from nearby Weymouth. 'Hopefully I can get there by one. I'll call you again and let you know what train I'm on.'

'You can send me a text.'

'I'd prefer to call you.' Marvik wasn't going to risk being tracked by his mobile phone even though he could use the mission mobile.

'As you wish. I want to . . . No, it can wait.'

Marvik sincerely hoped so and that whatever Lanbury had to say would give him some clue as to why that computer disk had been taken by the mysterious James Dewell.

CHAPTER EIGHT

Marvik reached the impressive building of the National Maritime Museum shortly after one thirty. He'd called Dr Lanbury on a public pay phone from Weymouth railway station to relay his expected arrival time and was pleased and relieved the trains had run to time. He wondered what Lanbury was so excited about. Perhaps simply the thought he could talk to Dan Coulter's son.

On the train, in the small area between carriages, and alone, Marvik had updated Strathen using the mission mobile. He'd relayed that he'd missed the fact, or rather the significance of the fact, that there was no record of what his parents had been working on from 1991 to the time of their deaths in 1997. Strathen said he had tried Culverham's mobile phone and the line was dead. That was worrying. 'Perhaps he's dropped his phone and smashed it.'

But Marvik knew that, like him, Strathen didn't believe that. Although there was nothing concrete to indicate Culverham was involved in whatever was going on, there was the fact that a picture of the distinctive boat he'd only recently purchased had been hidden on Freestone's premises, and that Culverham had changed the boat's name to something that could connect with Marvik's parents' fate. That might all be coincidence. And there was nothing to say that the man who had sold the boat to Culverham could be the one involved. For all Marvik knew, Jellicoe could be Dewell the computer disk thief. He wondered if he should have asked Professor Galt if she recognized the name. He'd ask Dr Lanbury.

Strathen also relayed that he hadn't heard from Jellicoe, but he'd managed to track him down to an address just outside Chichester. 'He's a company director, so getting his contact details was fairly easy. He's not answering his home landline, and the receptionist at his company says he's away on business. She declined to give out his mobile number but has assured me she'll pass on the message that I'd like to talk to him about his previous boat, the *Golden Fleece*.'

Aside from that there wasn't much more that Strathen could do. He could find no trace of Amber Tunstone or Stuart Craven, nor any online backup files for Marvik's parents, and he said he had some client work to attend to.

Marvik headed for the members' lounge. He was glad Lanbury had suggested it because it would be more private than the public Compass Lounge and the other cafés in the museum. Lanbury must be a member or a patron of the museum. Both Marvik's parents had been lifetime patrons and he had continued the tradition, something he saw no need to tell Lanbury or anyone else.

He'd been to the museum many times in the past but not in recent years. He was as impressed now as he had been as a boy and something of that same thrill ran through him, but this time tainted with a sadness at the memories of being here with his parents. Often he had been left alone to explore the collections while his father met a colleague and his mother carried out research in the archives. Something tugged at the back of his mind — was it a memory of being here with her or with his father? Or was it closer to the present, something to do with those missing years and that disk? He had no time to consider it further though as he had reached the lounge.

Studying the occupants, he looked for one of the two men he remembered from the memorial service twenty years ago. He identified Dr Lanbury as the portly man with grey hair in the far right hand corner drinking coffee. He was wrong. A member of staff pointed out a lean man, with untidy silver hair framing a suntanned and freckled balding pate. He was sitting hunched over a laptop.

As Marvik addressed him, he looked up, startled. His sharp, blue, prominent eyes rapidly took in the scars on Marvik's face before registering the name as Marvik announced himself and held out his hand. Lanbury jumped up, almost knocking over his half-empty coffee cup, and grasped Marvik's hand with both hands.

'It's a great pleasure to meet you,' Lanbury cried excitedly, seeming not to want to let go. The warmth of his welcome was genuine. 'Please sit.' Lanbury waved him into a seat. The coffee cup once again shook perilously in its saucer but remained upright. 'Coffee? Lunch?'

'Coffee would be fine. I had some sandwiches on the train.'

'Of course, of course.' Lanbury summoned the waiter and gave the order for coffee as Marvik glanced around the air-conditioned lounge. It was fairly busy and there were people at adjoining tables but there was enough space between them to ensure their conversation would be private. Marvik was keen to get down to business. Lanbury was even keener.

Sitting forward across the table, Lanbury, who Marvik calculated must be in his early seventies, seemed infused with the same impatient air as Professor Galt. Marvik found that surprising when their research must often be laborious and painstaking but then the man in front of him and Galt both exuded passion for their subject. Their impatient attitude was an expression of their enthusiasm. Lanbury's manner, though, wasn't as brusque as Galt's.

'I'm delighted you've got in touch, Mr Marvik — it is mister, isn't it?' he added, seeming concerned that he might have given offence by using the incorrect form of address.

'Yes, and it's Art, please.'

Lanbury beamed at him. 'Good, good. As I said on the telephone, Art, I've been trying to contact you. I hoped you would agree to see me and here you are.' He eyed Marvik as though he'd appeared like the genie from the bottle.

Marvik couldn't help smiling. 'Why have you been trying to contact me?' Marvik repeated the question he'd asked on the phone earlier, but had to wait for a reply as his coffee arrived.

When the waiter had left, Lanbury sat forward, an earnest expression on his lined, ruddy countenance. 'I wondered if you had any papers on your father's research.'

'Everything was given to the relevant organizations. You oversaw that.' Marvik knew what was coming next. He wondered if Galt had called Lanbury while he had been heading here.

'I did indeed. It's just . . .' He sat back, eyeing Marvik intently as though he was wondering whether to trust him. No, Marvik reconsidered, whether he would upset him. Lanbury ran a hand over his head, and seemed to come to a decision. 'Not all your father's research papers were present when I and Professor Ansler went through them. There was no record of what Dan was working on from 1991 until the time of his and your mother's deaths in 1997. I thought you might know where those papers were.'

He only wished he did. But he was struck by the fact that Lanbury was asking about them now. Maybe he had enquired about them over the intervening years. Colmead, under instructions from Marvik, wouldn't have passed that on.

Marvik said, 'I believe Professor Galt asked about that at the time with my solicitor, Michael Colmead.'

'She probably did. And as you have spoken to her you no doubt know that we were told the papers and disks could have been destroyed by accident.'

'Professor Galt contacted you today?'

'Yes. About an hour ago. She said she'd given you my mobile number and she hoped I didn't mind, although she wasn't as polite as that.' Lanbury pulled a face. 'She has a somewhat abrupt manner, doesn't tolerate fools very easily and anyone who doesn't think and act like her, or do as she says, is not up to the mark in her book.'

'Including you?' Marvik smiled to soften the remark.

'Especially me.' Lanbury returned the gesture to show he wasn't fazed by Galt's opinion of him. 'She considers me to be a bumbling old idiot. It's of no consequence. It's just the way she is. But I'm afraid it doesn't always endear her to people, including sponsors. Despite her formidable reputation as a marine archaeologist she's been overlooked for many prestigious explorations because of her inability to hold her tongue, but then she always used to say she didn't have time to pussyfoot around sensitive souls and pander to egos. They either took her on her merit, which of course is excellent, or they could . . . well, you know. You can't change people, can you?'

Marvik agreed you couldn't.

Lanbury continued. 'Professor Galt didn't enquire about your *father's* diaries with the solicitor, though. I did.'

'By letter?' Marvik didn't remember seeing any evidence of that in the index of correspondence in the archived file. Could that and Galt's letter have been removed by the solicitor, or by Dewell when he had paid a visit to the storage company, according to Julie? Or perhaps the fragments of burnt paper in Colmead's bedroom fireplace with those initials on it — were from one or both letters?

Lanbury dashed that idea.

'No, I spoke to him over the telephone while I was going through all the papers after their deaths. Your father always kept notes of his research, and his personal thoughts, in small, dark-blue hardback notebooks but there were none from 1991 onwards.'

There was one, thought Marvik, *with the pages torn out and a computer disk strapped to the inside back cover.* 'Perhaps he changed his method and decided to keep everything on his computer?'

'No.' Lanbury shook his head with vigour.

'Why so certain?'

'I knew your father. He would never have trusted the almighty computer as the guardian of his research.' He scrutinized Marvik with a disappointed and bewildered air. 'Does this mean you don't have the diaries?'

Should Marvik fob him off? Say he had them and would need a couple of days to retrieve them and see where that led? Or should he tell the truth? He thought the latter, if only to see Lanbury's reaction. And Lanbury's words had sparked several more thoughts. He should have asked Professor Galt if his mother had kept diaries, either hardback ones or on computer or both. Galt hadn't mentioned them, only the missing disks.

'The only diaries I have are from my father's university days.'

'Ah, yes, Cambridge,' Lanbury said wistfully. 'Dan was reading science and physics while I was reading mathematics and fluid mechanics, but we shared two common interests, the Arctic and ocean turbulence. Like me, Dan, was fascinated at how the restless oceans shape our world. He was intrigued by the drift of objects, not only icebergs but also marine life and how some objects can move more speedily in ocean currents that are predictable and steady rather than the opposite. And how those same currents that carry floating objects play a much bigger role in conveying heat over great distances and depths affecting our climate and global warming. He'd be appalled now at the rate of the declining sea ice in the Arctic.'

Marvik, after years of shutting out the past, found that listening to Lanbury talking about his father was more pleasurable than he had anticipated. He was beginning to see his parents more as living beings than dead people. Despite the complications of the case and the fact that possibly his life, and the lives of others, depended on finding the truth, he was finding relief and comfort in this process of becoming reacquainted with them and bringing them to life.

Lanbury leaned a little further forward across the table, almost knocking over the coffee cup. Marvik felt like moving it well out of his reach but resisted. 'The Arctic Ocean is unique, as you most probably know. It's the world's smallest ocean, centring approximately on the North Pole. Have you been there?' he asked, as though he was querying if Marvik had been to Scotland or Cornwall.

Marvik said he had. Lanbury hadn't asked his occupation, he was too wrapped up in his desire to find those diaries and that suited Marvik fine. Lanbury hadn't even asked about the scars but that was of little interest to the scientist in front of him, who had the single-mindedness of a man in love with his work.

'It is also the world's largest confined ocean and its sea ice makes it a hostile environment for research from many perspectives, including marine exploration, as both Dan and Eerika knew. Dan and I were working there when he met your mother in 1979.'

Marvik knew that. His mother had been thirteen years younger than his father. She'd been assigned to work with the team at the Arctic examining shipwrecks and their movements in the ice flows.

Lanbury was still on his pet subject. Marvik didn't mind. He found it interesting listening to him.

'The Arctic Ocean is not matched by any other, and because of its uniqueness and its recent dramatic changes, it gives us a clear insight into climatic change and global warming.' Suddenly Lanbury stopped as though something had occurred to him. His eyes held a vague quality as though he was trying to remember what it was he was trying to recall.

Marvik was about to speak when Lanbury physically shrugged as though to shake off what had occurred to him and continued. 'My experience, like Dan's, was in measuring turbulence in oceanic and coastal systems. We have both been widely published. Me more so because I have been fortunate to live longer than your father. More recently I've been researching wave energy, looking at harnessing the power of the sea either through creating tidal lagoons, such as that in Swansea, utilizing wave energy, or generating energy through offshore wind turbines.' He stopped abruptly and pulled himself up with a sheepish grin. 'Sorry, habit of mine, droning on about my pet subjects. You didn't come here to get a lecture on climate change and alternative energy sources, and that won't help you or me learn what Dan and Eerika were working on after 1991.' He paused, and again there was that distant look about his eyes. '1991 . . .' he repeated, as though there was some other meaning to it.

Marvik said nothing in case a memory or thought occurred to Lanbury. But after a few moments Lanbury sighed heavily and looked regretful.

Marvik said, 'As my parents were away for most of that period, 1991 to 1997, they could have stored their papers, diaries and computer disks elsewhere for safe keeping until they could retrieve them later. They might have been worried that they'd get stolen or lost in a fire. But I'm afraid, if they did, they never confided it to me.'

He wondered if, before going to the Straits of Malacca, his parents had placed their research documents and computer disks in a safe deposit box. Maybe they still languished there. But that didn't explain the disk that had been in Sarah's possession and been stolen from him. Could that possibly hold the key to the location of those missing files for 1991 to 1997?

'That's a great pity,' Lanbury said. 'I wrote to Colmead last week to ask for your contact details. He hasn't replied but I'm pleased to see that he passed my message on to you.'

Marvik hid his surprise. Colmead had not contacted him and furthermore Julie hadn't mentioned that correspondence. Perhaps she hadn't thought it important or hadn't seen it. Or perhaps it was the letter that had ended up in Colmead's fireplace. He didn't enlighten Lanbury of the fact that he hadn't spoken to Colmead, not since April anyway.

'My parents could have sent their research to a close friend or colleague,' he suggested.

'I would probably have been Dan's natural choice and Letitia Galt your mother's. When I spoke to Galt earlier today she said she hadn't seen hide nor hair of anything from 1991 onwards and Dan left nothing with me, and neither did he contact me during those years, or me him, but then I was busily engrossed on a project at Woods Hole, Massachusetts. Do you know it?'

Marvik said he didn't.

'It's an independent non-profit organisation founded in 1930. It was an excellent opportunity for me. I was involved in fascinating research right across the marine and sciences spectrum on ocean exploration and climate change. I spoke to Dan briefly before I left England in 1991, when he told me about the new boat *Vasa II*, and that was the last I heard from him.'

'You met up with my father?' Marvik asked keenly, wondering if this might lead him further in his investigations.

'No. He told me about it over the telephone. He was very impressed with it, said it was twice the size of *Vasa*. I joked and said he must have found a generous benefactor. He said he had but didn't tell me who that was. He just said he and Eerika were well-equipped for their next expedition. I asked where it was and he said, "Let's say we're returning to our roots."'

'The Arctic?' Marvik said, excited but confused, because they hadn't ended up there in 1997.

'Possibly. But between 1991 and 1997 I can't recall hearing or reading about their exploration there and when I asked Professor Galt, she said the same.'

'How about Professor Ansler, did you speak to him before his death?'

'No. I lost touch with him shortly after we'd sorted through Dan's papers. I asked that man, Davington, at the memorial service what your parents had been working on and why they were in the Straits of Malacca. He was sitting next to me at the front. In the row across the aisle from you. He muttered something about it being a leisure trip in the sun. I said it couldn't have been much of a holiday for him — he was as pale as a ghost. He said his tan had faded and he wasn't much of a one for the sun anyway. But I guess the poor man was already ill by then and didn't want to blab about it to strangers because he died shortly afterwards.'

'Did you know Davington before then? Did my father talk about him or did Davington accompany him or my mother on any other expeditions?' Marvik realized he didn't know enough about Davington. In fact he knew nothing about him, save that he'd been on board with his parents.

'I asked him that and about his background. He was vague. He said he had known them for a few years. He'd been in the army. I was surprised because I assumed army meant he didn't have a marine background and said so, but he said he had been a diver and helmsman. He'd been in the Royal Engineers. I wondered where Dan or Eerika had found him, but I didn't get the chance to ask him because the service began and he shot off after it very quickly.' Lanbury sat back with a weary expression on his lined face. 'Although I am very pleased to see you, Art, I am disappointed to learn that you don't have Dan's diaries for those missing years. Dan was always very methodical. There would have been a record somewhere.'

There had been, on computer disk, and now Dewell had that. Marvik wondered what he would do with it. He asked if either of his parents had mentioned Hugh Freestone to him.

'No. The first time I heard of him was after their deaths.'

'Who informed you of it?'

'Colmead. He was their executor, as you know. I only met Freestone at the memorial service. I didn't have any chance to talk to him as he was with you. And after the service when I went to pass on my condolences and to speak with you, he said you had to leave.'

And Marvik remembered he had been only too willing to get the hell out of there as quickly as possible.

'Letitia and I spoke about Freestone. She'd never heard of him before either. We assumed he must have been some kind of legal adviser to your parents from the past, unencumbered with a law practice as Colmead was.'

Marvik asked Lanbury if he knew Culverham or had heard his name in connection with his parents. The answer was no and the same went for James Dewell and Sarah Redburn.

'Would they have evidence of your parents' research?' Lanbury asked.

'No, they're just names I've come across,' Marvik airily dismissed.

Lanbury shifted in his seat. He looked a little uneasy. Marvik wondered what he was about to say, something delicate, judging by his manner. 'Your parents must have spoken to you about what they were doing.'

'I was away at school,' Marvik answered lightly, noting Lanbury's baffled expression. 'I didn't see a great deal of them.'

'But they must have written to you.'

'I got the occasional letter.'

'Posted from where?' Lanbury's tone was sharp with curiosity and eagerness.

'I don't remember,' Marvik said and got a sceptical look in return.

'A schoolboy always looks at stamps and postmarks,' Lanbury answered disbelievingly.

'Not me, sorry, sir,' Marvik replied. He recalled receiving a handful of letters. They had come erratically. He tried to envisage them but instead came the memory of the feelings associated with receiving them: hope that the letter would say he was to join his parents on board *Vasa II* or that they had finished their expedition and were returning to Britain and he could see more of them, swiftly followed by disappointment as he read on, and then anger. At first, he'd received the letters enthusiastically, ripping them open without noticing the stamps or postmarks, just recognizing his mother's or father's handwriting. As time went on, he'd barely wanted to bother opening them, knowing they wouldn't relay what he hoped for.

He seemed to remember that the letters had contained details of past expeditions when they had all been together. To Marvik it had been like rubbing salt into the wounds. They had asked how he was getting on, encouraged him to study, asked about his ideas for a future career and about their own choices and why they had made them. He didn't remember them writing about the new boat, *Vasa II*.

When he did get to see them it had been only a couple of times a year and, now that he considered it, during the last two years of their lives, 1996 and 1997, it had only been at Christmas and in the summer. They had never gone to the house on the Isle of Wight or on board *Vasa II*, which had disappointed him. His father had always made some excuse. Instead they had gone to a lodge in Sweden and to a hotel in Scotland, among other places, but always somewhere remote with lots of outdoor activities that involved just him and his parents. Looking back, did he sense their anxiety? Had they been nervous, distracted or occupied by their own thoughts and research? He'd been as self-absorbed as any teenager. He wouldn't have noticed, not unless they had shouted at him, burst into tears or been unusually demonstrative. They hadn't been.

'I'm sorry, Dr Lanbury, but I didn't keep any letters from them. When I joined the Marines, shortly after their deaths, I destroyed everything of my childhood. I wanted a fresh start, a new life. I was angry at them for dying.'

'A natural part of the bereavement process for many people,' Lanbury acknowledged.

Registering Lanbury's crestfallen expression, Marvik said, 'I'll see if I can find any reference to my father's diaries in the papers I have.' He knew there weren't any though.

Lanbury brightened up at that. 'That's most kind of you. I've been doing the same with my diaries and papers from the past, but I'm not as methodical as Dan, and they're in a something of a mess.'

'Can I ask why the interest now, sir?'

Lanbury looked slightly embarrassed. 'Didn't I say? I'm writing a book. I thought I mentioned it. I have an extremely competent young scientist assisting me, Dr Verity Taylor. It's not an academic tome. I want to bring to the populace's attention the fact that time is running out on the world's greatest experiment and that we might soon have the answer to it and that answer might not be a very pleasing one. Global warming,' he explained to Marvik's mystified look. 'We've been pumping CO2 into the atmosphere for years, and if that isn't enough, we've been infecting our planet and our seas with microbes from plastic, which will destroy marine life and therefore us.'

'It sounds like you have backing from an environmental group.'

Lanbury looked sorrowful for a moment. 'No, just my own beliefs. I have no sidings with any political party or environmental pressure group. Nobody will probably want to publish the thing anyway. I'm not concerned about that. I can always publish it myself. I wanted to bring into the book some of your father's findings, with full credit of course,' he hastily added. 'Which was why Verity and I started to wonder if there was anything relevant in those papers and diaries from 1991 to 1997 — which we thought you might allow us to read, but that's not to be, so it seems. Ah, here she is now.'

Marvik followed the direction of his gaze and with a shock found himself studying a petite woman in her early thirties with fine-boned, angular features. She was marching towards them with a confident manner. Her long, straight, black hair was tied back in a ponytail and her slanting chocolate-brown eyes were behind a pair of fashionable spectacles, but there was no mistaking who she was. The last time he had seen her had been in a car pulling away from Freestone's cottage. Then, she had gone by the name of Amber Tunstone.

CHAPTER NINE

Marvik stepped out into the frantic noisy London traffic and waited. He knew that Amber, or he should say Verity, would make some excuse to join him. Her expression had registered surprise when she had seen him, then irritation when Lanbury had introduced him, although Lanbury announced that he had called her to say that Art Marvik was meeting him. But clearly Verity had not expected it to be the man she had met and lied to in Freestone's garden. If she had known he was Professor Coulter's son then she would have latched on to him and asked him about his father's diaries. She showed no embarrassment over the lie though.

He'd briefly wondered if Lanbury had sent her to Freestone's house to search it for the missing diaries, then dismissed the idea. Lanbury had relayed to her the news that Marvik didn't have in his possession any of his father's diaries from 1991 to 1997 but was willing to look through his private papers for any references that could help them fill in the gaps in his parents' research during that period. Verity had expressed disappointment but Marvik was certain she had been faking it because she already knew that he wouldn't be able to help.

He didn't see any need to prolong the interview with Lanbury, and he was keen to speak to Verity alone, a fact he signalled to her with his eyes and, by the slight narrowing of hers, she'd read and interpreted. He made his farewells to Lanbury after taking down his address. He lived in the New Forest, not far from the River Beaulieu. Lanbury already had Marvik's mobile phone number.

It was ten minutes before Verity reappeared. 'Let's talk over there,' she said, striding out towards Greenwich Park.

Marvik fell into step beside her. He remained silent, waiting for her to open up the conversation. Perhaps she'd begin by apologizing, or explaining why she had given him a false name and lied about being the owner of Freestone's cottage. Perhaps she'd even tell him why she and Craven had killed Freestone.

Instead, in a sharp voice she demanded to know what Dr Lanbury had told him about her.

'That you're helping him with his research for a book he's writing.'

'I'm not a secretary,' she flashed.

'I never said you were. Anyway, what's wrong with being a secretary?'

'I have a Master of Science degree in Atmosphere, Ocean and Climate from the University of Southampton and a special interest in climate change and the Arctic,' she said stiffly. 'As a result of which I have studied all of Dr Lanbury's work, and Professor Dan Coulter's. I am a great admirer of both.'

'Why didn't you tell me this when we met?'

'Because I didn't know who you were.'

'You didn't ask. Instead you spun me a pack of lies.'

'Why should I have told a stranger anything?' she quipped.

'I take it your real name is Verity Taylor and not Amber Tunstone?'

'You can check with the university.'

'So why did you lie about Hugh Freestone's house belonging to you and all that bullshit about Stuart Craven being an estate agent.'

'As I've just said, I had no idea who you were. I had to think of something quick when I saw you in the grounds.'

She ran her dark eyes over his face. 'And you didn't look as though you were Professor Coulter's son.'

'How would expect me to look?'

She ignored that and all references to his scars. 'I thought you might be about to break into Freestone's cottage to—'

'Search for Dan Coulter's diaries from 1991 to 1997,' he finished for her. 'I saw you both. I was concealed in the grounds.'

He made no mention of discovering Freestone's bloated body wedged under the jetty. Could she have killed him? Was she capable of that? Freestone had been old and possibly weakened with cancer judging by that hospital letter he'd seen. She was petite and Freestone tall but perhaps he had been bending over, she'd struck him violently and then pushed him into the river. Or maybe Craven had done that.

He said, 'You suspect there are others who are keen to get their hands on my father's diaries?'

'Evidently,' she tersely replied and slowed her footsteps as they crossed the grass towards the Royal Observatory. The early afternoon was hot and the park busy. Marvik didn't think anyone was following or observing them but he took swift stock of the people around them.

'Why evidently?'

'There would be, wouldn't there,' she fudged. 'Is it true what you told Dr Lanbury, that you don't have your father's diaries or notes, or know of their whereabouts?'

'For that period, yes.'

She threw him a disbelieving glance. He wondered if she knew that he'd had one such notebook in his possession at one time. If she did that meant she could be working in conjunction with Dewell, and the notebook Dewell had taken from Marvik's safe deposit box hadn't given them the location of where the other notebooks and computer disks might be. Or, judging by her remark 'evidently', he wondered if she knew that Dewell was from a competing organization after the same thing. Perhaps that stolen computer disk contained an index of whatever it was his parents had been doing between 1991 and 1997, which could be connected with their possible search for the *Flor de la Mar* in the Straits of Malacca as Professor Galt had intimated, but not as Dr Lanbury had testified.

But if Verity Taylor was on the level and Dewell was a separate party after Dan Coulter's notebooks and the computer disks, and the stolen one *had* held the key to their location, then Marvik didn't think that he or anyone else would ever see them again.

She said, 'Didn't your father or mother tell you what they were working on before their deaths?'

'I was away at school. I didn't see much of them.' *And why the hell should I tell you anyway!* Tersely and a little sourly, he said, 'And if you recall, they died suddenly, without time to summon me and leave a dying confession of where their diaries were deposited.'

'Your mother kept a diary?' she said sharply and with surprise, picking up on his reference to both his parents. It had been a slip of the tongue, but her reaction was interesting.

'She might have done.'

'But you must know.'

'Why should I? Diaries by their very nature are private.'

'Professor Galt said Dr Eerika Marvik never kept a diary.'

'When did you speak to Galt?' Marvik rapped.

She looked disconcerted for a moment. 'Wednesday. Have *you* asked Galt about your mother's diaries?'

'I haven't spoken to her.' Two people could play the lying game, or three if you counted Galt, because she'd made no mention of an enquiry about Eerika's diaries to him. He also noted that so far Verity Taylor had made no mention of computer disks. He wondered why. Or perhaps that would come later. 'How did you know where to find Hugh Freestone?' he asked.

She let loose her hair and pushed her long slender fingers through it. It was a sensuous gesture and, turning her full gaze on him, he could see she was mentally calculating how much to tell him, or perhaps thinking up her next lie. If he had professed to have the diaries, he wondered what she would have done to get hold of them. Did she really believe he didn't know their location? Maybe she thought he was lying. Or perhaps she was considering that even if he didn't know where they were he might still be useful to her in locating them.

She gestured at a seat that had become vacant close to the Victorian bandstand. The crowd had thinned out. Marvik gazed around at the people in the park, noting if anyone took up residence on the grass close by or at a few yards' distance. Two people did, a scruffily dressed man of about twenty with a beard, who took some sandwiches from a rucksack, and a woman in her thirties with two children, one in a pushchair.

When seated, she said, 'I contacted Colmead on Dr Lanbury's instructions and asked for Mr Freestone's address.'

Lanbury had said *he* had telephoned Colmead and he hadn't mentioned getting Freestone's address.

'Colmead gave me Freestone's telephone number and I phoned and asked if I could visit him,' she went on. 'He agreed. I turned up, as arranged, to find you there and no sign of Freestone.'

'And you decided to break in.'

'The door was open.'

Not when Marvik had tried it.

'I thought Freestone might be inside, so went to check. For all I knew you could have attacked and robbed him. There was no sign of him.'

'So, worried, you called the police.'

'Of course I didn't. Did they show up?' she asked, suddenly alarmed.

'How should I know, you and Craven saw me off the premises.'

She played with her hair.

'How did you get to the cottage?' he asked.

'Eh?'

Marvik didn't repeat the question. She'd heard him all right.

'By car, of course, I didn't swim there,' she caustically replied.

'I didn't see your car.'

'It was parked down the lane behind the derelict barns.'

Another lie.

'Have you tried contacting Freestone since?'

'Yes. But he isn't answering his phone.'

He wouldn't. 'You left a message on his answer machine?'

'No. I didn't think it was worth bothering. Have you seen him?' she asked keenly.

Yes, but not alive. 'No.'

She looked as though she didn't believe him. 'Why were you there anyway?'

'Why shouldn't I have been? He was my guardian.'

'Then you knew that what I said in the garden was bullshit,' she protested. 'Why didn't you say?'

'Why should I?'

She pursued her lips together. 'Do you know where he is? Can you contact him?'

'No. On both counts.' That at least was the truth. The body could be way out in the English Channel by now and unless he was a spiritualist, he would have no further contact with Hugh Freestone.

'But he could help us.'

'Help *you*,' Marvik said.

'And Dr Lanbury.' Then with an exasperated air, 'Don't you want to know what happened to your father's diaries and what research he and your mother were engaged upon at the time of their deaths?'

'Why should I?'

'But you must have been at Freestone's for a reason.'

'I was.'

'And that was?'

'I don't see why I should tell you.'

She scowled at him, then relaxed and smiled sheepishly, though Marvik thought it was an act. 'Look, I'm sorry we got off on the wrong foot, but your father's diaries could contain very valuable information.'

'In monetary terms?'

'Yes, if what your parents discovered in the years before they died has major significance.'

'It's been suggested they were searching for the *Flor de la Mar* which went down somewhere in the Straits of Malacca.' But Marvik could tell instantly by her expression that this was not what Verity thought. Lanbury had told her about his last conversation with Dan Coulter and the fact he'd said he was 'returning to his roots', which were not the Straits of Malacca.

'I doubt that,' she replied. 'It's possible that your father's diaries could enhance someone's reputation in the field of oceanography.'

'Yours?' he said a little derisively.

'Why not? There's nothing wrong with ambition. And I wouldn't be *stealing* your father's research, I would give him full credit for anything he discovered.'

'I thought you were working for Dr Lanbury.'

'*With* Dr Lanbury,' she corrected, tight-lipped. Then, with the air of talking to a dim student, she continued. 'Professor Coulter was an expert on ocean turbulence, weather patterns, the Arctic and climate change. All of that is highly significant today.'

'But his work was carried out twenty years ago. Surely more recent research will have overtaken any of his studies. I can't see how they can be important.'

She seemed disconcerted by the fact that he'd given her a fairly intelligent reply. But she quickly recovered her composure. 'It's true that computer modelling has advanced considerably since the early 1990s, along with our data on global warming which, despite the facts, some people still seem to think is some kind of great conspiracy. And now we have far more sophisticated remotely-operated vehicles to study the oceans, but the sea is still a great mystery. And so is the fact that the diaries from 1991 to 1997 seem to have vanished.'

There was still no mention of a computer disk.

'Dr Lanbury said your parents never spoke of their expeditions when you were at school.'

'Correct.' She didn't believe him. Tough.

'When did you speak to Michael Colmead to get Hugh Freestone's address?'

'On Wednesday, just after I saw Professor Galt.' She again pushed a hand through her hair.

Another lie to add to all the others she had spewed forth. On Wednesday, Colmead was already missing.

'When can you check your paperwork to see if there is any mention of the diaries?' she asked.

'Soon.'

'Can you do it today or tomorrow?'

'Why the hurry?' he said lazily.

'Because I'm keen to know what they contain. I'd willingly help you go through them.'

I bet you would. 'They're at my cottage on the Isle of Wight,' he lied and watched for a reaction, wondering if she and Craven had already searched it and had been on that motorboat he'd heard take off on Wednesday night. Her expression was one of impatience. 'I'll call Dr Lanbury if I find anything.'

'Can you also call me? I'll give you my mobile number.'

Marvik punched it into his phone. He gave her his number.

She jumped up and turned towards the National Maritime Museum.

'Who is Stuart Craven? Why is he involved in this?' Marvik asked.

'He's just helping me.'

'If my father's diaries are as valuable as you seem to think then perhaps someone else has already asked Hugh Freestone about them. He could be in danger. He could be dead.'

'He can't be,' she asserted, but there was flicker of anxiety in the deep-brown eyes.

‘How do you know that?’

She snatched a glance at her watch. ‘I have to go. Call me if you find anything.’

He watched her march away while checking who walked in front, beside and behind her. Maybe someone was tailing her but whoever it was it wasn’t Stuart Craven. But then he’d have no need to. He’d know exactly where she was.

With only one glance back she disappeared inside the museum. Marvik knew she wouldn’t breathe a word to Lanbury about their conversation, and neither would she give up her quest to find the diaries. He didn’t trust her, and he didn’t believe her. Verity Taylor had lied consistently from the very first moment he had met her to the last.

CHAPTER TEN

On the platform at Waterloo Marvik called Strathen using the mission mobile and asked him to find out what he could about Dr Verity Taylor. He said he would call again when he reached Weymouth.

As the train stopped and started on its long journey south, Marvik had the chance to think over his conversation with Lanbury, but it was his own relationship with his parents that kept intruding on his thoughts, sparked by Lanbury's question about his parents' erratic contact with him during his school days. As the grey terraced houses of London turned into countryside, instead of viewing his despatch to an English boarding school as his parents' way of dumping him, he questioned if his parents' intention had been to protect him. Had their expedition been dangerous? Whatever they had been doing *had* resulted in their deaths. And now, over twenty years later, others had been killed, not to mention there having been the attempt on his life.

Had Stuart Craven killed Sarah? Had Verity Taylor enticed Sarah to a meeting with Craven because she believed, or knew, Sarah had that diary and computer disk? Sarah had packed it away in her belongings stored in a house in Eel Pie Island which he had discovered just before the house had been torched. Had that been Craven's doing? He'd got the information out of Sarah before killing her but arrived at the house too late? Or perhaps James Dewell was the murderer? Or perhaps neither of them were because the arsonist had wanted the disk destroyed and didn't care that he was also inside the house.

He shut his eyes, deciding to take the opportunity of the three-hour journey to get some sleep. It was the half-waking, watchful kind that he had perfected over the years when on operations. Despite that, it was still restful and helped to recharge the batteries.

When he alighted at Weymouth, he called Strathen as promised. 'Any luck with Verity Taylor?'

'She is what she claims to be, an oceanographer and a very clever and ambitious lady judging by the papers she's had published: land and ocean ecosystems; abrupt climate change; interactions between the ocean, atmosphere and sea ice cover, and more of the same ilk with some big words that I'd need a dictionary to understand. But I can't find where she's currently working.'

'For Dr Lanbury, if what she says is true, and most of what she told me isn't.' Marvik relayed the full extent of what had happened both with his interview with Lanbury and the ensuing one with Verity.

'Do you think she's a killer?' Strathen asked.

'It's possible if the stakes are high enough — and they seem to be. And Craven and Verity could have killed Freestone, but if they did, why return to the house?'

'Maybe they were trying to force information from him about the diaries and it went wrong and the poor soul died. That frightened them off from immediately searching the house, so they returned a few days later only to find you there so had to quickly devise a cock-and-bull story about selling the house.'

'She told me that she'd rung Colmead on Wednesday and spoken to him to get Freestone's address. So she can't know that Colmead is missing.'

'Or she does and she said that to see if you had been in touch with him.'

'Then she and Craven could also be involved in Colmead's disappearance. It would explain how they got hold of Freestone's address. They could have forced Colmead to give it to them. But that would mean they're not linked with Dewell who went to my safe deposit box.'

'Why not? He retrieved the disk and now they need the others. Or the information on that disk was corrupt so they still need to look for other sources, in particular the diaries, which have a longer shelf life. That could be why she is more interested in finding diaries than disks.'

That made sense because if the disk Dewell had taken had told everything, there would be no need for them to look for anything else.

Strathen said, 'Is Dr Lanbury on the level?'

'Yes, but the idea for the book probably came from Verity as a means of getting access to his papers in case there is something in them that can lead her to my father's research. She dismissed Galt's hypothesis that they had been searching for the *Flor de la Mar*. She also claims to have spoken to Professor Galt on Wednesday about my mother's diaries, but Galt never mentioned it to me. I'm going to see if that was another of Verity's lies.'

He took a taxi to Portland Marina. It was just after 7.40 p.m. and he hoped that Galt was on board RV *Oyster*. She was, but not in the best of tempers. She didn't look too pleased to see him but that was explained when she said it had been a long and frustrating day. 'Working with idiots doesn't help,' she snapped.

'Letitia, you can't blame the team,' Kranton tried to mollify her. He too looked frazzled. There were only the three of them on the boat.

'Can't I?' she snarled. 'They call themselves experienced divers, but they wouldn't know a snorkel from an aqualung — and as for being marine archaeologists!' She snorted and dragged a bony hand through her wiry grey hair. Her face was more drawn than earlier that morning and her eyes held a distant, slightly confused expression. She rounded on him. 'What is it now? There's nothing more I can tell you and I need a drink.' This time there was no invitation to 'sit'.

'I've been speaking to Dr Lanbury.'

Kranton said, 'I'll leave.'

But Galt flapped an arm at him. 'Not without me you don't.'

Kranton glanced at Marvik with an air of apology and enquiry. Marvik smiled to say it was OK with him.

Galt said, 'What did Lanbury tell you?'

'More or less the same as you did.'

She sniffed as if to say, 'I told you so'.

'But his assistant, or I should say his researcher, told me something more. Why didn't you tell me that Dr Verity Taylor came to see you and asked about my mother's diaries?'

'Because I sent her away with a flea in her ear.'

So for once Verity had told the truth. Marvik raised his eyebrows. Kranton gave him a pained look. 'You don't like her?'

Acidly, she said, 'She's an overly ambitious, pushy young woman, and I saw no reason to discuss with her the private affairs of Eerika and Dan. I suppose *she* tracked you down to ask you the same questions she tried out on me. I hope you weren't fooled by her prettiness.'

'Fooled into what?'

'Helping her to find out what happened to your parents' diaries, papers and computer disks, because I can tell you, Marvik, she would be quite capable of using whatever it took, including sex, to get her hands on their research and then she'd milk it for all it was worth.'

'You have evidence that she has done this before?' he asked, surprised.

'Letitia,' Kranton cautioned.

Tautly, she said, 'I'm warning you, Marvik, that girl is clever and poisonous. She'll steal anyone's research and put her own name to it.'

Perhaps Galt was right.

'Did Eerika keep a diary?' he said.

'Not that I am aware of, but then it's not the sort of question you ask. She would have kept notes of her work, as I've already told you. But as to writing down her innermost thoughts, I'd have said no. Eerika was a consummate professional and didn't waste time on emotions and musings.'

Galt's words added to Marvik's store of memories. He considered his mother's personality and accepted that Galt was right. It wasn't that his mother had been cold but she hadn't shown emotion, not to him certainly. It hadn't left him feeling unloved though. It was simply that his mother had a brusque, straightforward, practical manner — like Galt's, and perhaps that was why they had hit it off. Galt hadn't considered Eerika anyone's fool.

As he recalled his relationship with his mother with adult eyes, he saw that Eerika had treated him like an adult even when he was a child. It had been his father who had been the more emotional and demonstrative of the pair. That didn't mean she hadn't kept diaries though. Marvik didn't think Galt had been close enough to Eerika to pronounce so firm a judgement. But there had been none in his safe deposit boxes, nor listed by Bell, the solicitor's clerk.

'Dr Lanbury suggested that Eerika and Dan were returning to the Arctic in 1991. Do you think it likely?'

'No,' she declared firmly.

'Why so certain?'

'Because when I last saw Eerika in September 1990 she said nothing about that, and she would have done.'

'But she did tell you about their new boat, *Vasa II*.'

'Never said a word about it.'

But Marvik was beginning to wonder how reliable Galt's memory was. He was reading something in Kranton's expression. He wasn't certain what it was, but it looked like an apology of some kind. For what, though — Galt's behaviour, or her memory?

Galt said, 'And they couldn't have been going to the Arctic for six years because they would have needed crew and scientific personnel on board. You can't just set sail for the Arctic without support because of the demands of the terrain. Someone would have said something about it.'

'But you were in the Sargasso Sea for much of that time, miles away, and focused on your own exploration. You probably wouldn't have heard anything.'

'I was, but you can't keep that sort of expedition quiet. I'm right, aren't I, Guy?'

'Yes. I never heard anything about your parents being on an exploration in the Arctic but then I was working in the South Pacific for most of that period.'

'Lanbury's probably got it wrong. He often does.'

Marvik noted the scathing dismissive note in her voice and recalled Lanbury's explanation for it. But she had a point. Marvik had been on missions in the Arctic and knew that they required considerable resources because of the cold.

Galt locked up the boat, saying over her shoulder, 'As I told you before, my belief is that they were in the Straits of Malacca on and off for six years looking for the *Flor de la Mar.*'

'Who would have funded such an expedition?'

'They might have self-financed it. Your parents could afford it.'

Was that a slightly sour note in her voice? 'But surely not for six years. They weren't that wealthy.'

'Well they always seemed to get sponsors and commissions,' Galt replied as she climbed off the boat. Marvik and Kranton followed suit.

She continued, 'Nobody came forward to provide any information even though the tragedy was covered in all the broadsheets and the professional magazines. Can't help you more, Marvik. I need a drink.' She marched off.

Kranton turned to Marvik with an apologetic frown. 'She's not always so irascible,' he said. 'But she has been under considerable strain and her health isn't too good, not that she'd ever admit that, but it annoys her that she's not as fit as the youngsters on the team. I guess we all hate getting older.' He made as if to say more but Galt called out an irritable, 'For God's sake, Guy, hurry up.' He waved an arm at her and said to Marvik, 'Good luck with your research.'

Marvik returned to his boat deep in thought. Had his parents been looking for the *Flor de la Mar*? Had they discovered something that could help locate it? Could whoever had funded them have taken their research but hadn't been able to capitalize on what they had discovered for one reason or another? But the discovery of the wreck wouldn't have been of such great interest to Verity Taylor, an oceanographer, discounting its financial value. Perhaps Stuart Craven was a marine archaeologist and Verity had joined forces with him. If that was so, why hadn't Craven spoken to Professor Galt and left Verity to tackle Lanbury? And if Craven *was* a marine archaeologist then why couldn't Strathen locate him? No, he was certain the *Flor de la Mar* was a blind alley.

He climbed on board his boat and, using the sonar equipment Strathen had given him, checked it over in case someone had decided to plant another incendiary device or a tracking system in his absence. He found neither. There were so many questions and he didn't seem any closer to getting the answers. In fact, every step he took and every person he spoke to created more questions.

He opened the fridge and reached for a bottle of water. Drinking thirstily as the wind whistled through the masts of the yachts around him, he considered Galt's words about Verity Taylor. Was she ambitious enough to commit murder? Maybe.

So where next? Call Crowder and report what he had discovered even though this wasn't an official mission? Ask him what he knew about Sarah Redburn's death and the deaths of his parents? But perhaps Crowder knew little of it and even if he knew more, he might not disclose that to Marvik.

He mulled over the events of the day, starting and ending with his meetings with Galt, and as he did, a name came to mind that both Galt and Lanbury had mentioned and that, so far, he'd ignored, because the man was dead: his parents' diver operator, Fred Davington. Dead men don't speak. Or do they?

Eagerly he fired up his laptop. Lanbury had told him that Davington was ex-army, Royal Engineers, and that meant his friends and relatives could be traceable through the army network. One of them might know something — even if it was only a small thing — about Davington's last voyage with Dan Coulter and Eerika Marvik.

Marvik went directly to the Royal Engineers Association website. Soon he was scrolling through the 'In Memoriam' section, where, to his delight, he found a reference to Fred Davington along with his service number, rank, age and a notation that read, 'Sadly missed and fondly remembered by his close friend and former colleague 23 Amphibious Engineer Squadron, Gordon Hillingdon.'

Great. This was better than he had anticipated. Furthermore, there was an email address for Hillingdon. A telephone number would have been better but Marvik fired off an email asking if he could speak to Hillingdon. As he did so, he wondered if Dewell or Craven and Verity had followed this route. Marvik gave his personal mobile phone number. He didn't know where Hillingdon lived. It could be Cumbria, Cornwall or Caernarvon. He might be abroad, sick or in a nursing home. He might ignore the email, or let it linger in his junk mail.

Marvik reported back to Strathen, who said he had still not managed to speak to the previous owner of the *Golden Fleece*, Nigel Jellicoe. And he could find nothing on Roland Culverham. Marvik said he would stay in Portland Marina that night and tomorrow he would contact Verity Taylor and go in harder this time, facing her with the lies she'd spouted.

It was just after nine. Marvik thought about food. He could gatecrash Galt's party and head for the restaurant where she and her crew were eating, but he saw no point in that. Alternatively, he could make for The Cove Inn on the beach. In the end he decided he couldn't be bothered. Instead he made himself something to eat on board while his mind ran through the numerous questions plaguing it, but it still didn't yield any answers.

He'd barely taken two mouthfuls of his omelette when his mobile rang. It was a number he didn't recognize but he was amazed and delighted when the caller announced himself as Gordon Hillingdon. That was damn quick. Marvik repeated the request he'd made in his email, adding, 'I'd just like to know a bit more about Frederick Davington.'

'Happy to talk to you about Davvers. Do you want to meet up? Where are you?'

'Portland Marina, Dorset.'

'You have a boat?'

'Yes.'

'Can you make Shamrock Quay, Southampton tomorrow? Do you know it?'

Marvik said he did and that he could make it. This was far better than he had hoped, or ever expected, to have Hillingdon so close on hand and willing to talk.

'I'll meet you in the café there,' Hillingdon said. 'Ten o'clock be OK for you?'

'Perfect.'

He was tempted to set off for Shamrock Quay that instant but it wouldn't make the meeting come any quicker. If he left before 6 a.m., he would be there in time. He was keen to hear more about Davington. He was also curious to know if Hillingdon had been approached by anyone else over the years, and more recently, about his parents' last and fateful trip and their research in the years preceding it.

As he retired for the night, Marvik considered the fact that Davington had been the last person to see Eerika and Dan alive. He cursed his stupidity for not thinking of following this route before, because this was where he should have started.

CHAPTER ELEVEN

Sunday

It had been a while since Marvik had moored up at Shamrock Quay, a large marina not far from the city centre equipped with a bar, restaurant, café and shops. It also had a superyacht berth, which Marvik saw was empty, but on the visitors' berths close by a very sleek, large expensive motor yacht was moored.

He had made good time on the bright May morning. There had been a stiff south-westerly breeze and fast-scudding clouds. The forecast though was for rain by early evening. He didn't know what Hillingdon looked like but as he entered the nautical-themed café there was only one customer inside, a tanned, muscular man in his early sixties with a bald pate surrounded by cropped grey hair. He glanced up from his Sunday newspaper and, by his quizzical and expectant air, Marvik deduced it was Hillingdon. He was correct.

Marvik introduced himself. Hillingdon's handshake was firm and dry.

'Like a top up?' Marvik asked, indicating the empty coffee cup.

Hillingdon said he would and, after fetching two coffees, Marvik took the seat opposite the rugged, broad-shouldered man who eyed him curiously. 'So you're the son of Eerika Marvik and Dan Coulter.'

'You knew them?' Marvik said, taken aback.

'Only through Davvers — that's what we always called him. He was never a Fred or a Frederick, probably just as you were never an Arthur.' Hillingdon smiled. Marvik didn't enlighten him that his name had been registered at birth as Art.

'He was a great mate, a brilliant sapper and a bit mad, like we all were in those days, much like you if those scars are anything to go by. Judging by them, your build and bearing, I'd say you are in the services.'

'Was. Royal Marines.'

Hillingdon nodded as if to say, 'Thought as much.'

'My scars don't show unless I strip off my shirt and I'm not inclined to do that often at my age,' Hillingdon said.

Marvik thought even if he did, he had nothing to be ashamed of. His physique would put many younger men to shame.

'I served seven years with Davvers, from the age of twenty-one, and when you're in your twenties you're invincible, and you're never going to get old.' His expression clouded over. Marvik knew that he was mentally recalling those days with sadness because they were long gone.

He suppressed his own emotions. His life in the Marines now seemed as far away to him as Hillingdon's time in the army did to the older man. Like him, Hillingdon had enjoyed the adrenaline-fuelled brushes with danger and death. Crowder had given Marvik the opportunity to relive them in the National Intelligence Marine Squad, and he had grabbed that with both hands. In the Marines, he hadn't cared whether he lived or died. Now though, he found he did care. He didn't want to give the bastard who had killed Sarah, his parents and Freestone the satisfaction of gloating over another death. His.

He said, 'You kept in touch with Davvers after you left the army?'

'On and off. You know how it is. But that didn't matter. When we met up, we just picked up where we had left off as though we had never been apart. We were very close.'

'What did Davvers tell you about my parents?'

'That they were both nuts.' He grinned. 'But then who isn't when they're passionate about what they do? He meant it as a compliment.'

'When did he tell you this, Mr Hillingdon?'

'Gordon, please, although my moniker in the army was Dale. Hillingdon became over the hill and subsequently dale, as in the song, and I got lumbered with it. Could have been worse. We became Davvers and Dale. Sounded like a comedy duo and we used to ham it up, usually when we were pissed, which was as often as possible.' Hillingdon again smiled before his expression turned serious. 'Davvers said your parents had been killed in an underwater earthquake. It shook him up. I told him to get medical help, but he insisted he was OK. As it turned out, he wasn't. You must have been quite young when they died.'

'Seventeen. And I hadn't had much contact with them for the six years before then. I was away at school. Did Davvers tell you what they were doing in the Straits of Malacca?'

'No. I guessed on some marine exploration. Didn't they tell you? Or leave any record of it?' he asked, concerned.

'In all the confusion over their deaths it seems the Indonesian police seized those records and then inadvertently destroyed them.' He thought it was a good enough story so he might as well peddle it. It might actually have been the truth, except for that one computer disk that had somehow got into the hands of Sarah and now Dewell. 'What can you tell me about Davvers?'

Hillingdon looked wistful. 'He was a bit of a loner really. No family. When he died—'

'Who told you about his death?'

Hillingdon looked stunned for an instant at the suddenness of Marvik's question. 'I found his body. Didn't you know?' he added, seeing Marvik's expression. 'He'd contacted me, asked if I would come round, said there was something he wanted to discuss with me, something he needed my help with, but he gave no hint of what it was. He sounded very worried. I said I'd be round in half an hour, but I got held up in traffic and it took me just over an hour. There was no answer when I arrived. His car was in the car park. I grew concerned and broke in. I found him on the sitting room floor. He was dead — you know instantly, don't you? But I checked for a pulse to make sure, then I rang the police. No point in bothering the ambulance service.'

'Was there any kind of disturbance in his flat?'

'No, nothing out of place, as neat as ninepence, but then Davvers was always very tidy and meticulous. Thorough and damn good at his job.'

'Which was?'

'Construction, demolition, diving, bomb disposal, whatever it took to accomplish the mission. You'd know all about that.' He drank his coffee. 'We were combat engineers — technically minded, practical, skilled in turning our hands to whatever it took. Davvers left a tidy sum in his will to the Royal Engineers Benevolent Fund, but then he didn't have a wife or ex-wife and no kids to spend his money. He didn't own any property either. He could have invested in some and rented it out, but Davvers liked to be on the move. When he left the army — the same year as me, 1978 — he worked as a commercial diver for one of the major international cable laying companies, and for companies who needed divers with expertise in contaminated water, maybe it was that which kick-started his asthma, who knows?' He shrugged. 'He also worked for many different undersea exploration companies, which is where I guess his work with your parents came in. He liked working alone or in a small team, and he liked the challenge of different projects, the tougher the better. He was bit of an adrenaline junkie, always hankering after that fix we had in the army. I expect it was the same for you in the Marines.'

'A bit.' Marvik was beginning to get a very different picture of Frederick Davington from the one he'd conjured up from his memory of a gaunt, silent, ashen-faced man at the memorial service. He was about to ask Hillingdon a question, but Hillingdon was in full flow and Marvik wasn't about to stop him.

'He wasn't short of women either. Well, not when he was a sapper, and not that I'm aware of in the years afterwards. Although I believe there was one at the time of his death, and perhaps that was what he wanted to talk to me about but neither I nor the solicitor could find any reference to her among his personal belongings. And despite all the notices that were put in the local newspaper in Winchester where he lived, no female friend showed up at his funeral. I thought your parents' deaths and perhaps this woman chucking him over had sent him into a depression which caused his attack. She had an unusual name, that's why I remember it.' Hillingdon eyed Marvik curiously as though waiting for him to furnish it. His heavy brow knitted and after a moment he added, 'It was Fenella. I think it's Irish or Scottish. Maybe it was someone your parents knew,' he posited.

'Not that I'm aware of.'

'You never heard of it before?'

'No. Didn't he give you a surname?'

'No.'

Marvik was disappointed. A first name was no help at all.

Hillingdon continued. 'The post-mortem said Davvers died of heart failure, but then everyone dies of that. There was no evidence of cardiac disease, but it was believed it was caused by a severe asthma attack. I'd never known him to suffer from asthma, although I have been told you can develop it in your fifties and sixties and, as I said, maybe he got it from some of the specialized work he did, brought on by some toxic substance he'd been exposed to.'

'Was he on medication for it?'

'Apparently. He had an inhaler.' Hillingdon's bold-featured face looked troubled and he shifted uneasily as a noisy crowd of six entered the café, their laughter and voices at odds with the moment.

After a short pause, Hillingdon went on. 'He was really cut up about your parents' deaths. He said he felt responsible, even though it was a natural phenomenon. I suppose that could have brought on the asthma. Some say it can be triggered by stress but then they put every ailment down to stress these days. I'm sorry, Art, none of this is much good to you. He never said what he was doing out in the Straits of Malacca with them.'

'Have you any idea of how long Davvers knew my parents?'

Hillingdon shook his head. 'As I said, he wasn't a talker and if he didn't reveal it to me, then I doubt if he told anyone else.'

So another dead end, thought Marvik, disguising his disappointment. He thanked Hillingdon and rose. Unexpectedly, Hillingdon followed suit. Picking up his newspaper, he said, 'My boat's moored up here.'

They headed towards the visitors' pontoon and Hillingdon turned the talk towards boating. 'Gets in your blood,' he said. 'Where do you keep yours?'

'On the Isle of Wight usually, but I'm hardly ever there.'

'Bit of a nomad, eh? Can't settle after coming out of the Marines. I know the feeling. Took me a while to find what I wanted to do.'

'And that is?'

'Demolition. I blow things up. Nice craft,' Hillingdon said, coming alongside Marvik's motor cruiser. 'That's mine.' He nodded his head to the large, new slick, expensive motorboat Marvik had noted earlier farther along the pontoon. Seeing his surprise Hillingdon said with a grin, 'Not bad for an ex-sapper. I've got my own demolition company. It's done pretty good.'

Obviously, thought Marvik. He stretched out his hand and thanked him for his help. Hillingdon promised to call if he thought of anything that might help, but Marvik wasn't going to hold his breath. A woman's first name was impossible to trace even if Davington had said something to her about his parents, which was unlikely. He was left with several questions. He didn't know how long Davington had worked with his parents, why they had engaged him, or even how they had known him. And he wasn't ever going to know, not unless Crowder could, and would, get him that information via Her Majesty's Revenue and Customs, and the Border Agency. The first would hold employment and tax records, the second Davington's movements in and out of the country, except this was over twenty years ago, and Marvik wasn't certain there would still be records available to find. And perhaps it was of no significance anyway. If following up Davington was now out of the equation, where did that leave him? Back with Verity Taylor.

He made the boat ready and swung out into Southampton Water, making for Strathen's apartment at Hamble. The mission mobile rang as he reached the Solent, which meant it was Strathen.

'Where are you?'

'On my way to see you with precious little new information,' Marvik said.

'Then this might you cheer you up, or on the other hand, confuse you. I've just been speaking to Nigel Jellicoe, the previous owner of the *Golden Fleece*. He claims he's never owned a fishing rod and he's never stuffed a picture of his boat inside one, and neither, as far as he is aware, did his father, who owned the Fairey Swordsman before him. But that's not all. I asked him what he could tell me about the man he had sold the boat to, Roland Culverham. He said "Nothing," because he hadn't sold it to anyone called Culverham. In fact, he'd never heard of him.'

'But the Commodore of the Fairey Owners Club told us Jellicoe had sold it to Culverham.'

'No, he didn't. I asked the Commodore about the *Golden Fleece*. He told me Jellicoe had sold it to a semi-retired man who lived on the Isle of Wight. I rang around the marinas asking if they had the *Golden Fleece* moored there, and the guy at Shepards Wharf told me they had and it belonged to Roland Culverham.'

'So Culverham gave a false name to Nigel Jellicoe.'

'Yes.'

'And what was the name he used?' Marvik asked, picking up the intrigue and excitement in Strathen's tone.

'Yours. Jellicoe sold it to Art Marvik.'

CHAPTER TWELVE

'The boat was paid for by bank transfer in the name of Art Marvik,' Strathen continued while Marvik's head spun with this new twist on events. 'So, unless Culverham hacked into your account, there's another bank account somewhere in your name because the transaction went through without a hitch.'

'I can certainly confirm no one has hacked into my account. Why on earth should this man have bought a boat in my name?'

'Do you think he could have known your parents?'

'As I said before, his name doesn't crop up in any of the files and neither Galt nor Lanbury have heard of him,' Marvik said perplexed. 'And a petro-chemical consultant wasn't my parents' usual circle of acquaintances. But it confirms that the picture of the boat was put in Freestone's fishing rod deliberately in the hope that I would find it and that it would lead me to Culverham. Pity he's not around to ask.'

'Perhaps that's why he's not around,' Strathen said solemnly. 'Someone certainly doesn't want you to find out why your parents were killed. Freestone and Culverham must have been working together on this. They were told you'd been asking questions about your parents' research for around the time of their deaths.'

'By Colmead?'

'Or Bell. Remember that conversation Julie Pembroke said she overheard.'

Marvik recalled it: *Nigel Bell didn't tell Marvik anything . . . Because I asked Bell . . . Everything's as it was . . . I don't like this . . .*

'But what didn't Colmead like?' Marvik said, puzzled. 'From that it sounds as though he was talking to someone who wanted to hush things up and prevent me from finding out anything.'

'Then maybe Bell lied to Colmead. Bell might have told Freestone or Culverham you'd been digging up the past.'

'But why didn't one of them contact me directly?' Marvik said with exasperation. 'Why go through this elaborate charade of buying an expensive boat in my name and then putting a picture of it in a fishing rod? It doesn't make any sense.'

'It does if they both knew there were some ruthless parties after whatever information those missing research papers and disks hold. Just look at it, Art. Sarah Redburn was strangled, Hugh Freestone bludgeoned and drowned, Michael Colmead missing, Nigel Bell on an unexpected trip abroad — *if* he really is abroad — Culverham's phone dead. They couldn't be open about it because it would put them, and you, at risk.'

'They misjudged whoever is behind this then as far as they were concerned,' Marvik said solemnly.

'Yes. Although Culverham and Colmead might still be alive and in hiding somewhere. Whether they are or not, Culverham and Freestone ensured there was a trail to follow. Culverham saw to the purchase of the boat and the renaming of it, while Freestone bought a fishing rod and stuffed the picture down it. He was counting on the fact that if you showed up—'

'That's a big if.'

'Not really — he'd been told you'd begun to ask questions about 1997. He anticipated you'd come looking for him. You'd remember that he'd said he despised fishing, and you, thinking it strange that he would have such an item in his boathouse, would examine it in curiosity. The Fairey Swordsman was chosen deliberately because it is a distinctive and rare boat that can be easily traced. They knew you would do so.'

'But it's all pure chance, Shaun. I might never have gone to Freestone's cottage. I might never have noticed the fishing rod. Even if I did, I might have stuck it back in the corner and never looked inside it. Or, on finding the photograph of the boat, I could have tossed it away.'

'It was a chance they were prepared to take. If you didn't follow it up, so be it. Maybe they would have tried something different. Perhaps one or both of them know you better than you think.'

'You mean they could have been keeping an eye on my career.'

'Possibly and, as I said, you did kick-start things by asking Colmead about your parents' research papers. That gave them enough time to set this up.'

'I could have forgotten all about Sarah Redburn.'

'Crowder saw to it that you didn't.'

Marvik peered at the thickening cloud and grey sea as his mind grappled with the turn of events. After a moment, he said, 'This is a mission?'

'Probably, but unofficially as far as we're concerned. Crowder must have known that the notebook and disk existed and that it had fallen into Sarah's hands. He might even know what's on it, or suspect what it contains, and we are being detailed to find out. Crowder knew you would involve me and that you would follow through on it after he told you Sarah's death was somehow connected with your parents'. You approached Colmead and Bell, one or the other of them reported back to Freestone, who told Culverham. They had to devise a way of helping you get to the truth but without alerting Sarah's killer, because they knew that whoever is behind this is dangerous, as it has already proved with the incendiary device in your cottage, and Freestone's death.'

'And Culverham sold his sleek motorboat for a classic boat just for me?' Marvik said incredulously.

'His sleek motorboat is probably moored up elsewhere. He bought the Fairey Swordsman with your money, or, I should say, money in an account in your name. It would be interesting to know when that account was opened.'

'And why there is, or was, such a considerable sum of money in it. Just who is Culverham?'

'A highly paid civil servant like Freestone is my guess and not a petro-chemical engineering consultant. I haven't been able to find anything about him on the internet or the databases I can access. Perhaps we'll get some answers in his apartment. We might even find him there.'

Strathen didn't need to add, 'dead'. 'We're going to take a look?'

'Pick me up at Hamble Marina.'

'Almost there now.'

Strathen was waiting on the visitors' pontoon. There was a damp unseasonal chilliness in the wind as they headed across the Solent and moored up at the marina at West Cowes as before. They checked that Culverham's boat was still on its allotted berth. It was. And they found it exactly as it was before.

Once again, they made their way through the narrow streets of the town. The promenade in front of Culverham's apartment was deserted, because of the inclement weather, which suited their purposes perfectly. Strathen pressed his finger on the buzzer. There was no reply. He glanced up at the camera over the door.

'It's linked to the video entry system rather than a recording surveillance device,' he said, but they pushed down their sailing caps and averted their faces anyway to be on the safe side. Using an electronic device, Strathen found the frequency of the entry mechanism and it swung open easily. They climbed the stairs to the top floor. 'There'll be a camera in the lift and I need the exercise.'

Marvik wasn't going to argue, there was no need. Neither of them were the slightest bit out of breath when they reached the fifth floor, and if Shaun's leg pained him, he would never admit it. The carpeted corridor was silent. Strathen once again manipulated the lock and edged the door open. No alarm sounded. They stepped into a narrow hallway. No one rushed out to greet them and there was no smell of death.

Strathen took the door facing them while Marvik took the one to his right. He entered a spacious living room with a kitchen area beyond it. The rain was bashing against the wide windows, which faced onto a balcony. The room was comfortably furnished in a contemporary clinical style. Beside the glass-topped table in front of the windows was a telescope, which was about the only personal touch in the room devoid of books, magazines and photographs. Marvik thought it looked more like a holiday let than someone's permanent residence. But then this could be Culverham's second or even third property for all he knew.

He crossed to the kitchen and opened the drawers and cupboards. They contained the usual — kitchen utensils, tins of food, coffee, tea and sugar, cleaning materials in the cupboard under the sink and some good wine in the wine rack. Nothing perishable though and no letters or paperwork, no bank statements, bills or correspondence, and no phone or computer.

'No dust either,' he added to Strathen, who had joined him. 'He could have a cleaner. There's no note of who that might be, and I doubt anyone in this apartment block will know. Most of the flats are probably empty.'

'He's got some good-quality clothes, a couple of bespoke suits, made in Hong Kong or London, I'd say. I can look up the tailor's name on the internet and see if I can get more information on Culverham from them. There are also some casual chain-store trousers, shoes — size nine — underwear, shirts — three handmade, and two department store bought. Nothing in the pockets. About my height if the trousers are anything to judge by, but slimmer, lean. No books or photographs. Towels in the bathroom — clean, unused, shaving cream and shower gel, barely touched. No medicines. The second bedroom has a double bed, unmade. No clothes or any other items in it.'

Marvik turned to stare out at the Solent through the rain-soaked windows. A ferry was steadily ploughing in. The promenade was devoid of the usual Sunday midday strollers. He felt disappointed though not surprised by their findings.

Strathen said, 'Perhaps someone's tidied up after abducting him or luring him away. We don't know what car he drives, but there must be a garage or parking bay with this flat. Let's check it out.'

They returned to the ground floor and located a rear door at the end of the corridor. Marvik pressed a release button to the right and they stepped into a yard with allocated parking bays. In Culverham's space was a dark-blue saloon car.

'He hasn't driven off then.' Strathen noted the registration plate number. 'Nothing on any of the seats and probably nothing in the boot. Shame I can't unlock it without setting off the alarm.'

Marvik gazed around in the pouring rain and up at the windows of the flats. 'I doubt there's anyone around to hear it, and even if they do, they'll probably think it's gone off by mistake.'

'OK, here goes. Let's hope we don't find a rotting corpse inside.'

They didn't. In fact, there was nothing. They beat a hasty retreat before anyone got curious. Thoughts were running around Marvik's mind as they called in at one of the pubs for some lunch.

'I'd like to talk to Nigel Jellicoe and find out more about this bank account in my name,' he said.

Strathen relayed Jellicoe's phone number and a few minutes later, Marvik came off the line having arranged to meet Jellicoe on the visitors' pontoon at Chichester Marina at three. He hadn't mentioned anything about the bank account — he'd deal with that when he was face to face with the man. He'd simply said he had some questions to ask him about the *Golden Fleece* if he didn't mind answering them. Jellicoe had asked whether he could help over the phone, but Marvik had said he was on his way to Chichester Marina anyway and would be grateful if Jellicoe could spare the time to meet up personally. He assured him he was perfectly happy with the craft and there was no problem. 'I won't take up much of your time, Mr Jellicoe, but if it's inconvenient perhaps I could call on you, or arrange another time to meet up.' Jellicoe had agreed the 3 p.m. meeting with some reluctance.

After they'd eaten, Strathen gently pumped the staff in the marina office for further information on Roland Culverham, saying he was concerned as he wasn't answering his phone and wasn't on his boat or in his flat. No one had seen Culverham since the end of April, when he had arrived on the new boat. He never attended any of the marina functions nor was he particularly friendly with any of the berth holders. He was rarely there as he worked abroad a great deal. By their description he was a tall, slim, well-spoken man with grey hair.

Marvik postponed the thoughts that were troubling him about Culverham and, as they made for Chichester Marina in the mid-afternoon, he called Julie Pembroke on her mobile. He apologized for disturbing her on a Sunday and asked her if Michael Colmead had received a letter from Dr Lanbury in the last week enquiring about his whereabouts. She said that if he had, Michael hadn't mentioned it to her. Next he asked if she knew, or had heard of, Roland Culverham. She hadn't. It was as he had expected.

'Can you find out who Hugh Freestone has named as his beneficiaries? I know that's confidential but I can't get any response from Hugh Freestone and there might be something in his file that could give me some ideas as to where Michael is,' he pressed. He didn't believe that for one minute. He doubted Julie did either but as she was desperately worried about her boss, she promised to check in the morning and call him.

As they headed farther east on the rolling sea, Marvik recalled when he had done much the same with Helen Shannon on board. The thought made him smile, although their task to find her sister's killer hadn't been a happy or pleasant one. He remembered how she had gazed out at the tranquil waters of Chichester Harbour and the South Downs in the distance and had said, "It's nice here. Quiet too, except for those noisy seagulls." They were still noisy. But she had found a moment's peace.

They moved out of the rain, although the afternoon remained overcast. Marvik reached the marina with ten minutes to spare. As it was, Jellicoe didn't show for another thirty minutes.

The overweight man in his mid-forties stepped on to the pontoon. His eyes alighted on Marvik and away again.

Marvik stepped forward. 'Mr Jellicoe.'

'Yes?' he answered warily.

'I'm Art Marvik.'

Jellicoe's malleable round face registered surprise, then bewilderment, before suspicion swiftly followed. Marvik, who already had his passport in his hand, held it out. 'This will verify it.'

Jellicoe glanced at it apprehensively and then back at Marvik. 'Minus the scars,' Marvik said. 'It was taken before I got these. I'm a former Royal Marine and this is my colleague, Shaun Strathen. You spoke to him earlier on the phone.' Strathen had appeared on deck.

Jellicoe still looked bewildered. 'I don't understand.'

Neither did Marvik, but he'd like to. 'I know I am not the man who came to you and bought the *Golden Fleece*, but I'd like to know who did.'

Jellicoe ran a hand through his dark hair, which flopped onto his brow and almost over his right eye. He pushed it back as his slightly ruddy face paled. 'You don't mean this was some kind of fraud? I took that money in good faith.'

'It's OK, I know you did. No one's claiming you were swindled, and neither was I.'

'But I—'

'Would you like to come on board?'

Jellicoe looked alarmed. He took a step back. 'I really don't see how I can help you.' His eyes were darting around as though he would dearly love to escape. 'The man who bought my boat said he'd seen it up for sale on the club owners' website and had always wanted to own a classic boat. He came and viewed it here, made an offer there and then, didn't want to fuss with a boat survey and said he would arrange to pay me by bank transfer. He wanted the boat urgently.'

'Did he say why?'

'Only that he wasn't in the best of health, so he wanted to get some cruising in before it was too late. The money went through no problem. I called him to tell him.'

'He gave you a mobile number?'

'Yes.'

'Do you still have it?'

'Probably. It's on my phone somewhere, I guess.'

'I'd like it.'

Jellicoe hesitated. Marvik said, 'I'm happy for you to call him yourself while we're here and ask if he'd speak to me, the real Art Marvik.'

'No, you can have it.' Jellicoe quickly reached for his phone. It was clear from his manner and his expression that he wanted away from there as rapidly as possible. He probably thought they were two heavies out to find this interloper and question him. Within seconds Jellicoe was relaying the number to Strathen, who punched it into his own phone and left the deck.

Jellicoe shifted nervously. 'There's nothing more I can tell you. Once the money had gone through, he came and collected the boat.'

'So you met him twice?'

Jellicoe nodded.

'I'd like the bank details he gave you.'

'I'm not sure—'

'It *is* an account in my name and I'd prefer not to report this to the police.'

'I haven't got the details on me.'

'Then perhaps we could drive to your house and get them.'

'Now?'

'It would save me hanging around or returning.'

Jellicoe looked uneasy but agreed, probably because he saw it was the only way to get shot of him, Marvik thought. Within twenty minutes, Marvik had the salient details. He asked Jellicoe for a description of Culverham. It was similar to that the marina staff at Cowes had given them: about mid-sixties, silver-haired, lean.

With various thoughts tumbling through his head, Marvik sprinted back to the marina. Strathen was waiting for him in the main salon.

'It's a London branch of a national bank,' Marvik said, panting from his exertions. 'Jellicoe is correct, the account is in my name.'

'The phone number Jellicoe gave us for Culverham is not the same one the marina staff gave us. But it's dead just the same.'

'Which is what he is.'

'You don't know that for certain.'

'I do,' Marvik replied with conviction. 'Because I fished him out of the River Arun. Roland Culverham is Hugh Freestone.'

CHAPTER THIRTEEN

'The description Jellicoe gave us could fit any number of men but it's Freestone all right,' Marvik said with conviction. He took the seat opposite Strathen across the table in the salon. 'It all adds up to being him. The empty, impersonal flat, the fishing rod, the picture, the absences.'

'Which means there is a lot more to Freestone than a reclusive retired civil servant.'

'Yes. Neither Galt nor Lanbury knew where Freestone sprang from, and there's nothing in the files to indicate he was named as my guardian, but someone appointed him. Was that my parents verbally before they died or someone else after their deaths? Who would do that?' It was a rhetorical question because ideas were already flying through Marvik's mind and had been for a while. He knew Strathen would be thinking along the same lines.

He voiced Marvik's thoughts. 'The British government. And they also made sure to remove your parents' computers, disks and notebooks from the boat and their house after their deaths.'

'Except one, which they overlooked. Either Davington managed to get it off that boat, or my father or mother gave it to someone before their deaths. And that person was not

Sarah Redburn but somehow she got hold of it. I can't see Freestone having it in his possession all these years and then giving it to Sarah. He would have known the information was dangerous and wouldn't have put her life at risk.'

'Maybe she stole it from him.'

Having met her, admittedly only the once, Marvik didn't see her as a thief. But then, as Galt had said of Verity Taylor, professional ambition can drive people to extreme lengths.

Strathen said, 'There are another couple of possibilities. One, Freestone was not only working for the British government but for another one, or another party, hence his dual identity. He, on behalf of one of his masters, was very keen to get hold of the missing disk. By becoming your guardian, he had access to anyone who approached you and he could intercept your mail. But the missing notebook and computer disk never showed up, and there was no reference to it in your belongings, so when you said you were joining the Marines, he was glad to let you go. His assignment was ended until earlier this year. Sarah Redburn approached you and someone knew she had come into possession of that computer disk.'

Marvik thought that made some sense and it echoed the ideas that had occurred to him while running back to the boat.

'The second option is that your parents were working for a rival government or party.'

'And were taken out by British Intelligence?' Marvik wasn't so keen on that theory.

'Maybe it was an accident, or perhaps they *were* targeted. Their deaths meant a swift search of the vessel and their house, and the seizure of all information relating to whatever project it was they were working on.'

'But what could they have been doing?'

'Whatever it was, and whoever it was for, it required both your parents' subjects of expertise, marine archaeology and oceanography. And I certainly don't think it was the search for the *Flor de la Mar*.'

'Neither do I. One of their colleagues must have seen them during those years,' Marvik insisted with exasperation. 'They must have put in somewhere and corresponded with some of their friends and fellow professionals.'

'You say that both Galt and Lanbury claim they didn't — can we believe them?'

'Well Lanbury certainly seems keen to get his hand on their research. Verity Taylor may have approached him, or it could be the other way around, that he approached her because he needs someone to do his running and he asked her to contact Galt and visit Freestone. But I just can't see him using it for any lucrative, illegal or dubious professional means. I'd say he's strictly honest and on the level. Not so Verity Taylor.'

'Was there a coroner's inquest on your parents?'

'There must have been, but there's nothing in my papers or in Colmead's archived files about it, although that's not necessarily suspicious. I'd only be given a copy if I requested it.'

'I bet you don't even know where the inquest was held?'

'I assume the Isle of Wight, that being their formal address.'

'Were their bodies flown home there?'

'I never asked. I don't even know the extent of their injuries or how they were identified. I accepted what I was told and forgot it for twenty years.' He rose and turned to the helm.

'You might learn something from that bank account in your name.'

'I'll go up to town tomorrow.' Marvik started the engine. Strathen cast off and Marvik made for Hamble. Strathen offered him a bed for the night and this time Marvik accepted. Before he retired to the spare bedroom he again went through the papers he'd taken from his safe deposit box. There was, as he'd already stated, nothing about the inquest. Galt had told him she had organized the memorial service. Freestone must have organized the scattering of the ashes at sea but what about the service at the crematorium? Had there been one? He certainly hadn't gone to one and there was nothing in their wills about not wanting a service. Strathen said he'd contact the Isle of Wight coroner's office and the crematorium in the morning. He'd also try the mainland crematoriums in Portsmouth and Southampton.

Early the next morning, Marvik moored up at Ocean Village Marina in Southampton and walked briskly to the railway station. Julie Pembroke called him while he was on the train to London.

'I've looked up Mr Freestone's will,' she said. 'His estate is left to the Sailors' Society, the Shipwrecked Mariners' Society and the Fishermen's Mission.'

Marvik knew all three. Their offices were based along the coast. He hadn't expected to be named but he considered the fact that Freestone had chosen three charities connected with the sea. Maybe it meant nothing. Or perhaps Freestone had chosen them because he had worked in a field connected with the marine industry, another small factor that matched up with his parents. Julie's next comment also quickened his interest.

'This will was made last July.'

The time of Marvik's discharge from the Marines. But that didn't necessarily mean anything.

She confirmed there was still no sign nor sound from Michael Colmead and that Donald Merstead had told her he'd call the police to report Michael's disappearance if there was no news by the end of the day. *Still putting it off*, thought Marvik, but he wasn't complaining. It suited him fine.

Two and a half hours later, Marvik was in the London bank, where, after showing his passport and waiting what seemed an interminable time for someone to see him, and then even longer for another person higher in authority to provide him with the information he required, he finally learned that the account had been opened in 1991, in his name. The bank couldn't say who had initially opened the account. They claimed there was no record of that. Large sums of money had been deposited until 1997, after which smaller amounts had gone in, designed, Marvik thought, to keep the account open, until the money stopped altogether in 2001, but the account had never been closed and it had accrued interest.

The payment for the Fairey Swordsman hadn't cleaned it out. There was several thousand pounds left but not a fortune. The account address was Culverham's in Cowes and, although the account was in Marvik's name, Culverham was also nominated as a signatory. So even back in 1991 his parents had known Culverham, or rather Freestone, because Marvik was still convinced that Culverham and Freestone were one of the same. And over the years since 2001, Freestone, aka Culverham, must have replied to correspondence from the bank, who would have intermittently checked on the account to ask if it was still required, there not being any activity on it. Culverham had ensured it had stayed open and that the interest was credited. And he must have notified the bank when he'd changed address, or had he owned that apartment at Cowes since 1997?

As Marvik headed back to Waterloo Station he considered the information he'd gained. The money paid into the account between 1991 and 1997 looked as though it had been payment for his parents' services, whatever that might have been. They had chosen for it to go into an account in his name, overseen by Freestone, who then became his guardian on their deaths. So in 1991 they had known that their mission was dangerous and had wanted provisions to be made for their son in the event of not coming through.

The thought disturbed him. He tried to pin down how he felt about them and their deaths in light of all this new information. It was, he thought, a mixture of guilt because he had been unjust to them all these years, and of anger directed at the dead Freestone and his masters, who had kept the truth from him. OK, so as a teenager he might not have been able to understand and handle it but for God's sake, he'd had years since then when he could have taken whatever it was they had been engaged upon on board. How much longer would the secret behind their deaths have been contained if it hadn't been for Sarah's death and him discovering the disk?

Forever was the answer, he thought angrily. But anger wasn't going to get him anywhere. He had an objective to achieve, to find the truth, and only a cool head and rational thought would make that happen. The time for emotions was later. If there was a later.

He turned into the railway station, mulling over what the bank had told him, which wasn't much. They couldn't tell him who had made the payments because it was so long ago and there was no way of tracing the transactions. Marvik didn't believe them. There would be a way, but what they were really saying was that it would take too long and be too much effort. Marvik suspected that wherever the money had originated, the account and its source would now be defunct.

He wondered if someone was monitoring activity on the account. If so, they would have seen Culverham's transaction and followed the same trail as Strathen had to the boat renamed *Phorcys* in Cowes. From there that person — or organization — might have discovered Culverham's dual identity, or perhaps they were already aware of it and Freestone had been silenced. So perhaps Stuart Craven and Verity Taylor hadn't been involved in Freestone's murder. And now that Marvik had made enquiries at the bank would that activate another alert? Was someone from British Intelligence or perhaps Crowder's National Intelligence Marine Squad tailing him?

He surveyed the crowded platform but it was too difficult to spot anyone who might be. Should he face Crowder with what he had? Did Crowder already know that Freestone was dead? And perhaps Crowder also knew that Colmead was missing.

On the train he considered all he had learned, which left him with a string of questions and concerns over what to do next. Then he thought of his task in Crowder's unit, which was to stir up trouble, ask questions, provoke a reaction, flush out assassins. His visit to his safe deposit box last Wednesday to retrieve the disk had sparked the incident of the incendiary device in his cottage, had led him to Colmead's office and then to Freestone's cottage, and had flushed out Craven and Verity Taylor. Nothing had happened after his visit to Professor Galt or Dr Lanbury. Did that mean they weren't a threat to whoever was behind this, or that no one knew he had called on them?

And what of his discovery of this account and his visit to the bank today? Would this prompt a reaction? He'd been wondering where to go next with his investigations but perhaps that was the wrong way of looking at this. He didn't have to go anywhere or do anything. Someone would come to him. How long would he have to wait? Not long, he expected. And if nothing happened then all he had to do was use a lie as bait — he'd claim he had found the missing research and call three people: Verity Taylor, Professor Galt and Dr Lanbury, and see which one of them responded with some kind of action. Would that be an attempt on his life? Not before whoever it was made sure they had the research in their hands. He'd give it until tomorrow and if nothing happened, he'd make those calls.

Alighting from the train, he called Strathen and relayed what the bank and Julie had told him and his decision as to the way forward.

Strathen agreed. 'Your parents were cremated in Southampton and the inquest was held on the Isle of Wight. I've made a request for the report but it could take up to four days to reach me. But I don't think what it has to say will make any difference to what we know. If their deaths were suspicious and there has been a cover-up, which we know is the case, then requesting the report has probably already triggered an alert.'

'So between us we've set off more than enough alarm bells to make someone crawl out of the woodwork.'

'They'll do more than crawl, Art. Be careful.'

Marvik said he would.

He rang off and turned into the marina car park, but he'd hardly gone a few paces when his name was called. Startled, he swung round. Caroline Shaldon, the owner of Nautilus, was climbing out of a white Audi.

'I wonder if I could speak to you for a moment,' she said, drawing level with him. 'It's about Sarah Redburn.'

CHAPTER FOURTEEN

'Would you like to come on board?' Marvik invited.

'I thought a drink over in the bistro.'

'Fine.'

They made for it in the drizzle that had started to fall. She was wearing a yellow sailing jacket and black trousers and there were slightly dark shadows under her brown eyes that he was certain hadn't been there at Sarah's funeral.

'How did you know where to find me?' he asked lightly while his mind was racing with this sudden new development, one he had not foreseen. Or perhaps he had. He and Strathen had expected action but Marvik certainly hadn't anticipated it being so soon and in the form of Sarah Redburn's former boss. His mind was full of suspicions that he couldn't articulate, not even silently, because he couldn't see how she could be involved in all this.

'Letitia told me.'

Marvik eyed her, surprised. 'Professor Galt!'

'Oh, not that you were here. She didn't know where you were, but she gave me the name and make of your boat and I called the marinas along the coast, both west and east of Portland, until I located you. Of course you could have travelled further afield, or moored up where you live, wherever that is, but I thought it worth a try and it paid off. The marina staff told me you hadn't paid for the night and that you weren't on board so I drove on from Portland and waited.'

He remembered that Professor Galt had said that Caroline Shaldon was due to visit RV *Oyster* as the dive boat was owned by her company, but Marvik hadn't told Galt anything about *his* boat. Galt must have taken a look at it on the visitors' berths while he was on board and he hadn't seen her. Or maybe she had enquired about it at the marina office. Why would she though? Was it just curiosity, or was Caroline's remark the lie? She'd gone to a lot of trouble to track him down.

'Why didn't you phone me?' he asked.

'I did, but the number was unobtainable. I obviously put in the wrong digit when you gave it to me at Sarah's funeral. And I didn't ask Letitia for it because I already had it. Besides, I didn't know if you had given her your phone number.'

It could be the truth.

'Sounds a bit feeble, doesn't it?' she said, as though reading his thoughts. 'But when I saw you at Sarah's funeral I was under a lot of pressure, which was why I was short with you. I had to rush off to meet a prospective client. It was an important project and a lucrative one. That, and Sarah's tragic death, not to mention that awful committal — so few mourners, so sad — I just wasn't thinking straight. I'm sorry.'

'No need to apologize.' Marvik pushed open the door and they entered the bistro. It was relatively quiet given it was early evening and a miserable wet Monday. He didn't know much about her background, only what he had researched on the internet after Sarah's death and before the funeral. She'd set up Nautilus Marine Consultancy ten years ago in response to a demand for maritime archaeological contractual services on the south coast of England and had rapidly expanded nationally and internationally. Her client list was impressive and included renewable energy companies, ports, marinas, harbours, utilities, pipelines and mineral extraction companies. The projects were equally imposing: environmental assessments, diving and marine surveys, planning, and maritime heritage, the latter of which was Professor Galt's area of expertise and had been Sarah's.

She pushed down the hood of her sailing jacket to reveal her short, dark hair. There was an air of self-confidence about her and behind the tired eyes a sense of humour. He caught the scent of her perfume; it was spicy and intoxicating. She led the way to a table in the window. He'd have preferred one at the back.

'Were you waiting long for me?' he asked, as she pulled off her jacket and hung it over the back of her chair.

'No. I thought I might miss you but I checked and your boat was still there. I did some work while waiting and made some calls, never like to waste a moment,' she said brightly.

'It must be important what you have to tell me.'

'I don't know. You might make some sense of it and . . . Well, first I need a drink. Letitia Galt is not the easiest person in the world to do business with.'

Marvik put his rucksack on the floor under the table and pulled off his leather bomber jacket as he beckoned to an anaemic-looking, listless waiter. Hanging his jacket on the back of the chair, Marvik scanned the boardwalk. There were only a few people hurrying by. After a brief consultation over the drinks menu Marvik ordered two glasses of red wine. He asked if she would like something to eat. She agreed with alacrity. The waiter gave them the menus to peruse and left to fetch their drinks.

Marvik noted the other occupants in the bistro, just two couples, who didn't seem interested in him and Caroline. He knew no one had followed them here, and there was nowhere directly outside where someone could have them under surveillance, but he couldn't be certain that Caroline wasn't equipped with a recording device. It sounded a bit over the top but Sarah Redburn and Hugh Freestone had been murdered, and there was Colmead's disappearance.

'Did you get those on account of being in the Marines?' She pointed to his scars. She seemed in no hurry to divulge what it was about Sarah she wanted to say, perhaps because they now had a couple of hours to fill. He was in no rush either. Just very curious. Let her tell him in her own time. And, despite his suspicions, he found himself attracted to her.

'Those and a couple of other injuries. Nothing serious,' he dismissed. Talking about his career in the Marines and his injuries was the last thing he wanted to do, and besides there was much of his career he wasn't permitted to speak about anyway. The Official Secrets Act saw to that.

'Didn't you ever consider a career in the same fields as your parents?'

He had done once but after going away to school he'd become steadily more opposed to the idea. He'd blamed their professions for taking them away from him. He wasn't going to tell her that, though. 'I needed something with more action,' he said.

She laughed. He liked the sound of it. 'You'd be amazed at how much action there is in the maritime consultancy business.' He didn't mistake the double meaning in her words.

The waiter returned with their drinks. When he had again departed with their food order, Caroline said with a thoughtful look, 'Have you or the police got any new information about Sarah's murder?'

'If the police have, they haven't told me.'

'But you've got more?'

'No.'

He watched her play with the stem of her wine glass as she eyed him steadily. She was building up to tell him something, but would it be of significance? he wondered.

'You believe that Sarah's death is connected with your parents, don't you?'

He hadn't told her or any of Sarah's former work colleagues the real reason for his interest, the finding of the notebook and computer disk in Sarah's belongings, but he had asked Caroline at the funeral if Sarah had ever mentioned either of his parents. It seemed as though Galt had told Caroline that he'd come enquiring about his parents' missing research and had at the same time asked about Sarah Redburn. It wasn't difficult for an intelligent woman like Caroline to put the two together. How much to tell her though? What did she already know? As he had considered on the train, if he wanted results, then he'd have to start pushing for them. No time like the present. But there was no reason to tell her the whole story, only part of it.

'The last time I saw Sarah—' *and the only time*, he added to himself — 'she asked me if I knew why my parents had been in the Straits of Malacca when they were killed. I didn't then and I still don't know. I thought that Professor Galt, being a close friend of my mother's, might have known what they had been working on. Sarah mentioning them and then shortly afterwards her dying made me feel . . .' He hesitated.

'Guilty?' Caroline furnished. 'You shouldn't.'

He didn't, only angry and determined. But perhaps showing vulnerability might draw more information from Shaldon as to why she had been so keen to seek him out. 'I feel a sense of responsibility. Perhaps if I find the answer to what my parents were doing, I'd feel better about Sarah's murder.'

'But it's not your job to find her killer. Surely the police have the resources to do that.'

'They seem to have come to a dead end. She didn't deserve to die or to be killed like that.'

'No one does. But what can you do?'

'What I *am* doing — asking questions — except they don't seem to be getting me anywhere. Professor Galt mentioned they might have been looking for the *Flor de la Mar*.'

'It's possible, I suppose. And that would have been something that would have interested Sarah, although she never mentioned it to me. But then why should she have?'

'I think that whoever killed Sarah might have known her. It seems she went to meet them willingly, but I have no idea who that was or why she was killed. Sarah was far too young to have worked with, or known, my parents.'

'She might have been researching Dr Marvik for a thesis or paper.'

'Possible.' And that was an area that Marvik hadn't checked, but it would be easy to do so. He could ask at the universities where Sarah had obtained her degree and search the internet. He said as much, but Caroline shook her head.

'There was nothing published. I've seen her full CV, remember. But it could have been an ongoing project that never saw publication.'

Marvik thought of Sarah's files that had been burned in the house fire on Eel Pie Island. He'd only briefly checked through them because the notebook with *Vasa* written on it in his father's handwriting had sidetracked him — that and the fact the house was on fire.

Their meals arrived. It was some minutes before Caroline picked up where they had left off. 'I've never heard any word of what your parents were engaged on during that time and, as I said, Sarah didn't mention them to me, but she might have done to Letitia.'

Marvik sat up at this new information. 'Professor Galt claimed not to know Sarah.'

'She lied to you. Oh, I don't think it was deliberate,' Caroline hastily added. 'Letitia is hopeless at names. It's what I came to tell you, as well as the fact that it prompted my own thoughts about Sarah.'

'Anything you can tell me might help.'

She nodded and after a moment continued. 'Over lunch today Letitia told me that she and Guy had met you and you were curious to know what had happened to your parents' research papers at the time of their deaths. When Letitia left us to take a call on her mobile, Guy told me you had asked about a marine archaeologist called Sarah Redburn and that Letitia had denied knowing her.'

Marvik recalled that Kranton had been with him and Galt in the salon when he had enquired. 'Guy never said anything.'

'Perhaps because he didn't want to embarrass Letitia in front of you.'

'Galt doesn't look the type to be embarrassed.'

'Not normally, no.' She hesitated and looked concerned. 'But Guy's worried about her. He thinks she might have early onset dementia. Oh, not just because she forgot a name, but he says there have been other incidences.'

'Such as?'

'Repeating herself.'

'Don't we all?'

She smiled, then looked more serious. 'Guy says Letitia's been making mistakes with her work and getting more agitated and more irritable. I told Guy not to worry, but he will. He's very fond of her, though God alone knows why. She treats him abominably.'

'How long have they worked together?'

'For ever. They met on a marine exploration in the 1970s. Kranton, ex-navy, was the bosun on a ship that Letitia was working on as a young marine archaeologist, RV *Acionna* off the coast of Namibia in search of the *Vento Do Mar*, a sixteenth-century Portuguese ship rumoured to have sunk with thousands of pounds of gold and silver coins on board. It's never been found. Letitia's relationship with Guy seems to be more platonic than romantic, although it could have been the latter at one time, I suppose. I don't really know, and I've never picked up any gossip about them being an item. In fact, I've never heard of Letitia having any affairs or romantic entanglements with anyone.'

'And Guy?'

'No amorous liaisons, as far as I'm aware, but there could have been many, for all I know. He's very charismatic and attractive in a brutish sort of way. But aside from being about twenty years older than me, he's not my type.'

He wondered if she wanted him to ask who her type was. But he remained silent and continued eating, while into his mind came Helen with her blunt manner and her purple hair.

After a moment, Caroline continued. 'There was someone once, three times in fact, but only one with whom I walked up the aisle. The first one. Divorced after eighteen months, nine years ago. I was very young when I married him. I'd just got my MSc in marine archaeology. He was a pharmaceutical rep who thought more of his drug portfolio than me. God alone knows where he is now.'

'And the other two?'

'Do you really want to know?'

'No.'

She laughed. 'Wise man. What about you?'

'No one.'

'Has there been?'

'Not really.' Which was the truth. There had been girlfriends both steady and fleeting but no one he had wanted a commitment with. He said, 'To get back to Letitia and Sarah . . .'

She gave him a look that said, 'It's OK with me if you don't want to get personal.'

'After you had left Letitia and Guy,' she said, 'Guy told me he asked Letitia why she had denied knowing Sarah Redburn. She said she couldn't remember every marine archaeologist she has ever worked with. It was eighteen months ago that Letitia and Sarah worked together, before Sarah worked at Eastbourne on one of my projects.'

'Did Guy know Sarah?'

'No. He wasn't on that project, but he remembers Letitia talking about her.'

'What did she say?'

Caroline continued eating. Was she considering her answer or was she, like Verity Taylor, thinking up a plausible lie? He said nothing but ate without really tasting the food. He was too preoccupied for that.

'Letitia thought highly of Sarah's work,' Caroline resumed. 'And coming from her, that was praise indeed, which was why Guy was worried that Letitia didn't recall her. Sarah was engaged to assist Letitia for three weeks. Letitia was overseeing a coastal heritage project on the Isle of Wight, examining the impact of development on the coastal population. Sarah was seconded to Letitia's team, working from our office here in Southampton. She was assigned to pull together the digital data collected from the various maritime and heritage databases. They liaised by email and phone with one meeting at the beginning of the project and another before the final presentation. Letitia is extremely focused on her work. For her, it's the results that count, not who actually made those results happen, which could be why she forgot the name.'

'Not a team player then? I'd have thought she'd have to be in her field.'

'She's good at directing a team. She very much likes to be in charge. Some scientists and skippers find her difficult to work with.'

He thought of Galt's acidic barbs about Lanbury and Verity Taylor. He could well imagine her scorn for those she found lacking in her own field. 'So Kranton soothes things over.'

'Yes. Guy is a saint and worth his weight in gold. He's very good at easing any tensions between her and the team, especially the younger members. If Letitia is engaged on a project for Nautilus, I have to choose the team carefully. But having her on a project is very prestigious. She has a formidable reputation. Discovering the *Cessabit* in the Sargasso Sea just off Bermuda in 1996 made her a household name in marine archaeological circles.'

Marvik had read as much when he had researched her on the internet.

Caroline pushed away her empty plate. 'Guy's remarks made me think about Sarah and the last time I saw her, which was in February. I know I didn't tell you this at the funeral,' she added when she must have seen his surprised look. 'But then we didn't really get much chance to talk. Looking back on it now, Sarah didn't seem her usual self. Generally speaking, she was a shy, quiet woman, clever and knowledgeable and passionate about her subject. But that time she seemed edgy and distracted. I thought she might have been having second thoughts about working for us on the Gibraltar project for Jason Marine Exploration, a private deep-ocean exploration company specializing in locating shipwreck treasures and artefacts.'

But Marvik knew the source of Sarah's disturbed state, which had nothing to do with her forthcoming project but was connected with her father's disappearance in 1978 and her efforts to find out what had happened to him. He wasn't going to tell Caroline that. It wasn't really relevant anyway.

'Sarah had just returned from Scandinavia.'

That was news to Marvik but it didn't necessarily mean much. 'Whereabouts?' he asked.

'Sweden. She was based in Stockholm.'

But that did mean something. Stockholm was the home of a museum named after a ship that had capsized and sunk there in 1628. The story of how it had been discovered and salvaged had inspired his mother to become a marine archaeologist. It had also been the reason why his parents had chosen to name their boats after it, *Vasa*. He brought his attention back to Caroline while desperately trying to postpone fathoming out the significance — if there was one — of this latest piece of information.

'Sarah was one of a team of marine archaeologists engaged by Norvol Exploration, who were laying a pipeline in the Baltic Sea, and at the same time wanted to record and make sure they protected the many shipwrecks there. Sarah was working on desk research and cataloguing for three months, from November through to the beginning of February. It's not one of our projects. She was working directly for Norvol.'

'You say "our" projects. You have other directors?'

'No. It's just a figure of speech. Nautilus is my company, but I never think of it like that. I engage so many talented professionals in the marine industry that it really is "us". If ever you are looking for a new job or a new challenge . . .'

'I'll know where to come,' he finished for her.

Galt had lied to him. And Sarah had worked in Sweden. Did either fact mean anything? There was also the matter of Galt not telling him about Verity Taylor asking about his parents' papers. Was it really a case of forgetfulness or the early signs of dementia, or was there more that Galt was deliberately hiding?

'Seriously, though,' Caroline broke through his racing thoughts, 'what do you do now you're out of the Marines?'

It took him a few seconds to pull himself up. 'I tried a stint at maritime security.'

'A growth area. It didn't work out?'

'No.' He wasn't going to tell her about his failure, that he'd let a man die. Even though it hadn't been his fault, it had happened on his watch. 'I'm not sure where I go from here.' He also wasn't going to mention working for Crowder and the National Intelligence Marine Squad. That was highly confidential. His remit was to work undercover. Not even the rest of Crowder's team knew about him and Strathen.

'Well if you fancy a contract, I could always do with someone with your expertise.'

'You don't know what that is.'

'The Marines means you are an expert diver, you understand how the sea behaves, you're used to working alone or in a team, you're disciplined, fit and can look after yourself. You're also trained to be cautious but take risks.'

Her words made him think of Fred Davington. The same could be said of Gordon Hillingdon, Davington's former buddy and fellow sapper.

'Do you fancy writing my CV?' Marvik joked.

'Any time,' she said solemnly, then smiled broadly, leaving him in no doubt as to what part of his CV she might be interested in writing, and it had nothing to do with his professional career. He found himself flattered and a little excited. Oh, to hell with it — more than a little. He left a short pause before asking her if she would like a dessert.

'No, but I'll have coffee on your boat, that is if the invitation to go on board is still open, and if you're not rushing off anywhere.'

It was and he was glad she'd taken it up. He called for the bill. On leaving the bistro he made sure to check who was leaving at the same time. No one. And no one followed them. The pontoons were deserted.

It was dark. The rain had ceased, leaving behind a damp, dull night. The sea was slapping against the boat, which rocked gently on its berth.

'Lovely boat,' she said. 'How long have you had it?'

'Since July. It was a present to myself when I left the Marines.'

She raised her dark eyebrows. He knew she was thinking, 'Expensive present', but he didn't own a property and his parents had left him extremely well provided for financially. Now it seemed Freestone had bestowed an expensive gift on him.

She climbed nimbly on board. But then she was used to boats in her line of work.

'I'll give you the guided tour.'

It didn't take long. Soon they were back at the central helm. He made a coffee. As he handed her the mug her hand brushed his, sending the electricity flying between them. Carefully, she put the mug on the table. He knew what was required of him. He didn't need any prompting. The smell of her was intoxicating, her softness exhilarating, and when he kissed her, she responded hungrily.

Huskily she said, 'I think that coffee will have to wait.'

He had no objection and kissed her again. His mobile phone rang. He cursed. Pulling back from her, he made to answer it, but her hand stilled his.

'Leave it,' she said, eyeing him with such desire that he thought he would leave Rome burning if she asked him to.

He kissed her slowly. Her eyes were a smouldering brown, the shadows under them enticingly sexual. He wasn't on an official mission. His time was his own. What difference would a few hours make? His phone fell silent.

CHAPTER FIFTEEN

Tuesday

It was just after 2.30 a.m. when Marvik quietly slid out of bed. Caroline didn't stir. Leaving the master cabin, he picked up his rucksack and made his way to the upper helm. Inside the rucksack were his three phones — the mission mobile Strathen had given him, the one Crowder had issued to him, and his personal one. It was the latter that had rung earlier, which he'd ignored. If it had been either of the other two he would have answered it. If Strathen had anything to report, or had been concerned about his safety, he would have rung through on the mission mobile, and Marvik would not have been able to ignore the ringtone of Crowder's summons. Marvik wondered if it might have been Julie calling him, although the late hour made that seem unlikely unless she had managed to get in touch with Michael Colmead, or perhaps his body had been found.

But Marvik saw with a start that the call had been from Dr Lanbury. He cursed silently. He'd been an idiot to ignore it. But maybe it was nothing, just Lanbury chasing up to see if he'd found any of his father's papers or notebooks. It was far too early in the morning to return the call but Lanbury had left a message.

'Marvik, I need to see you urgently.' Lanbury's eager voice throbbed with excitement. 'I know where your parents were in 1991 and have an idea what they were doing during the years before their deaths, which might . . . Well, I'll tell you when I see you. Most intriguing. When can you get here? Doesn't matter when it is, I never sleep well anyway. Most extraordinary.'

Marvik's self-loathing deepened. He cursed himself for letting his loins rule his head. How could he call Lanbury at this hour of the morning? He couldn't. He would have to wait until at least six before trying, but he was too impatient and too angry with himself for being so easily distracted. And from Lanbury's tone of voice the discovery he had made sounded genuine and was extremely significant. He could at least ring now and leave a message on Lanbury's voicemail.

Marvik turned to face the choppy dark sea and rang, waiting anxiously for the voicemail to switch in, ready to say that he could be contacted any time Lanbury picked up the message. He was amazed and heartily relieved when Lanbury himself answered and, judging by his voice, he didn't sound at all tired or as though Marvik had woken him. Marvik apologized all the same but Lanbury brushed that aside, interjecting before Marvik had finished.

'How soon can you get here? I'm at home,' he said excitedly.

'What have you discovered?' Marvik asked eagerly and as quietly as he could. The upper helm was as far away as he could get from the master cabin where Caroline was, but she might nevertheless hear him if she woke.

'I can't tell you over phone. When can you get here?' Lanbury insisted.

Marvik recalled that Lanbury lived in the New Forest close to Bucklers Hard Yacht Harbour. It would take him about thirty minutes by car, but as he didn't have a car he'd go by boat and then on foot to Lanbury's house. It was only a short trip back out to the Solent via Southampton Water and then up the twisting Beaulieu River to Bucklers Hard

Yacht Harbour, but there were speed restrictions and he could hardly turf Caroline out of bed. Or could he? Perhaps she'd understand if he woke her saying he had been called away urgently. He couldn't return to sleep now.

'I can try and be with you by six.'

'You know where to find me.'

Marvik said he did, but he was impatient and hungry for information, which he would already have had in his possession if he'd been stronger willed. 'Can't you give me any idea of what you've discovered?'

'It's remarkable. It goes back to 1976. It was . . . But it's far too complicated to explain over the phone. I'm not sure I understand it anyway. I might have got it wrong. I'll tell you when you get here.'

Lanbury abruptly rang off. Marvik's excitement was compounded by his frustration at Lanbury's mutterings and from not being free to set off immediately. What did he mean it goes back to 1976? What did? How did that year have any connection with his parents? They hadn't even met then. Or perhaps Lanbury was referring to what his father had been working on in 1976. But even then Marvik couldn't see what impact that would have had twenty-one years later in 1997. Where would his father have been in 1976 at the age of thirty-five? Marvik didn't know but he hoped that he would soon find out. He was also concerned that Lanbury had voiced this to Verity Taylor, his so-called researcher, but as he returned to the galley he thought that Lanbury would have considered it too late last night to disturb her and certainly too early this morning to contact her. The sooner he reached Lanbury the better.

There was no movement or sound from the master cabin. Caroline was still sleeping. He made himself a coffee, more for something to do and to think than because he needed one, and took it back to the upper helm. There he surveyed the marina in the dark early morning. The breeze was picking up. The forecast was for a strengthening wind and a low pressure front moving from the west. How fast it would hit here the forecasters hadn't said yesterday, because they didn't know. Maybe by now they did. And perhaps in a few hours he'd know what his parents had been doing during those missing years. If only Lanbury had said, but then perhaps he was right to be cautious and it was too important and complex to explain over the phone.

He drank his coffee without tasting it and fired up his laptop computer. He looked up events for the year 1976. There had been the usual political shenanigans in the UK. Harold Wilson had resigned, and James Callaghan had become Prime Minister. The IRA had set off bombs in the West End. There had been a fire on the Royal Navy's latest guided missile destroyer while it was being fitted out at a shipyard near Newcastle-upon-Tyne, killing eight men. The Cod War, as opposed to the Cold War, was still raging between Britain and Iceland over fishing zones, and there had been violent clashes between black demonstrators and police in Soweto. Three Britons and one American had been killed by firing squad for their part in the murder of fellow mercenaries in the Angolan Civil War. The water crisis in the UK had deepened because of the prolonged drought, and there was the usual Royal story — Princess Margaret and Snowdon had split. Aside from this there were prison riots, fights, thefts and huge earthquakes in Italy and China. The list could go on. But he couldn't find any reference to shipwrecks being located in 1976.

He shut down his computer. His thoughts veered to Caroline and last night. He took a breath as he recalled their lovemaking. It had been intense at first, then gentler but equally as passionate and fulfilling. His suspicions about her possibly having been sent by someone returned. Had her task been to encourage pillow talk and get information from him on his investigations into his parents' deaths and their missing research? Galt had implied that Verity Taylor would use sex to achieve her aims, perhaps Caroline did too. And he had fallen for it.

He felt the boat rock and turned to see her emerge on the upper helm. She was fully clothed. He hadn't heard her get up or move about, a thought that depressed him because it was the second time recently that he'd been taken by surprise — first by Verity creeping up on him at Freestone's cottage and now Caroline. He'd been too deeply engrossed in his thoughts. He disguised his depression at the thought he was losing his edge and said brightly, 'You're up early.'

'Later than you though.' She eyed him, concerned. 'That call last night, was it important?'

His brightness hadn't fooled her. Was he that transparent? Obviously. Perhaps she had feigned sleep as he'd crept out of the cabin and overheard his conversation with Lanbury. Or perhaps, he thought with growing despair, she had checked his phone while he'd slept and he hadn't sensed or heard her. But no, he was certain he would have known that. He was a light sleeper even after sex. She could clearly see he was worried about something and she could easily surmise it had something to do with the call he had failed to take last night.

As dismissively as he could, he said, 'Not specifically, but it means I need to get going.'

She moved towards him and put her arms around him, looking up at him with unease, or was it puzzlement? He returned her embrace, but she must have sensed his gesture lacked genuine warmth because she quickly withdrew. Her eyes were slightly bloodshot and seemed to hold a hint of sorrow. Or was that how he felt? A sadness that his tough days in the Marines were now a thing of the long and distant past. It was another life and all his training was slowly being drained from him.

She turned away. 'Then I'll leave you to it.'

His coldness had hurt her. 'Do you want something to eat first?'

'No. I'll wait until I get home.'

Which was where? He didn't know. And he wasn't going to ask. He followed her out on deck, where she hesitated and turned to face him.

'Will I see you again?'

'Of course.'

She just smiled and nodded knowingly. He should tell her he wasn't giving her the brush-off, but then he was. Not solely because he suspected her motives, and not simply because he was disgusted at himself for being so easily fooled. He had also realized Caroline meant nothing to him, whereas someone else did.

'What are you going to do next? About Sarah, I mean?' Caroline's voice broke through his disturbed emotions.

'I'm not sure,' he answered evasively, which was the truth. It all depended on what Dr Lanbury had to tell him.

'Art, I—' But she pulled herself up, smiled again and said, 'Take care.'

He watched her leave with part of him wanting to call after her, but the anger at himself for not taking that call last night and his eagerness to get away was stronger. Hurriedly he made the boat ready and cast off. When he was in Southampton Water, he called Lanbury and said that he should be with him by 5.30 a.m. All Lanbury said before ringing off was, 'Good.'

The wind was whipping up the Solent but soon he was in the more sheltered waters of the Beaulieu River. He slowed as he approached Buckler's Hard Yacht Harbour. The Harbour Master's office wasn't open until 8 a.m., but Marvik moored up on a vacant space on the visitors' pontoon and, after consulting his Ordnance Survey map for the area, which he then pushed into his rucksack, he set off on foot. Dr Lanbury's house was about a mile across country.

It was just after 5.20 a.m. The sun would be rising soon but he used his torch to light the way. The countryside was deserted. As he headed towards Lanbury's cottage the few houses that he passed petered out, leaving a couple of low-level farm buildings, sheds and stables until they also disappeared. His anxiety increased as he drew near to the small detached flint cottage thinking of the similarity between Lanbury's house and Freestone's. It was set back off the lane and isolated. And, as in the case of Freestone's cottage, Marvik knocked and received no answer. There were no lights showing. A sickening feeling churned his stomach.

Perhaps Lanbury had fallen asleep. He knocked again, harder. Still no reply. Marvik stepped back and gazed up at the house. There was no sign of life and the curtains weren't drawn.

He ran around to the rear and noted with deepening concern that the back door was wide open. He cursed vehemently. The signs were ominous. He caught a sound behind him and spun round but there was no one there. He froze, tense, listening and watching. There was nothing. But yes, there it was again, a moaning. No — a groan. It could be a trick to lure him deeper into what looked like a wilderness of a garden, but sod that. He'd handle it.

The groan came again, and Marvik could tell it was no act. Whoever it was was in a great deal of pain. Marvik made for the source and drew up horrified. Lanbury was lying face down on the wet grass behind some bushes.

He swore out loud and rushed to him. Lanbury's sodden jumper was bloody. Some bastard had shot the old man in the back.

Quickly, Marvik wrenched off his jacket and, easing Lanbury over, spread it over his chest. Then gently, Marvik lifted Lanbury's head and cradled it and his shoulders in his arms.

'It's Art Marvik,' he hastily reassured the badly injured man. Lanbury's skin was deathly grey. 'You'll be OK. I'll get an ambulance.'

But Lanbury had enough strength to shake his head and his hand reached out and forestalled Marvik. 'Too late,' he said, clearly mustering all his strength.

With a stab of guilt and self-loathing Marvik felt the remark as a rebuke, even though he knew that Lanbury was meaning it was too late to save him. The reproach though was fully justified. He *was* too late. But the time for recriminations was later, for now he had to get help and to do that he would need to use the phone in the house. He didn't want to give his mobile number or risk it being traced — he couldn't get involved, because how the hell did he explain what was going on?

'I have to leave you to get help.' Marvik made to move but Lanbury again took hold of his arm.

His eyes were wild and imploring. 'Dan . . . found . . . not Arctic Circle . . . Barents Sea . . .' He tried to say more but nothing except air emitted from his bloodless lips, not even a whisper. His lips formed again but no sound came from them. Marvik could see that Lanbury was making a superhuman effort to speak but even that wasn't enough.

'It's OK, take your time,' he said softly while his brain urged the opposite.

Lanbury seemed to shake his head, though the movement was barely perceptible. Then another word vanished into air before he managed to whisper, 'Edinburgh.'

Marvik's brain raced with thoughts. The Barents Sea . . . Edinburgh. These two locations resonated with him, not because of his parents, but because of what he'd learned while undertaking a mission off the Norwegian coast in the Marines. HMS *Edinburgh* was the wreck of a British warship that had been struck by two torpedoes from the German submarine U456, and again by a German destroyer. It had sunk in 1942 and two officers and fifty-six ratings had lost their lives. It had been carrying a very valuable cargo, Soviet gold bullion, in payment for weapons.

'Do you mean HMS *Edinburgh*?'

Lanbury tried to speak but the last of his strength was ebbing away.

'Who did this? Who attacked you?'

'Phorcys.'

Marvik started with shock. It was the last word he had expected to hear from anyone, let alone the lips of a dying man. 'Who is Phorcys?' he urged.

Lanbury made no sound. His breathing faded. He was weakening. For a moment his eyes held Marvik's with pleading in them, not for life but for his understanding. Lanbury's words had cost him a supreme effort. His knowledge, his death. Did his attacker also know what Lanbury had told him? Did he know more?

'What did my father find?'

Lanbury tried desperately to speak. It was clear to Marvik that he was in terrible pain. His heart went out to the poor man and anger coursed through his veins at the bastard who had done this. Marvik leaned closer to catch the words that were nothing more than a breath. Just as Marvik was about to speak, Lanbury whispered, 'Ninety-one.'

'The year?'

But there was no answer. Speech was beyond him. His eyes closed. He was slipping away. Marvik knew he didn't have much time.

'You mentioned 1976, is that connected with what happened in 1991?'

Again, no answer.

'Hang on in there, Dr Lanbury. You'll be fine,' Marvik gently reassured, knowing it was a lie. He'd seen too much death not to recognize it coming. 'I'm returning to the house to get help.' But even as he spoke, he knew that Lanbury was beyond help. He heard the soft, gentle sigh of death, then nothing.

CHAPTER SIXTEEN

Marvik straightened up, removed his jacket and stared down at the body, feeling a deep sadness and uttering a silent vow to get whoever had done this. He checked Lanbury's pockets. There was nothing connected to their conversation and nothing to indicate who Lanbury's killer was. There was also no mobile phone and nothing in the dead man's hands. Marvik scoured the area. Only Lanbury's footprints and his own were there, prints the police would take impressions of, and they would find his hairs on the body and fibres from his jacket on Lanbury. The National Maritime Museum staff would be able to give a description of him and when the police traced Lanbury's calls they would find him. He'd be prime suspect. Motive? Perhaps someone would come forward to provide one connected with his parents' past.

Crowder would know he wasn't guilty of murder. Crowder knew that his parents' deaths weren't accidental. How much more did he know? With a stab of guilt Marvik thought if he'd told Crowder about the notebook and disk then Freestone and Lanbury might still be alive. He should have reported to Crowder and he should have examined that disk instead of shoving it away.

His thoughts had taken him to the house. He entered through the open door into a rear lobby that contained some wellington boots and muddy walking shoes, a few outdoor jackets and a mackintosh. Swiftly, Marvik searched the pockets, wondering if Lanbury's killer was watching him and waiting, not to kill him, although that was possible, but to pick the right time to call the police. Finding nothing of relevance, Marvik headed into the untidy, cluttered kitchen. Rapidly, he opened drawers of the dresser and built-in units finding just utensils, circulars and other miscellaneous items. The narrow hall was crowded with heavy furniture on which there were stacks of books, which were also piled on the stairs and on the telephone table to the left of the staircase.

Marvik covered his hand, lifted the receiver and dialled for the last call made. It was a number he didn't recognize, not his own. Lanbury must have used his mobile phone for that.

In the front room more books were strewn around and photographs of Lanbury on expeditions and with family members were on the shelves and mantelpiece. Briefly, Marvik wondered about Lanbury's family background while he examined the pictures in case his father appeared in any of them. He didn't. His parents hadn't been one for photographs but there had been some. Although none after 1991.

Marvik quickly examined the back of the pictures taken on expeditions. There were nine in total. The dates Lanbury had inscribed on the reverse didn't tally with his parents' missing years. Lanbury must have other photographs around the house, perhaps in the loft. But if one of them had contained the secret, and Lanbury had unearthed it, it was sure now to be in the hands of his killer.

Marvik entered the back room, which was clearly Lanbury's study. Here the chaos was even greater. It was as though Lanbury had decided to turf out every book, every paper and file and go through them. Perhaps he had, or perhaps his killer had done that, searching this house just as Marvik was now.

Through the musty smell of the books, Marvik caught the hint of another scent. It reminded him of Christmas. Cinnamon perhaps, and there was the vague lingering odour of tobacco, which he'd also smelled on Lanbury. That was explained by evidence of a pipe on the desk. There were scraps of paper littered around — notes, scribblings, doodles and some fragments of paper as though Lanbury had been in the process of going through some documents and tearing them up. Two scraps caught Marvik's eye and he frowned as he tried to think why they had pulled him up. He stuffed them into his pocket, not quite knowing why but feeling he needed to make the connection between why the letters on them seemed familiar before discarding them.

He gazed around. Had the killer taken whatever it was that Lanbury had found? Or had Lanbury seen or read something here that had prompted his memory? Marvik didn't have time to go through everything in detail but he checked the top of the desk and cabinets and again the backs of the five pictures in the room. Nothing.

Marvik repeated the same process upstairs waiting for the telltale sound of the sirens or an approaching car but none came, and nothing resulted from his search. Admittedly it was only cursory. Perhaps what Lanbury had found wasn't physical evidence but something he had read, seen and connected with a memory. Had the killer extracted that information from him before killing him? He'd been shot in the back in the garden attempting to flee from the killer. Or had he, like Freestone, entered the garden willingly, lured there by a phone call or a shout and then shot?

This had Verity Taylor's and Stuart Craven's fingerprints all over it. Lanbury could have told the killer what he had discovered because it was a person he trusted, Verity. After eliciting the information, she had given Craven the nod to kill Lanbury and they had executed it while Marvik had been on his way here by boat.

He descended the stairs and hurried through to the kitchen, but as he did, he caught the sound of movement outside. He stepped back into the shadows and waited. Yes, there it was again — footsteps, and they were heading towards him. They stopped just for a few seconds. He imagined whoever it was pausing to listen. Then came a few more steps, a light tread on the crunching path.

Marvik froze and waited. He could hear the soft panting of the newcomer as they stepped inside. Marvik was on him in an instant with his arm around the neck.

The small body stiffened and a scream rang out. Marvik loosened his grip and put his hand over the mouth. He waited for a few moments, straining his ears for any sound from outside. Then he waited a few more as the person tried to struggle free.

No one came and there was only the sound of the wind outside. He released his hand and spun the figure round to face him while keeping a firm hold.

He was looking into the wide, frightened dark eyes of Verity Taylor.

'What the hell do you think you're doing?' she blazed. 'Let me go immediately.'

'Not until you tell me what you're doing here.'

'Why should I?'

'Because I'm asking, and because Dr Lanbury is lying dead in the garden, but then you already know that.'

Her skin paled. If it was an act it was a good one. Alarmed, she eyed him fearfully. 'You killed him!'

'Why should I have done that?'

She tried to struggle free of him but couldn't. If he let her go, she would run. He knew he could catch her, but he didn't see why he should go to all that bother. But he did want to get away from here, and soon.

Defeated in trying to release herself, defiantly, she said, 'Because you don't want the truth about your parents coming out.'

'And what is that truth?'

'I don't know.' She averted her eyes.

Maybe she didn't but she damn well knew something. 'You're lying,' he said roughly.

Her head came up and her eyes flickered with fear. Despite that, she pursed her lips together and renewed her efforts to break away. 'You're hurting me.'

He knew he must be bruising her arm with his solid hold on her. 'I'll ask you again, what are you doing here?' He tightened his grip.

She cried out and grabbed hold of his fingers with her free hand, trying to prise them from her arm before trying to reach up to his face, but his hold was too strong and he was too tall. She could kick against him but didn't. Perhaps she was smart enough to see it wouldn't make any difference.

'I see no reason to tell you anything,' she cried.

'OK then, let's go.' He pulled her towards the door.

'What are you doing? Let me go.' But his grip remained firm, and half pulling, half pushing her, he dragged her, protesting, into the garden to where Dr Lanbury lay.

'Are you responsible for that?' he shouted, pushing her round so that, in the pale light of dawn, she was forced to stare down at the dead, wet, stiff grey body of the elderly man.

'My God!' She put her free hand to her mouth. Her eyes widened with horror and her skin went ashen. 'What the . . .' She glanced up at him and swallowed. 'You think I . . .' But the words died in her throat. Then almost breathlessly, she repeated, 'You killed him.'

'If I did then I don't hold out much hope for you. But no, I didn't kill him. Perhaps your friend Stuart Craven did.'

'He couldn't.'

'Unless you want to be handed over to the police as an accessory to murder, you'd better start telling me what the devil is going on.'

She stared down at Lanbury's body, then back up at him. 'Can we get away from here?'

His thoughts exactly. Keeping a firm grip on her, he swung her round and strode off across the garden towards the road, forcing her to run to keep up with him.

'For God's sake, let me go. I won't run off.'

'Even if you did I'd catch up with you.'

'Then there's no point in trying to leave your fingerprints on my arm permanently.'

His eyes scanned the deserted road. 'How did you get here?'

'My car's parked farther down the lane.'

'Why?'

'What do you mean why?'

'Why not drive it up to the front of the house?'

'Because there's a layby just opposite the entrance to an old barn just before the bend, and it's easier to park there than negotiate this narrow lane where you can't turn round for about half a mile.'

'You've been here before?'

'Of course. You know that I was helping Dr Lanbury with his book.'

And searching for references to Dan Coulter. Parking her car down the lane by a barn was exactly the same yarn she'd spun him about Freestone's cottage. Was Craven suddenly going to appear? Marvik wondered. But Craven had had plenty of time to make an appearance. Maybe he was waiting for a signal from Verity.

'Give me your phone.'

'I — It's in my jacket pocket.'

She indicated the pocket on the side Marvik was holding her. With his free hand he delved into it and, retrieving the phone, switched it off and shoved it in the pocket of his jacket. She looked as though she was about to protest then pressed her lips together. He pulled her across the road to a gap in the hedge that also boasted a public footpath sign.

'Hey, where are we going?' She looked longingly down the road in the direction of her car. If it was there. Or for Craven in his.

'You'll find out soon enough.'

'But . . .' She followed him. She had no choice as he was pulling her across the edge of the field. 'Please, can't you let me go?'

'No.'

'I had nothing to do with Dr Lanbury's death.'

He didn't answer.

'I promise I won't run away.'

'Your promises mean nothing, Verity. You've lied to me right from the beginning.'

She eyed him sullenly but gave up struggling against him, seeing she had no option as they tramped across the muddy field north-westwards. The mud didn't bother Marvik, or his boots, but Verity's flat shoes were caked in it, as were the bottom of her trousers. It made their progress slightly slower than he hoped. The marina wasn't very far though and soon they came on to a tarmacked road. Marvik headed west, still holding on to Verity.

Several minutes passed. 'What are you going to do about Dr Lanbury?' she asked.

'What do you expect me to do?'

'But you can't just leave him there.'

'Why not? I can't bring him back to life. He doesn't know any different.'

'That's obscene!' she cried.

'Yes, and so is murder.' He rounded on her.

She made no further comment. After a quarter of a mile Marvik turned on to the road that led to the boatyard. The light was stronger but it was still early for anyone to be about. Soon they were at the marina, and, holding on to her, he said, 'Walk normally. Don't say anything and don't do anything to attract attention. If you do, I won't hesitate to push you into the water.'

'You wouldn't dare!' But she could see that he would. She tightened her lips and glared at him but did as he asked.

As he came up beside his boat, he quickly scanned the area. No one was about and no one was stirring on the neighbouring yachts. He noted her curious and bewildered gaze as, still holding her, he loosened the lines at the aft and the stern.

'We're going out?' Her voice held a tremor of fear. He guessed she was afraid he might dispose of her overboard. He said nothing to allay her concern. In fact, he thought it might finally make her tell him the truth.

He pushed her into the seat next to him at the helm and ordered her to stay put as he started the engine. She made as though to make a dash for it but within seconds the boat had swung away from the pontoon and they were on the river. 'You'll get very wet if you decide to take a walk,' he said.

She scowled at him and sat down again.

Marvik could still smell Caroline's scent. He wondered if Verity could, not that she would know it was Caroline's, and he didn't care what she thought anyway. The smell of Caroline disturbed him though, not in any lustful way but because it reminded him of his gross error of judgement last night. If he had responded to that call, Lanbury might still be alive and he might have learned more about those missing years.

'Where are we going?' Verity asked, nervously.

'Where we can talk.'

She swallowed hard. 'How do I know you're not going to kill me and throw me overboard?'

'You don't, but maybe you'd very much like to know what Lanbury told me before he died.'

His remark immediately hit home. She eased back into the seat and fell silent.

He took the curving River Beaulieu at a steady speed. Theirs was the only boat moving on it and soon he was in the Solent and making towards the Isle of Wight in the direction of Newtown Harbour, where his cottage was located. Long before that though he veered eastwards towards Osborne Bay. There were no boats moored there. He dropped anchor and stilled the engine.

Clouds were bubbling up in the west. The breeze was picking up and the water slapped against the boat but not yet strong enough to cause any irregular movement. He turned his seat to face Verity, wondering if she was capable of double murder, Freestone and Lanbury. Yes, perhaps she was.

She shifted under his candid gaze but returned it with defiance and eagerness in her eyes. 'What did Dr Lanbury tell you?'

'You first. What were you doing there?'

'How do I know you're going to tell me what he said?'

'You don't.'

She considered for a moment, then began. 'I got a call from him asking me to come quickly. He said he had something important to tell me.'

Was that the truth? 'What time?'

'Just after four thirty this morning.'

As Marvik had speculated earlier, when he had been traveling to Lanbury. But her telephone number wasn't the last number on Lanbury's landline. 'Did he ring you on his mobile?'

'Yes.'

'And you always answer your calls at that time in the morning?' he said, sceptically.

'Depends who's calling. It woke me and when I saw that it was Dr Lanbury, I knew it had to be important.'

'How did he sound?'

'Excited, breathless.'

Was that because he had grabbed his mobile and was trying to make his escape from his killer?

'Did he say he was in danger?'

'No.'

And Lanbury clearly hadn't said that Marvik was on his way, or had he? But Verity had seemed genuinely shocked to find him there. Perhaps though that was because he was alive. Had she known that Lanbury was lying in the garden shot in the back? By her initial reaction when he'd made her look at the body, he'd say not. But as he'd considered before, she could be a very good actress, and she was a liar.

'Did you tell your boyfriend, Craven? Lanbury's killer.'

'No, of course not. That's impossible. Stuart couldn't have killed him,' she insisted.

'Why not?'

'He's just not the type.'

'You know a lot of killers then?' he said, scathingly.

She flushed but remained silent.

'You and Craven searched Freestone's cottage. How do I know Craven, or you, or the pair of you didn't kill Freestone?'

'He's dead?'

'Oh, come on, don't say you didn't know.'

'But how?' Then her eyes widened. 'You mean he's been killed like Dr Lanbury.'

'That's a very dangerous boyfriend you've got.'

'He's not my boyfriend,' she hissed. 'Stuart wouldn't kill anyone,' she repeated, but she was beginning to sound less convinced. 'You're lying. How do you know Freestone is dead?' she challenged. 'I haven't heard anything about it on the news.'

'And what about Michael Colmead, have you or Craven killed him too?'

'What do you mean?' She fingered her mouth nervously. Her eyes looked troubled.

'You didn't phone Colmead, the solicitor, to get Freestone's address from him and then call Freestone to arrange an appointment as you told me because Colmead is missing and has been for eight days.'

She didn't even look shamefaced at the lie.

'So how did you know where Freestone lived?' he asked.

She stared at him for a long while. Marvik watched the expressions cross her face: bewilderment, doubt, and finally resignation. 'You're right, I didn't phone Colmead. Stuart Craven told me he did.'

'Why would Colmead blithely give out Freestone's address?'

'I don't know. Stuart says he did.'

Perhaps Craven had threatened and tortured Colmead into giving it. Craven was not Dewell but Craven and Dewell could be working together along with Verity. Or had Craven lied to Verity?

'And you believe everything he says?'

She opened her mouth to reply, then closed it again. She was possibly wondering if she had been played for a sucker and she didn't much like the thought of it. Or maybe she was still lying.

'So he told you that Colmead had given him Freestone's address and you thought that you would stand a better chance of getting information from Freestone, only he wasn't going to give it to you. You lured Freestone into the garden, as you did Lanbury, and then Craven killed Freestone, took his house keys, and pushed his body in the river.'

'No! I didn't know he was dead.'

So Craven had lied to Verity and said he hadn't harmed Freestone. But Marvik didn't really believe that.

'You and Craven should have searched Freestone's cottage then, but something prevented you from doing so. Or you couldn't find what you were looking for at first, so you decided to return and I happened to be there.'

'I swear I'd never been there before. It's the truth,' she added at his dubious look. 'We believed there might be something that could tell us what your parents had been doing in 1997.'

'Only then?'

'Yes.'

But he knew that was a lie.

'What did you think you'd find?'

'Notes, letters, diaries, computer disks, anything that might have belonged to or come from your parents. Hugh Freestone was your guardian, which means he was a close friend. He must have known what they were doing.'

'Then why didn't you simply ask him? Why lie about arranging to see him and illegally searching his house?'

'Because we knew he wouldn't tell us. Why should he when he'd kept quiet about it for years? After the initial speculation that your parents had been on the trail of the *Flor de la Mar* in the Straits of Malacca, there's been nothing. No press coverage, no rumours as to what happened, a complete media blackout, and no one's ever hinted at anything or even mentioned them and their previous research. It's as if they never existed. Don't you find that strange?'

He hadn't because he hadn't thought about it over the years. But she was right — normally someone in their circle would have written something about their past research and accomplishments.

She said, 'After you'd gone, Stuart got in through the back door. I thought he used some kind of skeleton key. He said we wouldn't be disturbed because he had seen Freestone go out.'

So who was the liar, Verity or Craven?

'I'll talk to Craven.'

'If you can find him,' she said sourly. 'I haven't seen him since that day, and I can't get hold of him on the number he gave me.'

'Try it.'

'Now?'

Marvik nodded. He handed her back her mobile and watched her carefully. As she lifted the phone to her ear, Marvik grabbed it from her, causing her to cry out. There was no answer. And no name logged against that number. He scrolled through her address book. No Stuart Craven, but then that name was phoney. Checking through her log of calls there were none listed for that number and none for or from Lanbury.

'I deleted them,' she said, holding his critical gaze.

He switched off her phone and pushed it into his pocket.

'Hey, that's mine.'

Rubbing at the scars on his face, wearily he said, 'Let's try again, Verity. The truth this time, or we're going to be on this boat a very long time, and you'll get nothing from me.'

He could see her weighing it up. After a moment, she nodded.

CHAPTER SEVENTEEN

'Let's start with how you discovered Colmead was my parents' executor and Freestone my guardian,' Marvik said.

'I simply went through the press coverage on your parents' memorial service and found references to Dr Lanbury, Professor Galt and Professor Ansler as being your parents' closest friends. I contacted a colleague and friend of mine who works for the Scottish Association of Marine Science, and he told me that Professor Ansler had died while on exploration in the Arctic Sea in 1999. So that left Dr Lanbury and Professor Galt. Galt was easy to find because she has such a high profile in academia and in the media. I read she was working on a marine archaeological project off Portland. I went to see her, as I told you before.'

And Galt had finally confirmed that after Marvik had faced her with it.

'I got the impression she disapproved of me — probably does of every female because she sees us as rivals, even though she's ancient enough to know better. I asked her for Dr Lanbury's contact details, which she wouldn't give me, but she grudgingly promised to call him and pass on my mobile number. I was amazed she did.'

Galt hadn't told him that. Maybe she had forgotten and it was symptomatic of the medical problem Caroline had told him of. Or was this another of Verity's lies? She must have been able to track down Dr Lanbury because they both worked in the same field, and she would surely have been able to get his contact details from the National Oceanography Centre in Southampton.

Verity was saying, 'Dr Lanbury called me. He was much more forthcoming and because we were both in the same line of work, we immediately gelled.' She paused as she suddenly remembered the body on the wet grass. Or, Marvik thought, that was just his interpretation of her frown, and she was remembering something else.

She continued. 'I suggested that Dr Lanbury write a book pulling together all his own thoughts, findings and research and that of your father's. Dr Lanbury jumped at the idea. He told me about the gap in your father's research and the mystery of the missing years between 1991 and 1997 and that he'd written to Colmead, the solicitor, for access to you when you were seventeen and under Freestone's guardianship, but he'd received a negative reply. Dr Lanbury told me that he thought Freestone lived on the south coast somewhere.'

'And you teamed up with Stuart Craven, who got the address out of Colmead.'

'He couldn't have used violence and I'm sure Stuart has nothing to do with him being missing.'

Marvik would reserve his opinion on that. 'How did you meet Craven?'

'Can I have a drink of water?'

Was she stalling for time while she thought of a story to concoct? He rose and crossed to the fridge, where he retrieved a bottle of mineral water. From the cupboard beside it, he took a glass and put both on the table. She poured a drink before continuing.

'I met Stuart in April at a conference in London on oceans and climate change. He's a marine biologist with expertise in the Arctic.'

Not according to Strathen's research.

As though reading his thoughts she hastily added, 'He's been working in the Arctic Circle and only returned to the UK in March. We hit it off immediately.'

She looked down and Marvik thought she'd hit it off with Craven in the same way as he and Caroline had last night. He only wished he hadn't.

She continued. 'Our beliefs and concerns about climate change and the effects on marine life are the same.'

So too must have been the majority of the delegates at that conference, thought Marvik cynically, but didn't say.

'The Earth's climate has been changing throughout history, most of which can be attributed to the very small variations in the Earth's orbit, which affects the amount of solar energy our planet receives. But the current scenario of climate change is at alarming levels and most of it is human induced. And we have proof that it is happening. We can see satellite images taken over a period of time, and we also have data gathered by underwater sensors deployed by the Royal Navy, who have been measuring the Arctic's temperature and salt content. Professor Coulter would have noticed a frightening change from his research in the 1980s.'

She studied him to see if he was following her. He was, though he didn't know where she was leading him.

'The disappearance of Arctic sea ice will have an effect on the ocean circulation, turbulence, chemistry and biology. My interest is primarily on the first of those two aspects, Stuart's on the latter, but I am as concerned as he is about the effect on marine life because that has a huge impact on our lives. I'm not sure how your father's name came up, but when I started talking about the research conducted by Dr Lanbury and Professor Coulter in the 1980s on ocean turbulence and deep circulation in the area of the Greenland Sea, the Barents Sea and the Arctic Ocean, Stuart became very excited.'

Marvik recalled Lanbury's dying words but showed no reaction to Verity's mention of the Barents Sea and the Arctic.

She continued, 'Stuart claimed that Professor Coulter and Dr Marvik, your mother, had discovered something that was highly controversial and that they had been on the verge of exposing it when they'd died in the Straits of Malacca.'

'How did he know this?' Marvik hid his surprise but not his scepticism.

She looked as though she was weighing up how much to tell him. Either that or she was making this up as she went along.

'He said someone had told him there was written evidence of the work they'd been engaged upon in the early 1990s in the Barents Sea that could have major international implications, but he wouldn't tell me who gave him this information.'

'Very convenient,' muttered Marvik.

'He tried to follow it up, but he'd been contacted by email, there was no phone number or address, and when Stuart checked out the IP address, it had been sent from a cybercafé in Sweden.'

Marvik disguised his interest in this latest piece of news. Was it possible that, at last, Verity was telling the truth? He recalled that Caroline had told him Sarah had been working there. 'Why did this person contact Stuart Craven?'

'Because, as I've just said, Craven is an expert on marine life of the Arctic Circle.'

But Strathen had found no record of that and Verity would have checked it out in the same way, so clearly she was lying. Marvik held sway on saying so. Several thoughts were racing through his head. For a start, why had Craven roped in Verity?

There were two answers to that question. One, Stuart Craven had singled her out, possibly because her expertise was needed to interpret Professor Coulter's findings, *if* they found them; and two, Verity was the ideal candidate to charm her way into Lanbury's life with the offer of helping him to write his book based on his research and diaries, in order to find a reference to Dan Coulter's research.

Alternatively, she was spinning him total bullshit. For all he knew she could have hired Craven to kill Freestone, abduct and kill Colmead, and kill Lanbury. But there was this connection to Sweden, and Verity wouldn't have known Sarah had been working there. So far he had avoided mentioning Sarah. But then he realized it didn't mean Verity didn't know about Sarah and the manner of her death. Craven could have killed Sarah to get hold of the computer disk, which this anonymous person in Sweden had told him about. Perhaps Dewell was working independently and had beaten Craven to it. Or, as Marvik had previously considered, maybe they were working together and had discovered there was nothing on the disk, or the information it had held had been corrupted.

He said, 'You believed Craven's story?'

'Why shouldn't I? And he was right. There was something going on, because there is no reference to what your parents were engaged upon between 1991 and 1997.'

'Maybe they were on holiday.'

'For six years?' she said incredulously. Eagerly she sat forward. 'What did Dr Lanbury tell you before he died?'

Marvik remained silent.

'Did he say anything?' she pressed, her tone slightly harsher.

He rose. 'Coffee?'

She looked startled, then furious. 'You lied just to get me talking! He didn't say anything, did he?'

Marvik could say that Lanbury hadn't but that wouldn't take him any further forward. He didn't trust her, but he needed to see what she did with the information Lanbury had given him and where she went with it. Would she go running to Craven? She could have another number. She could even have another phone with it on — after all, he had three phones. Or perhaps they'd pre-arranged a meeting.

Maybe Lanbury's words meant nothing, but a dying man hardly uses his last breath to utter nonsense. And the only way to see if they meant something to Verity Taylor was to gauge her response when he told her. But he wouldn't reveal everything.

Abandoning the coffee, he resumed his seat. 'It wasn't much. Lanbury just managed to utter the words, "Dan . . . found . . . not Arctic Circle . . . Barents Sea."'

She looked disappointed and distrustful. 'And that's it?'

'He *was* dying,' Marvik stressed. He was going to withhold from her the two dates, 1976 and 1991 — if he had meant that date in those breathless words. Marvik would also withhold the fact that Lanbury had mentioned Phorcys. He wanted to know a great deal more about that before he let it loose on Verity.

'But he must have known more. Why else was he killed?' she said with exasperation.

'There was one other thing.'

'Yes?' She could barely contain her excitement.

'Edinburgh.'

She looked nonplussed and confused, and then he saw something creep into her eyes, but he couldn't quite interpret its meaning.

'The Barents Sea?' she repeated.

'Yes.'

'It doesn't mean anything to me, does it to you?'

'No,' he lied, just as she had done. She knew very well that Lanbury could have been referring to the discovery of HMS *Edinburgh* and its gold bullion in 1981 and that not all of it had been recovered. Five gold bars were unaccounted for. Was that what she and Craven were after? But it didn't quite tally. Why would an oceanographer and a so-called marine biologist be so obsessed with finding the remaining gold bars?

Then he mentally amended that. Why *wouldn't* they? Especially if they believed they could benefit from the discovery, not only personally but professionally. But why had Lanbury said 1976? Had he meant 1986, because twenty-nine gold bars had been brought up in that year? Had Marvik's parents been looking for the lost gold? They'd had the right vessel for such an exploration, *Vasa II*, but HMS

Edinburgh was a Commonwealth war grave and therefore no longer explored, not even in 1991. If they had been in that region he was certain someone would have been suspicious and word would have leaked out.

'Are you sure you have no idea what they were doing?' she persisted.

'None. I'll take you back to the marina.'

She remained silent while he released the anchor and manoeuvred the craft. He sensed her unease and behind it, he thought that she was troubled.

When they were almost back at the yacht harbour she said, 'What will you do now?'

'About Lanbury?

'No, about your parents.'

'Why should I do anything,' he tossed at her. 'I haven't been interested in them for the last twenty years. Whatever it was they were doing, it's the past. History.'

'But it might not be. It could be . . .' but she quickly added, 'Hugh Freestone's death and Dr Lanbury's isn't history.'

That wasn't what she had been about to say. Marvik didn't press her. 'I have only met Dr Lanbury three times in my life — once at my parents' memorial service, the second time at the National Maritime Museum and the third as he lay dying in his garden.'

'Don't you care?' she said, confused.

He shrugged.

'But you'll have to report it to the police,' she insisted.

'I'll leave that to you.'

'But *I* can't.'

'Why not? You were working with Lanbury on that book he was writing. It would be natural for you to show up to help him, and not finding him in the house you grew concerned and discovered him in the garden.'

'I don't want to get involved.'

'You are involved, Verity.' *Right up to your pretty eyes and beyond*, he added to himself. 'The police will want to talk to you and if they come looking for me, I will certainly tell them about you and your boyfriend. Oh, sorry, he's not your boyfriend.'

'I have no idea where he is. You saw that his line is dead.'

'Perhaps you can trace him through the conference you both attended.'

'Maybe.' But she looked away. And Marvik knew that was just another one of her lies like the many that had come before it.

CHAPTER EIGHTEEN

It was two hours later that Marvik, in the operations room of Strathen's apartment, relayed all that happened including his encounter with Caroline Shaldon, without going into all the details. Strathen had enough imagination and more for that.

Marvik had dropped Verity at the marina. She'd made no further mention of HMS *Edinburgh*, but something had been preying on her mind. Perhaps the fact that Lanbury was dead and therefore a dead end as far as her investigation went.

He had given her a head start and then set off after her. She'd made for Lanbury's house, paused for a moment outside it, then hurried on. For once she had told him the truth about her car being parked farther down the lane. Keeping out of sight, he saw her press her mobile to her ear for the third time on her journey. Obviously with the same result. There was no answer. She zapped open the car and threw her phone on the passenger seat and had sped off down the lane.

'Verity looked annoyed at my suggestion that Craven killed Lanbury, but I think it was because she was beginning to suspect Craven might have used her and now he's got what he wanted from Lanbury, he's ditched her. Hence her failure to get hold of him on the phone. After she'd gone, I searched around some more for his mobile but couldn't find it.' He had also called the police from Lanbury's landline, curtly announcing there had been an accident and giving the address before replacing the receiver. 'Craven could have been using Verity to get close to Lanbury. Lanbury telephoned her to say he'd found something, she told Craven and he got there first, killed Lanbury and took away the evidence.'

Strathen said, 'Lanbury's phone, both his landline and mobile, could be tapped. Perhaps Craven was already on his way *before* she phoned him. *If* she did. I'm surprised she didn't offer to join forces with you.'

'Me too. But perhaps she was eager to get back and report in, either to Craven or possibly to another party. I wish to God I'd answered that call last night,' Marvik said, angry at himself. 'I let myself be sidetracked.'

'You're only human.'

'Yeah, and stupid and weak.'

'Don't beat yourself up, Art. It's done.'

'Yes, but was it done deliberately? Was Caroline Shaldon sent to prevent me taking that call? But that doesn't make sense because she couldn't have known that Lanbury would phone me.'

'Let's examine what Lanbury managed to utter before dying.'

Marvik had been thinking a great deal about that as he'd headed for Strathen's place. Now he expressed some of those thoughts, eager to have Strathen's take on them.

'Lanbury could have been referring to the discovery of HMS *Edinburgh* and its missing gold bullion. My father was an expert on ocean turbulence and currents, my mother on wrecks — a perfect team to locate the gold on behalf of the British government. It would explain why they were given *Vasa II* and why there is no paperwork on the purchase and sale or lease of the boat in my parents' files . And why there is no logbook.'

Strathen nodded. 'Go on.'

'Although *Edinburgh* was sunk in the Norwegian sector of the Barents Sea, my parents could have located the missing gold in the Russian sector on board a vessel that got caught in one of the maelstroms off the Norwegian coast. The tidal currents there are among the strongest in the world, and the maelstrom of Saltstraumen one of the Earth's most powerful. If a sunken vessel with its gold was discovered in the Russia sector my parents would have been detailed to keep it quiet so the Russians didn't lay claim to it. They were paid handsomely for their work, into that bank account in my name, which was opened in 1991, and from which Freestone aka Culverham bought the Fairey Swordsman and renamed it *Phorcys* — hidden dangers of the deep. Freestone worked for the Ministry of Defence, knew all about the mission, and maybe that my parents were silenced when they wanted to tell what they'd discovered.

'But my father wrote an account of it, which he must have given to Lanbury in some shape or form, perhaps a letter, or a note in a book, or a code, which Lanbury finally stumbled on. It was also backed up on a floppy disk. If the information is readable then Dewell and his masters know the gold was found. Now, having got the location, they're going to mount an exploration to go after it. But Dewell and his boss aren't the only ones after that gold; Verity and Stuart Craven want it. Verity told me that Craven had received an email from someone in Sweden who claimed to have made a major discovery. And Caroline told me last night that Sarah had been working in Stockholm on a project from November to February for Norvol Exploration, who were laying a pipeline and wanted to record and protect the shipwrecks in the Barents Sea. Being a marine archaeologist, Sarah couldn't have resisted visiting the Vasa Museum, and because of her profession was given access to the archives. The email that Craven received came from a cybercafé in Sweden. Coincidence? Maybe. Or perhaps not. My father wrote on the outside of that missing notebook, the word "*Vasa*".' Marvik knew that Strathen was keeping pace with him, if not already ahead. 'I thought it referred to their research vessel but if my father and mother had wanted to hide a notebook and disk where it couldn't be easily located, intending to retrieve it later, where would they have hidden it? Where do you hide a notebook so that no one will find it, where it will blend in and look like any other notebook?'

'In a museum.'

'Yes. It would have been a natural hiding place for such information for my parents. They couldn't risk having it on their boat or sending it to anyone, except that my father must have managed to get some kind of message out to Lanbury, who was in America. Perhaps he received this message, didn't really register its significance because it was coded, and tucked it away. My parents thought that they could retrieve the disk later and give it to someone they could trust, but they never got the chance because they were killed in the Straits of Malacca.'

'But why go there?'

'I don't know. Perhaps they were on holiday. Or perhaps they were detailed another assignment.'

'The search for the *Flor de la Mar*?'

Marvik shrugged, but his mind raced. 'It could have been used to entice them there, in order for them to be killed many miles away from their real mission, so that no one would guess it. And if anyone got too nosy they would believe the *Flor de la Mar* was the real quest. Their computers were seized, probably not by the Indonesian government, but by whoever authorized their killing, or rather his operative.'

'And Sarah discovered the notebook and disk at the museum.'

'Yes, either in the presence of someone, a work colleague or friend perhaps, or she confided in someone.'

'Who said they had access to a hard drive that would open the disk for her.'

'Yes. And when this other person read what was on it, he, or she, realized its worth. Let's assume it was a he, for now. He told Sarah that the information was corrupt and returned the notebook and disk to her, but he had already copied the contents on to a USB stick and possibly saved it online. Then he set about finding the highest bidder for the information.'

'And he contacted Stuart Craven who possibly had access to an interested party.'

'Who is not Verity Taylor but together they're working with someone who is. I need to speak to the museum and find out if Sarah was given access to the archives.' Marvik reached for his phone.

His name granted him a swift audience with the curator, Dr Hilda Eklund, who was only too delighted to talk to Dr Eerika Marvik's son. She had taken him at his word. She had no need to doubt him. It was an honour to speak to him; his mother's reputation and work were well known and highly respected throughout Scandinavia. Dr Eerika Marvik had visited the museum many times in the past, although that was before the curator's time and Dr Marvik had been a patron, like her parents before her. Marvik hadn't known that but it provided another reason why the notebook could have been deposited there.

'Yes, Sarah worked in our archives voluntarily for three weeks over the Christmas period,' Dr Eklund announced after Marvik had asked her if she knew Sarah. He didn't say why he was enquiring. He felt a frisson of excitement. He'd been correct. Strathen was listening in to the call.

Dr Eklund continued. 'Sarah was assisting Orion Wellby by cataloguing and scanning correspondence and material for the period from 1990 to 2000.'

This was even better.

'Sadly, Orion was killed in a car accident in mid-February.'

Why did Marvik get a bad feeling about this? He dashed a glance at Strathen, who was looking dubious.

'Orion skidded off the road, hit a tree and his car burst into flames. Such a tragic waste. He was a very talented computer specialist and marine archaeologist.'

This had to be the person who had emailed Stuart Craven from a cybercafé. 'How did he come to be working for the museum?'

'It was because of his work on the *Mary Rose* in Portsmouth. He created a virtual reality programme for it, which visitors can access to see and feel as though they were living on board in Tudor times. We asked him to create the same for us for our ship, *Vasa*.'

'He worked freelance?'

'No, he was attached to the Centre for Maritime Archaeology at Southampton University.'

Was he indeed? Another connection, but this time with Verity Taylor, who had studied there.

'We work closely with them and they with us and our own centre for maritime archaeological research, MARIS at Sodertorn University. As you must know, the Baltic Sea is one of the best places in the world for maritime archaeological research. Because of the cold, brackish water, shipwrecks and other artefacts can survive nearly intact for hundreds of years in the dark at the bottom of the sea.'

He asked her if either Sarah or Orion had found anything unusual or significant in their cataloguing. Her answer said they hadn't, or if they had, Marvik thought, they certainly hadn't shared it with her.

'Did the police investigate his death?' he asked.

'Only in that it was an accident. No other car was involved.'

But Marvik wondered what had caused him to skid off the road and if the vehicle had been examined for faults. 'What happened to Orion's personal effects?'

'They were sent to his sister in Wales.'

'Including his laptop and mobile?'

'I think they were on him when he was killed.'

Convenient, and highly suspicious, as far as he was concerned.

'They weren't here in the office,' she added.

Marvik would need to check with the sister, if by any chance they had been sent to her, which he doubted. He didn't want to distress her, but he knew he would have to make sure. He'd also need to ask if Orion had sent anything to her or mentioned anything about Sarah Redburn or his parents' last expedition.

'His sister didn't come over?' he asked.

'No. Arrangements were made to fly the body back to Britain.'

Dr Eklund agreed to email the sister's details to him. He asked her if the museum held any papers, notebooks or any material supplied by either of his parents. The answer was in the negative, which was what he had expected, but he had another question. 'Do you have records of who visited the museum archives in the 1990s?'

'We do. They have been digitalized. That was one of the things Sarah was working on.'

Was it indeed! This had to be how Sarah had come across the notebook and computer disk.

'Could you check to see if Dr Marvik or Professor Coulter visited and had access to your library and the archives anytime between 1991 and 1997 and let me know?'

'Of course.'

She didn't ask why. He was glad of that. He thanked her warmly.

'Was Orion's death an accident or made to look like one?' he posed to Strathen.

'I don't think we need three guesses to come up with the answer to that. Dr Eklund is right.' Strathen pointed at his computer screen. 'According to the glowing obit on the university's website, Orion Wellby was very talented in the fields of marine archaeology and information technology. Originally from Wales, aged thirty-two, survived by his sister.'

Marvik wondered if the police or Crowder had traced Sarah's movements back to Sweden and put her death in early March alongside that of the death two weeks before of the man she had worked beside. If Crowder had then, true to form, he'd not mentioned it.

Strathen said, 'It sounds as though your idea about Wellby opening that disk is correct. Sodertorn University would have had the ancient hard drive to take it.'

'He must have known Stuart Craven. We don't really know who Craven is, because it's obviously not his real name.'

'Or perhaps Orion contacted Verity,' Strathen said. 'He would have known her from the Centre for Maritime Archaeology.'

'But how did Dewell know about the disk?'

'As you said earlier, Art, maybe Wellby contacted more than one party, saying he would sell the information to the highest bidder, but one of them managed to locate and kill him before he could do so.'

'Would they have discovered he'd backed it up elsewhere?' mused Marvik.

'Maybe he held out on them.' Strathen sat forward. Eagerly, he continued. 'Or maybe he told them that your father's computer disk had given him details of where your parents had backed up the information online and the password, but he gave them the wrong information. By the time they realized that, he was dead — they'd eliminated him. But Dewell and his masters were told by Wellby that Sarah had the notebook and floppy disk. Someone was sent to retrieve it from her. She told them where it was before she was killed only you beat the killer to the disk.'

Marvik rapidly picked up the theory. 'But they didn't know that, because everything was destroyed in a fire. They thought that was the end of the matter until I went asking questions at Sarah's funeral.' He thought of Caroline Shaldon. 'And then I contacted Colmead and Bell and started making enquiries about my parents' research in 1997. Colmead reported back to them and told them about my safe deposit box. He gave Dewell access to it, either willingly or under duress.'

'I think Wellby wiped that floppy disk clean. Dewell soon discovered he'd been lumbered with a dud, so the hunt continued. Hence the search of your cottage and the incendiary device to take you out of the picture. He could have been behind the murder of Freestone and the search of his property before Craven and Verity showed up.'

Marvik sat back deep in thought, his brow knitted. 'Davington must have known what my parents were doing during those years. Was he working for or against them? He was certainly silenced when it looked as though he might tell. But by whom? The British government or a rival party? Perhaps the gold's already been retrieved. Davington could have been made to tell of the location before he was killed.'

'Then there would be no need for the information contained on that floppy disk.'

'And if the gold had been found by my parents, then surely the government would have mounted an expedition to recover it.'

'Not unless it is in the Russian sector, as I said.'

'But if Craven, Verity and Dewell believe there is still a chance the gold is where my parents located it, they'll need time and money to mount an expedition.' Would Caroline Shaldon provide the resources for that? Her company was well equipped to do so. Had Professor Galt really lied about not knowing Sarah Redburn? Was she really suffering from memory loss or early stage dementia, as Caroline had told him, or was that a pack of lies? Had Caroline given him the information about Sarah having worked in Sweden to see his reaction? Maybe she thought he had some information that could help her and Dewell locate the gold. He needed to check her story.

He voiced his concerns to Strathen while dialling the number for Portland Marina to find out if RV *Oyster* was still there. It wasn't. It had left for Town Quay, Southampton, an hour ago. That gave Marvik plenty of time to reach there. Strathen's phone pinged.

'Damn, I've got to leave. It's a client confirming he needs my expertise urgently.'

'That's OK.' Marvik felt a little guilty at intruding on Strathen's time. This wasn't a formal mission for the Squad, it was personal. Strathen didn't need to help him, though Marvik knew he always would, just as Marvik would lay his life on the line for Shaun if it came to it. He hoped it never would.

Strathen said he would be in touch as soon as he could, adding that if anything urgent occurred to call him on the mission mobile. 'I'll get to you as soon as I can, but the client is based in Bristol.' Which meant a two hour drive. 'There's always Crowder,' Strathen added, concerned.

Marvik hastily reassured Shaun that he'd be fine and a few minutes later set off for his boat and Southampton.

CHAPTER NINETEEN

Marvik waited impatiently for RV *Oyster* to arrive. While he did, he received one message and one telephone call. The message was from Dr Hilda Eklund, who had sent over a photograph of Dr Eerika Marvik's signature, showing that she had signed in to access the archives in December 1996. That was all the confirmation Marvik needed that the notebook containing the computer disk had been deposited there. The call was from Julie Pembroke.

'Donald is reporting Michael's disappearance to the police tomorrow morning,' she said, her voice filled with anxiety.

So he had still put it off. 'Has Donald said anything to you about me?'

'Well yes, I . . .'

'He's told you that he thinks it best if you don't mention that Colmead gave a letter of authority to a dead client to illegally access and steal from my safe deposit box.'

'He said he would speak to you about it. He'll contact you later today.'

It would be interesting if he did and to hear what he had to say.

Marvik could see RV *Oyster* approaching. At the helm was the bearlike figure of Kranton, but there was no sign of Professor Galt. Marvik hoped Kranton hadn't dropped her off at another marina en route. But, as the craft drew closer, the lean figure of Professor Galt appeared on deck. She didn't glance at his boat, though she must have recognized it because she had told Caroline the name and make. Or had that been a lie?

He watched Galt nimbly alight as Kranton brought the vessel alongside and she expertly tied off before climbing back on board. She exchanged a few words with Kranton. Then she threw two substantial holdalls on to the pontoon before again alighting. Marvik watched her let loose the line. Kranton reversed and swung the craft round and out into the marina with a wave of his suntanned, muscular arm.

Marvik alighted. 'Can I give you a hand, Professor Galt?'

She spun round, startled. 'What are you doing here?'

'Waiting for you.'

'Why?'

'Because I'd like to know why you told me you didn't know Sarah Redburn when you worked with her not very long ago.'

'I might have worked with her, Marvik, but I didn't *know* her.'

'Oh, come on.'

'All right, so I forgot her name. I forget a lot of people's names. It's never been my strong point. I've met hundreds of starstruck young marine archaeologists, one seems very much like the other to me.'

Perhaps that was true.

'Sarah assisted me on a project. I'd forgotten her until Guy reminded me.' She picked up one of her holdalls. Marvik reached down and lifted the other. She looked about to protest, then struck out along the pontoon.

'What did Sarah tell you when she got in touch with you in February?'

She tossed him a bewildered glance. 'Tell me? Nothing, because she hasn't spoken to me.'

'Not even about my mother?'

'Not about that or anything. Are you still trying to find Eerika's papers?'

'Yes. Are you?'

'No. I *was* interested and curious in 1997, as I told you. But there's no point now.'

'Why not?'

She studied him, exasperated. 'Because, as I told you, some idiot and incompetent fool of a clerk, or the Indonesian police, lost or destroyed them, and no one's going to admit it. They didn't twenty years ago and they're certainly not going to now.'

'You really believe that was the case?' he said incredulously.

She halted and looked hard at him. 'Why? Have you heard something different? Do you know where they are?' There was a new tone of interest in her voice and in her eyes.

'No.'

'Or what they were doing?'

'No.'

'You're a liar, Marvik.' She walked on.

It takes one to know one, he thought. But was she involved? He wasn't sure. It was time to force the issue, to tell something of the truth and see where it led him. 'Sarah Redburn was killed because she had in her possession something belonging to my parents from those missing years of research between 1991 and 1997.'

That brought her up sharply. Her surprise seemed genuine. 'You mean some notes?'

'And a computer disk.'

Her grey eyes narrowed as though she wasn't sure whether to believe him. She walked on.

'Since then, not only has my former guardian, Hugh Freestone, been killed, but early this morning when I went to visit Dr Lanbury, at his request, I found him dead.'

'Dead! But I only . . . You mean, not from natural causes?'

'He was shot in the back.'

Her steps slowed but he could see her mind racing with this latest shocking news.

'He said he had some information about what my father was engaged on during those missing years. Do you know what it was that Dr Lanbury wanted to tell me?'

'No.'

But Marvik caught an unaccustomed hesitation. She seemed preoccupied and troubled. He ventured a guess based on the fact that she had said, 'But I only—'

'He phoned you before calling me, didn't he?'

Her head swung round. 'He can't have been killed because of Eerika and Dan,' she insisted. 'He has no more idea of what they were up to than I have.'

'He must have because someone saw fit to put a bullet in him.'

'Haven't you got this computer disk that you say Sarah Redburn had?'

'If I had there wouldn't have been any need to kill Freestone and Lanbury,' Marvik quipped.

They had reached the car park. She turned to face him. 'All right, Lanbury did call me last night but he didn't make any sense. He asked me if Eerika had ever mentioned anyone called Fenella.'

Marvik's heartbeat jumped. My God, that was the name that Hillingdon said Davington had mentioned to him.

'You look startled, Marvik.'

'Puzzled. Have you heard of her?'

'No, but evidently your father had because Lanbury said he'd written the name in a letter, which he'd unearthed from the depths of his papers.'

And that letter was what the killer had been after. What else had it contained aside from the name Fenella? Perhaps the words *Phorcys*, Barents Sea and Edinburgh, along with the years 1976 and 1991.

'What else did Lanbury say?'

'Nothing. He just said, "What does Fenella mean to you?" I said bugger all. Eerika had never mentioned her.

Then he rang off. Does that make any sense to you?' she asked keenly.

Only in that Davington had apparently told his former army colleague Hillingdon that he wanted to talk to him about Fenella, but Marvik wasn't going to tell Galt that.

Maybe Galt had forgotten the conversation — she wasn't the world's best listener. And with her memory weakening, maybe she needed some help remembering if Lanbury had mentioned any of the other things he'd uttered in his dying breath to Marvik. 'Did he mention the name Phorcys to you, or do you remember my parents mentioning it?'

'The ancient sea god of the hidden dangers of the deep. No. Why?' She looked at him strangely.

Should he fob her off? She would know if he did. He wasn't concerned what she'd think of that. But as he'd already decided it was time to force the issue, he'd push it further and see where it led. 'I think both names have a bearing on why my parents were killed.'

'Killed? You mean deliberately?'

'Yes.'

'But that's ridiculous. What could have been so dangerous?' she cried in frustration. Then her eyes narrowed. 'Do you have any idea?'

Maybe. 'Before Dr Lanbury died, he mentioned the Barents Sea and Edinburgh.'

'The wreck?' she said instantly.

'Could they have been looking for the missing gold bullion?'

'You know about that?' she asked, surprised, then recalled his former career and his parentage. 'Yes, of course you would. No, not the *Edinburgh*,' she said in a determined voice with a shake of her head, and Marvik instantly saw what Lanbury had been trying to say. In the breath he had taken before uttering the word 'Edinburgh' he had been struggling to say *not* the *Edinburgh*. Dan and Eerika had been in the Barents Sea for another reason.

Galt said, 'I would certainly have heard about that, everyone would. And there would have been no need for the secrecy.'

'Perhaps they found it and wanted to keep the find to themselves,' he ventured, although he no longer believed that was why his parents had been there.

'Impossible. They would never have stolen the bullion if they had even found it.'

'It could have been in the Russian sector.' He ventured the theory he and Strathen had discussed, but Galt was shaking her sparrow-like head.

'I'm sure they weren't after that. Besides, that doesn't explain why they were in the Straits of Malacca.'

'What else could they have been doing in the Barents Sea?' he asked.

'There are other wrecks there.' And by her expression, she was trying to recall which of those his parents might have gone in search of. 'Lanbury probably got it all wrong. He often does. What will you do now?' she asked. It was the same question Verity had uttered to him.

'Keep looking.'

'I suppose you must, although you're a fool to do so. It's the past, Marvik. You can't bring them back, and you can't change it.'

'But I can find out who killed them.'

'*If* someone did. It was an underwater tremor.'

'It might have been, but someone has since killed Sarah Redburn, Hugh Freestone and Dr Lanbury, and their deaths were not accidents.'

'Then let the police deal with that.'

He said nothing.

After a moment, she said, 'Stubborn, like your mother. I'll go through my old files and see if there is anything from Eerika that might help, but don't bank on it.'

A taxi pulled into the car park.

'Did you tell Caroline Shaldon about my boat?' he asked.

'Eh?'

'It doesn't matter.'

She lifted the holdall he had deposited on the ground and paused. 'Eerika was a good friend to me. If you're right and she was killed then let me know if and when you find who did it.'

He watched her climb into the taxi and waited until it had turned out of the marina before heading back to his boat. Three women, Verity Taylor, Letitia Galt and Caroline Shaldon — which of them was lying? Were they all? It seemed so. Was one of them a ruthless killer?

On board he checked the internet on his phone for any news of Freestone's body being found. There was none, but he noted with interest that a body had been washed up on the shore at Milford-on-Sea, over seventy miles in the opposite direction to where Freestone had lived, and closer to Colmead's house. The police said that as yet it was unidentified. He wondered if it was Michael Colmead.

His mind ran on . . . Colmead . . . the burnt fragments of paper in his grate, a C or O, Y and S — Phorcys? Possibly.

He turned his attention to the information that Galt had given him from Lanbury, the name, Fenella. Did Hillingdon know more than he'd revealed about this mysterious woman whom Davington had mentioned to him before his death?

Only one way to find out. He needed to talk to the former sapper again.

CHAPTER TWENTY

A large four-by-four vehicle was parked outside the front of Hillingdon's demolition company. By its personalized number plate it was clearly Gordon Hillingdon's. It was the only vehicle there. The company had been easy to find. From its website Marvik had seen that it was a far more substantial business than he had anticipated, although, after seeing Hillingdon's sleek expensive motor cruiser in Shamrock Quay, he should have guessed. He also saw that Hillingdon specialized in marine demolition. He hadn't mentioned that when they had met. Still, there was no reason for him to have done so.

The company was situated to the north of Shamrock Quay, farther up the River Itchen sited between Saxon Wharf and a scrap metal yard. It backed on to the quayside, where, according to the website, Hillingdon kept a crane barge when it wasn't being used on location, a coastal tugboat, a multi-cat with winches and a crane, a dive boat much like RV *Oyster*, two RIBs, and other land-based equipment such as cranes and diggers. He also provided teams of divers and underwater engineers experienced in inshore diving and underwater engineering including pipeline installation work, underwater cutting and welding, surveys and salvage activities. Hillingdon had done well.

It being just under two miles away from where Marvik was moored up at Town Quay he walked there in thirty minutes hoping that he would find the former sapper there. It was just after 6 p.m. when he rapped on the door. Unless Hillingdon was asleep or deaf he'd have to come to investigate, and soon the bulky figure appeared with a cross look on his lined, tanned face, which changed to one of surprise when he recognized Marvik.

'Where's the fire?' he said, opening the door and studying Marvik with curiosity, and some apprehension, Marvik thought.

'I'm sorry to bother you again but we need to talk.'

Hillingdon stepped back to let Marvik into a small lobby bedecked with large photographs of some of Hillingdon's demolition projects: oil platforms, marina buildings, port terminals.

'Come through,' Hillingdon said, reluctantly.

Marvik followed him down a short corridor to a spacious office at the rear. It was untidy, with papers strewn across a tatty old desk, equipment and clothing dumped on the grimy floor, and a sturdy safe by a scratched grey filing cabinet. Through the salt-spattered windows, Marvik glimpsed moored up alongside the quay a research and diving vessel similar to that of RV *Oyster* and a powerful RIB. He caught the sound of a boat's engine in the marina to their right, a superyacht by the tenor of it.

'Is this about Davvers?' Hillingdon gestured Marvik into the seat across his desk.

Why was Hillingdon so uneasy? wondered Marvik. Because he had disturbed him in the middle of some technical or difficult work, or because he'd returned to ask more questions about a subject he thought he had laid to rest.

'Did Davvers say anything to you about the Barents Sea?'

'Probably,' Hillingdon said evasively, with a smile that didn't quite touch his eyes. 'I expect he worked on it or under it at some stage.'

‘With my parents?’

‘Not that I can remember. But then I don’t know what he did for them, or what they were engaged on. As I told you, Davvers and I only picked up our friendship occasionally after we’d left the army.’

‘Did he mention HMS *Edinburgh*?’

‘The ship that went down with all that gold bullion on board? No. I don’t think I can help you, Art.’

‘But he did mention Fenella?’

Hillingdon shifted and ran a hand over his chin. ‘Yes. Like I told you, it was a woman he’d got involved with.’

‘In 1976?’

Hillingdon looked startled for a moment then picked up a pen and began to fiddle with it. ‘He could have said Nella.’

‘What happened to Davvers’ personal effects?’

‘I don’t know.’

Oh, but he did. And Marvik was guessing that Hillingdon had gone through them. Had he found something that he had conveniently forgotten for twenty years such as a note or letter from Davvers saying what he had been doing on *Vasa II*?

‘Who organized the funeral?’

‘The solicitor, who was his executor, with a bit of help from me. I guess he sorted through Davvers’ belongings. The only things the solicitor gave me were Davvers’ army discharge papers, and they were no good to anyone. I burned them.’ He pointedly consulted his watch and stood. ‘I’m sorry but I’m going to have to throw you out. I’ve got an estimate to finish for a prospective client and I’m already behind with it.’

‘Of course.’ Marvik rose. The look of relief on Hillingdon’s face was evident. ‘I’m sorry to have taken up so much of your time.’

‘That’s OK,’ Hillingdon said, now magnanimous at the thought that he could get rid of his guest. Marvik’s suspicions were growing by the minute. If Hillingdon had nothing to hide, and no knowledge of what Davington had meant by Fenella, then why so eager to get shot of him? Maybe he did have work to do but since their meeting in the café on

Sunday, Hillingdon's easygoing manner had evaporated and Marvik was looking at a very troubled man. As he showed Marvik to the door, Hillingdon said, 'It's tough losing your parents, but I'm afraid I can't help you.'

'I was just hoping.' Marvik smiled sadly. 'It's just that two names have been mentioned to me in connection with my parents — one being Fenella and the other Phorcys.'

Marvik hadn't really expected a reaction unless it was a blank stare but what he got was considerably more and stunned him. Hillingdon visibly started. His skin paled. He struggled to pull himself together.

'Does the name Phorcys mean anything to you?' Marvik asked, hiding his excitement.

The natural reaction for Hillingdon — unless he was an expert on Greek mythology — would have been to say something along the lines of, 'Strange name, never heard of it, what does it mean?' But he cleared his throat and said with false breeziness, 'Not a thing. Like I said, I'm sorry I can't help you.' His eyes held Marvik's for a moment then quickly looked away.

'Thanks anyway.' Marvik stretched out his hand. Hillingdon took it. His handshake was as firm as before but sweaty, matching the perspiration on his brow.

Marvik walked briskly away. Once out of view, he halted. The streets were quiet. The industrial units around him were closed, its workers having left for the day. Only a few cars were parked in the marina's car park. It was clear to him that Hillingdon had heard of Phorcys and equally obvious the name terrified him. He'd been correct in thinking the letters in Colmead's grate had spelt Phorcys.

How was Hillingdon involved? Had Davington confided in his mate in 1997 before dying? Or had Hillingdon, after finding his buddy's body, searched the flat and found a record of what had occurred on *Vasa II* in 1997 and under the sea in the Straits of Malacca? If so why didn't Hillingdon tell him?

The answer was because it put his dead mate in a bad light. Davington had been a sapper, which meant he'd been an expert in explosives, and underwater ones at that. Had Davington killed Dan and Eerika? Is that what Hillingdon knew?

Marvik caught the sound of a powerful RIB starting up. He thought of the one that he'd seen moored on the quayside outside Hillingdon's office. Was it his? If so, perhaps Hillingdon just fancied a sea trip to clear his head. Perhaps he was delivering that estimate to the client. But Marvik doubted both of these explanations. He had rattled Hillingdon. He cursed himself for not thinking that Hillingdon would take to the water and raced through the marina, reaching the waterside in time to catch sight of Hillingdon on his RIB making his way towards the Itchen Bridge and out to sea. Where was Hillingdon going? Was he heading for the Fairey Swordsman in Cowes in the belief he would see Culverham there? Or was he running to Dewell or Craven or whoever it was behind all this? There was only one way to find out.

Marvik ran back to his boat in Town Quay Marina and was soon heading across the Solent. The sea was growing choppier with a forecast for a stiffening wind from the west. The sun had set, and the heavy cloud obscured any sign of emerging celestial light as he made his way into Cowes. He scanned the pontoons for signs of Hillingdon's RIB, but it wasn't there, and made his way along the pontoons to *Phorcys*. There was no one on board and nothing more Marvik could do here. He decided to return to his cottage.

The peace and tranquillity of Newtown Harbour seemed at odds with his swirling thoughts and emotions. There were only a handful of sailing yachts moored up in the trots, it being early in the sailing season and a weekday, and soon they petered out as Marvik made his way up the quiet inlet towards his private pontoon and cottage. He could moor up on it blindfolded and although it was dark, an unexpected break in the clouds revealed a moon that bathed the wooden jetty in a silver beam.

As he brought the sturdy motorboat alongside, Marvik scanned the horizon and grasslands around his cottage in the near distance. There didn't seem to be anything untoward.

He jumped off, expertly tied off and silenced the engine. Picking up his rucksack he headed for the cottage. His Land Rover was where he had left it and there were no signs of anyone having been here. He unlocked the door and stood inside for several seconds as he had done before, listening.

Again, only silence greeted him. He rapidly checked each room but knew that no one had been inside, not since the last time. Then a sound caught his attention. He stiffened and listened. Yes, there it was in the distance, an outboard engine. Suddenly it ceased and his nerve ends tingled.

Stealthily, Marvik made his way through the garden and grassland towards the jetty, taking care to keep low. It was an hour off high water and the wind was now rustling through the reeds and sending the sea slapping against the dark shape of his boat. Both were familiar sounds to him, but in among them was another, barely discernible, but it was there.

He eased forward and watched as a figure clad in a wet suit climbed on board his boat. From its build and the way it moved he was certain it wasn't Hillingdon. Had Hillingdon despatched someone to deal with him? Dewell perhaps? Marvik couldn't see the RIB in the harbour — it was too dark — but he was convinced it was there and maybe Hillingdon was on board.

Marvik put his full attention on the figure on his boat, his adrenaline pumping. The man was making for the foredeck. He ducked down and leaned over the for'ard before straightening up. Then with a glance around, he made his way back to the cockpit.

Marvik moved rapidly and silently. Leaping on to the boat before the figure could drop over the side into the water, Marvik was on him. He thrust a strong forearm around the man's neck, making it impossible for him to move without strangling himself, and, with his other hand, Marvik wrenched off the black diving cap.

'OK, Dewell, so let's have a look at you,' Marvik said gruffly, releasing his grip and spinning the man round. But it wasn't Dewell. It was Stuart Craven.

CHAPTER TWENTY-ONE

Marvik rapidly recovered from his surprise. From the tightness of the wet suit Craven couldn't be concealing a gun and there was no knife about his person. He wasn't going to take any chances though. He balled his fist and rammed it into Craven's midriff before the man could move. Craven doubled up with a cry of agony and fell to his knees on the deck.

'Let's start with your real name,' Marvik hissed.

Craven, still clutching his stomach, didn't reply. Marvik stepped forward. Craven looked up alarmed. 'Stuart Bradshott,' he quickly mumbled, gasping.

'Are you alone?'

Bradshott nodded. Marvik could make out the dark shape of a RIB in the channel. He couldn't see another figure on board but there could be someone crouched down in it. If so he would be a sitting target for a shooter if they had a gun with night vision, or if the clouds didn't obscure the moon. He hauled Bradshott up and made certain to stand in front of him and slightly to the right where, if there was a shot, he could duck into the cabin with Bradshott in his grip. But perhaps Bradshott had come alone as he claimed. Still keeping a firm grip on him, Marvik said, 'Who sent you?'

'No one.'

Marvik let that go for now. 'What are you doing here?'

Bradshott swallowed hard. But didn't answer.

'I'll ask you once more before I beat you to a pulp.' Marvik balled his fist.

'I was looking for a computer disk.'

'In a wet suit over the side of my boat?' Marvik scoffed. 'But we'll leave that aside for the moment. What computer disk?'

Bradshott eyed him fearfully and with puzzlement. 'The one your mother deposited in the Vasa Museum in Sweden.'

'How do you know I've got it?'

'You must have it.'

'Why?'

Bradshott's eyes were darting about alarmingly. 'Look, can we talk somewhere else?'

'No, this is the perfect place. Maybe you'd just better start talking quickly. Did you kill Sarah Redburn?'

'I haven't killed anyone. I wouldn't.'

'Had much experience in planting explosive devices on boats, have you?' Marvik sneered.

Bradshott dashed him a fearful glance. 'It's not a bomb.'

'Then what is it?'

'A tracking device.'

'Who ordered you to put it there?'

'No one.'

'Oh, the idea just sprang into your head, did it?' Marvik said with heavy sarcasm. 'And you thought I might lead you to discovering what was on that disk.'

'Do you have the disk?' he asked eagerly.

'Why are you so interested?'

'Orion said it could be used for our cause.'

'Orion Wellby.'

'Y-You know him?' Bradshott stammered.

'I know he's dead, killed in a car accident in Sweden, but I can see from your expression you knew that too. A lot of people seem to be dying because of that disk. What cause?' Marvik barked out the last.

'The environment. It's true,' Bradshott quickly added to Marvik's scornful look. 'The fishing stocks are declining alarmingly because of pollution and global warming, and the fish and marine life is stuffed full of plastic shit.'

'And how will what my parents discovered help that?' Marvik said scathingly. His first thought had been that Bradshott wanted the *Edinburgh*'s missing gold to fund an environmental group and an international media campaign, but this wasn't about gold. It never had been. And neither was it about a Portuguese wreck called the *Flor de la Mar*. A fact that Bradshott confirmed with his next words.

'Orion said it had something to do with a deadly bacteria that the British government had deliberately dumped at sea.'

Marvik eyed him closely. Questions raced through his mind at this new twist. He was certain that at last he'd heard the truth. Mention of the British government tallied with what he and Strathen had discussed. *Vasa II* had been given to his parents, and their mission had been cloaked in secrecy. Freestone had worked for the Ministry of Defence and had a dual identity. But how and why had his parents become involved in a search for bacteria?

'Can we go now?' Bradshott said fearfully.

'You enlisted Verity Taylor's help to try and discover what this deadly bacteria was and where it could have been dumped. Did she send you here?' Marvik wondered if she could have planted a tracking device on his boat while on board yesterday. He hadn't swept it since before Caroline's nocturnal sojourn on board. Careless of him.

Bradshott ran a tongue over his lips but didn't speak. Marvik grasped the wet suit at Bradshott's throat and balled his fist.

'All right, I'll tell you. Just don't hit me and for Christ's sake, can we go inside?'

His fear evidently meant there was someone on that RIB out there. Marvik nodded and released his hold, but as he did, he caught the barely perceptible whoosh of a bullet.

Quickly he ducked down as he witnessed Bradshott's shocked expression before his body slumped to the deck.

Then, in the quiet of the night, came the roar of the RIB's engine. Marvik leaped up to see it speeding out of the harbour. He could chase after it. He had a powerful fast boat.

But by the time he'd cast off and started the engine he knew the RIB would be swallowed up in the dark of the Solent. Even if he went in search of it, it might have ducked into a nearby bay or creek.

Swiftly, Marvik checked for a pulse, knowing he wouldn't find one. It was clear that Bradshott had been shot expertly from a high-velocity rifle in the back of the head. The bullet might have exited but Marvik wasn't about to spend time looking for it. He had a more pressing matter to attend to and that was to see what Bradshott had been told to plant over the side of his boat, and he didn't think it was a tracking device. He might have only minutes before his boat, and he, and Bradshott, would be dispersed into tiny pieces.

Within seconds he had stripped off, grabbed his waterproof torch and was lowering himself into the cold water, thankful that it was May and not the frozen depths of February. He also had the advantage of knowing where the device was located, having seen Bradshott put it there, and it would be just above or slightly below the waterline. How long did he have? Time to disarm it before whoever it was on that RIB set the trigger? He had no intention of becoming a marine accident statistic as he had a domestic fire victim at that house on Eel Pie Island when he'd discovered the notebook and disk. Or the incendiary device planted in his cottage. Had that been Bradshott's doing? He'd never got the chance to get that far with his questions. Time was paramount.

His mind flitted to Hillingdon, an explosives expert whom he had spooked very recently, and who had taken off on a RIB. A man who was probably an expert shot having been trained by the army. But how would Hillingdon have known where he was? Simple. He knew the name and make of his boat having seen it at their Sunday meeting. Hillingdon, after taking off on his RIB, had seen that Marvik wasn't moored up in Shamrock Quay. He'd taken a gamble that he had to be in either Town Quay or Ocean Village Marina nearby. He'd located the boat and had planted a tracking device before Marvik could reach it. Hillingdon wouldn't have the time to plant an explosive device, and neither would he probably have wanted to take a dive into cold water when he had a much younger man to do that for him. He'd quickly arranged to pick up Stuart Craven, or rather Bradshott, returned to his office, collected a wet suit, gun, and an incendiary device while noting on his phone or computer where Marvik was heading.

Marvik considered that this explosive device, like the one planted in his cottage last Wednesday, would probably be rigged to detonate on contact or by movement — magnetic, acoustic or seismic pressure — or a combination of some or all of those things, common signatures of waterborne craft. Perhaps it had been constructed with both timer and movement triggers, the latter determining that the boat was on the move before setting off a timer for the bomb to detonate, thereby guaranteeing that he would be on board somewhere at sea and unlikely to be close to other shipping. Not that Hillingdon cared about casualties, but it would be far better for Marvik's boat to suffer an explosion at sea that might then be explained by the possible rupture of a feed to the engine or the gas cylinder.

With his blood pumping fast, Marvik's eyes locked on the spherical object. Even before removing it, he recognized it. He'd planted some very similar devices on missions in the Royal Marines in far-flung places and some not so far with the object of creating confusion, distraction and extricating people — not always successfully, as the scars on the right hand side of his face reminded him. It made him even more certain that Hillingdon, an ex-Army Royal Engineer, had devised the explosive and got Bradshott to plant it. Bradshott must have known what it was, hence his nervousness that it might be detonated while he was on board. Well, he didn't have to worry about that anymore, or the marine environment.

With care, Marvik lifted the device from the hull, holding his breath. This could be his last moment on this earth. He'd die in the water just as his parents had. Killed by the same hand? he wondered. Had Hillingdon planted an underwater device on a submerged structure where Dan and Eerika had been diving? Had Davington told him where that was?

Time to consider that later. With his heart pumping, he counted the seconds. He was still alive, and he was damn cold. The explosive device wasn't movement sensitive, which meant it had to be triggered remotely.

He had two options. One, hurl it into the water as far as he could and wait for it to explode or two, dismantle it. He climbed back on board and, recalling all his training, with his heart thudding, but with steady hands, he opened the casing and was relieved and pleased to see it was simple enough to defuse, for him anyway. And simple enough for someone of Hillingdon's expertise to construct. Hillingdon would have had the basic ingredients to hand given his occupation. He'd had the training, both with the Royal Engineers and in his ensuing career as a demolition expert. And Hillingdon had kept his hand in with guns. But why come armed with the high-velocity rifle equipped with night vision when the plan was to kill him in a boating explosion? But Marvik had the answer immediately. Because Stuart Bradshott had also been the target after he'd successfully planted the device. That didn't bode well for Verity Taylor unless she was in on this with Hillingdon.

It took Marvik barely a minute to disable the device, but it was a very long minute. With a great sigh of relief, he stood back. He didn't have time to relax though. He threw on some warm clothes. Returning to the deck, he glanced down at Stuart Bradshott's body. He couldn't take him with him. Summoning up his strength he lifted the dead weight and managed to get the body over his shoulder in a fireman's hold. He alighted from the aft of the boat on to the jetty and then into the reeds, away from the wash of the tide, where he placed the body and ran back to his boat.

His mind teemed with questions as he made his way out of the tranquil harbour and across the Solent to Southampton. His intention was to pay another call on Hillingdon, who might either be on his boat at Shamrock Quay or at his office. He could, of course, have returned to his home. Marvik didn't know where that was but an internet search would give him that. Being a company director, his address would likely be public.

First, though, he put in at Shamrock Quay. There was no sign of Hillingdon, but his large motor cruiser was there with its tender on board and no sign of the fast RIB he had taken off on from his office. Marvik lowered his tender, a small RIB with a powerful engine and oars, perfect for the short journey up the River Itchen to Hillingdon's quayside.

Before reaching it, he stilled the engine and took to the oars. Hillingdon's RIB was there and a light was shining in his office. Good.

Leaping off, his blood pumping, he tied up and, keeping low, made his way to the rear door, which was slightly ajar. He entered the small back lobby and crept towards the open door of the office where five hours earlier he'd sat talking to Hillingdon about Phorcys and Fenella. Hillingdon was at his safe with his back to Marvik. There was a hastiness about his actions but no sign of the rifle beside him, or on his desk, and it hadn't been in the RIB. Could he have ditched it in the Solent? Unlikely. He'd probably hidden it somewhere here, or in an outbuilding. Or perhaps he had stopped off at Shamrock Quay and had stashed it on his motor cruiser.

Marvik stepped inside. 'Going somewhere?'

Hillingdon spun round with a cry. 'Jesus, you scared the shit out of me,' he cried, clutching his heart. 'What the hell are you doing here?' Then, without waiting for an answer, he physically crumpled. 'I knew it was a test. I won't say anything. I've kept my mouth shut for over forty years. I'm not going to squeal now.'

'No, you're killing people instead.'

Hillingdon looked flummoxed. 'I haven't killed anyone except in combat and that was years ago.'

'Then what was that episode tonight — a fantasy, or were you sleep walking?' sneered Marvik.

'I don't know what you're talking about.' Hillingdon ran a hand across his wide, perspiring forehead.

'You didn't think you would see me again. Handy with explosive devices, aren't you?'

'Eh?'

'The one you got Bradshott to plant on my boat.'

Hillingdon's eyes widened. His face paled. 'I swear to you I haven't been near your boat. And who the hell is Bradshott?'

'Cut the act.' Marvik stepped menacingly forward. 'Where's the rifle you've just used to kill a man.'

Hillingdon's skin turned ashen. His brow furrowed. 'I haven't killed anyone, and I don't have a rifle.'

Hillingdon could be bluffing. Or maybe he hadn't killed Bradshott. If so, who had? Verity? Marvik had certainly known some female crack shots in his career. In fact, women were often better shots than men. And Verity had a nasty habit of being around when people were murdered, Freestone and Lanbury for instance.

'Where did you go on your RIB?' demanded Marvik.

'Out. I just needed to think.'

Marvik eyed him disbelievingly. 'Wrong answer.' He stepped forward.

Hillingdon stepped back. He was almost pressed up against the open safe. Marvik couldn't see inside it on account of Hillingdon's bulk. There could be a gun inside.

'I needed to think,' Hillingdon hastily repeated.

'About murder?'

'No. About what to do. I swear I'll say nothing. I'll leave the country and stay away.'

Hillingdon was genuinely terrified. In his hand he had his passport and money. He looked ill, possibly on the verge of collapse. 'Can I sit down?'

Marvik nodded. 'Hands on the desk. No sudden movements. I can reach you faster than you can move.'

Hillingdon moved around to his desk sat down heavily. Dejectedly, he said, 'I knew you'd come back.'

'And that was why you tried to take me out.'

'No! I thought you'd come to take *me* out. You have, haven't you?'

'Why should I do that?'

'Because of Phorcys.'

CHAPTER TWENTY-TWO

Marvik's eyes stayed riveted on Hillingdon looking for the trick, but he saw that he might just be telling the truth. 'Tell me about it.'

'But you must know.'

Marvik swiftly recalled what Bradshott had told him, *Orion said it had something to do with a deadly bacteria that the British government had deliberately dumped at sea.*

'Bacteria.'

Hillingdon nodded. His big face was a picture of misery.

Marvik's brain raced to put this with what Lanbury had said to Professor Galt and his dying words. It was beginning to make sense. He, by no means had it all, but he hoped that Hillingdon would fill in the many gaps.

Marvik said, '*Fenella* is not a woman but the name of a boat.'

'Yes.'

'Which sunk in the Barents Sea in 1976.' Lanbury's words. *It goes back to 1976.*

'It sunk in 1976 but it was in the Norwegian Sea, or at least, that's the official version.'

'Who was on board?'

Hillingdon inhaled. His big-knuckled hands twitched on the desk. Somewhere a clock struck one a.m. His body slumped and he looked half the size he had done earlier in the evening. Marvik knew he was finally about to hear the truth.

Hillingdon slowly began. 'Davvers, myself and Carl Woolmer, another sapper, were a unit. We went everywhere together, got drunk together and got into fights together. We always ended up doing extra duty or being slammed in the cells. One night we went too far, and we found ourselves up on serious charges. We were sentenced to the glasshouse but at the last minute were given another option. We could participate in an experiment at Porton Down.'

Marvik's pulse quickened. Porton Down was the government's Wiltshire research laboratory, which, up until the 1950s, had been involved in developing chemical and biological weapons. After that the focus had changed to developing effective countermeasures to such catastrophic weapons. They produced small quantities of chemical and biological agents, which were disposed of when no longer required. They also ran a human volunteer programme and had done so since 1916.

Hillingdon said, 'I'm talking 1976 when we had the Cold War and conflicts all over the ruddy place — the Sahara War, that madman Pol Pot in Kampuchea and his killing fields rule, slaughtering millions of people, the Angolan Civil War, the Lebanese Civil War, Argentina's Dirty War following the coup by the Argentine armed forces. I could go on for ever. The world then, now and always, has been a fragile place, as you know only too well from your time in the Marines.'

Marvik did. And he'd looked up the events of 1976 because of what Lanbury had said.

Hillingdon continued. 'The UK had to keep up with the weapons used by these parties and others, including chemical and biological weapons and that's where Porton Down came in. The project we were on was called Phorcys, after some Greek god who had something to do with the sea.'

So, a code name. 'Was it a chemical that could be used at sea? You need to tell me,' Marvik insisted when Hillingdon hesitated. 'I believe my parents were killed because of it. Did Davington kill them? Did he plant an underwater explosive device that buried them at sea?'

'He swore he didn't, and I believed him. He'd worked with your parents for six years trying to locate the *Fenella*.' Hillingdon wiped his head and glanced around nervously. 'Are you sure no one can hear us?'

'Positive.'

'Davvers accompanied your parents not only to assist them but also to protect them, or so he thought. But someone killed them and then killed him. I've got no proof of that, and even if I did have, I certainly wouldn't shout about it. I found him dead like I told you. I searched his flat for anything that mentioned the *Fenella* and Phorcys but found nothing. I reported his death to the police, but never uttered a word about the project. As his death wasn't deemed suspicious there was no inquest and it was very quickly forgotten. That suited me fine. No one came after me. I kept my mouth shut and my head down.'

'Then why did you mention Fenella to me?'

Hillingdon ran a hand over his face. 'It was stupid, but you said they were your parents and I believed you. I wanted to see if it registered with you. I didn't know how much you knew. It looked as though it was nothing, then you came back and I thought that bit about you being their son was bullshit and you'd been sent to see if I was a liability, if I would squeal. I went out on the RIB, like I told you, to think what to do, and decided that clearing out for a while might be the best option. I came back for my passport and some money, and I was going to take off on my boat tonight.'

'Who gave the orders to take them and Davington out?'

'I swear to you, I don't know.'

'Was it Carl Woolmer, the third man who was with you at Porton Down?' Marvik pressed. 'Was he paid to kill them?'

'No.'

'Now he's resurfaced and is wiping the trail clean. Is that why you're so scared? You met with him recently and he told you to mention Fenella to me to see what reaction you got. He needs to know how far I've got with my probing. And then, after reporting back to him, he told you to take me out.'

'No. It's not him,' Hillingdon said.

'Why so sure?'

'Because Carl Woolmer died in my arms in the water tank at Porton Down.'

Marvik eased back and studied the grey-haired man. He could see it was the truth. Hillingdon looked haggard. He'd aged about ten years in the last twenty minutes. 'Connected with Phorcys?'

Hillingdon nodded.

'Go on.'

'Our job was to enter this massive saltwater tank wearing diving gear. We were told the wet suits had been coated with a new chemical to protect us in case of the release of an underwater biological or chemical weapon. We did it several times with no ill effects. Then one day something went wrong. Carl started struggling. He was in trouble. I went to him and indicated we needed to get him up, but nobody did anything. Davvers came over and tried to help. Carl was unconscious by then.

'Me and Davvers grabbed hold of him and took him to the surface. When they realized he was dead, there was a bit of a panic. Someone said, "Get Zueker up here, quick." That was Professor Zueker, who was in charge of the experiment, but the man who came was his assistant, Dr Greyman. And he looked bloody grey to me, so did Davvers, no doubt I did too. I heard Greyman say something about a bacteria having an effect on humans. It was the first I'd heard about any bacteria being in that tank. But then there had to be something in there for us to have been spun the yarn about the protective coating on the diving clothes.'

'You didn't believe that.'

'I believe that two of us had some kind of protective coating on our gear but that Carl didn't, or if he did it was a different kind of coating.'

'Have you any idea what this bacteria was?'

'None.'

'What happened next?'

'Davvers and I were medically checked and were told we were OK. They said that Woolmer had had a heart attack. Davvers and I were pulled off the experiment and posted to different places for the eighteen months prior to our discharge from the army. We were warned never to speak of the experiment for the sake of national security. We were both bound by the Official Secrets Act anyway. But it was also made quite clear that for the sake of our future health we'd do well to forget all about the experiment called Phorcys and Woolmer's heart attack, and get on with our lives. That suited me fine. I wanted to forget the whole thing and I have until now.'

'OK, so tell me what you know about the *Fenella*.'

'Only what I read up in the marine investigation accident report.'

'And what Davington told you when you met up with him in 1997, shortly after my parents died and just before he died.'

'Yeah, OK.' Hillingdon rubbed his large hand across his forehead. '*Fenella* was a fishing boat which set off from Lossiemouth in Scotland on the 9 October 1976 with its Scottish skipper, Douglas Gillmour, and three Englishmen, including Professor Able Zueker and Dr Peter Greyman. Davvers told me that Zueker was an aquaculturist, whatever that is.'

'An expert on marine life,' Marvik answered, and as such could have developed a deadly parasite, which, if released into the oceans, could have had devastating effects on marine life and the food chain. And that connected with what Bradshott had told him.

Hillingdon said, 'The other crew member was listed as being Carl Woolmer when both Davvers and I knew it couldn't have been him, or if it was, then it was his body.'

'And a good way to dispose of it was to ditch it at sea.'

Hillingdon nodded. 'He had no relatives, and Davvers and I weren't encouraged to ask about a funeral. The official line, if you were to read the report, is that Carl Woolmer of the Royal Engineers was accompanying Zueker and Greyman on a scientific expedition, but the *Fenella* was caught in a maelstrom in the Norwegian Sea and went down, all hands lost. The coastguard mounted a search and rescue operation, but it was never found.'

'Until my parents located it in the Barents Sea, not the Norwegian Sea.'

'I guess they did, but I don't know that for certain. Davvers said to me that he wanted to talk to me about the *Fenella* but he was dead before he could tell me what he and your parents had discovered.' Hillingdon's eyes shifted. He looked drained and scared. 'I don't want to end up the same way as Davvers.'

'You won't, not by my hand anyway,' Marvik answered grimly. 'But maybe you are right to clear out because someone doesn't want it coming out.'

Hillingdon swallowed.

'Why were my parents asked to search for the *Fenella* in 1991?'

Hillingdon hesitated.

Marvik pressed, 'You've gone this far, you might as well tell me the rest.'

Hillingdon lowered his voice. 'Davvers said the government were scared that what had killed Carl was leaking out of the *Fenella*. There had been some dead harp seals washed up on the Norwegian coast in 1990 and no one could identify what they had died of. I don't know anything more. I swear it. I just want to clear out for a while.'

After a moment, Marvik nodded and stepped back. Hillingdon scrambled up. He made to head for the safe, then turned. 'What are you going to do now?'

The answer was flush out a killer and stay alive long enough to do so. He said, 'Keep asking questions.' And one of those questions concerned the man he was staring at. Why was Hillingdon still alive when the others were dead? Were his days numbered? They had to be when he had served his purpose but what purpose was that? But perhaps the party after the disk hadn't made the connection between Davington and Hillingdon. Or if they had they believed it to be immaterial.

Marvik returned to his tender. As he made his way back to Shamrock Quay, he considered those involved, their roles and their subsequent fates. Michael Colmead's purpose had been twofold: one, to give Dewell access to the archived files on Marvik's parents so that he could search for and remove anything incriminating, and two, to get the letter of authorization and the code to the bank's safe deposit box and remove the notebook and computer disk, before being abducted and most probably killed.

Marvik still had no idea who Dewell was or whether he was working independently or for someone. Was that the same person Stuart Bradshott aka Craven had been working for, after all, either he or Verity Taylor had got Freestone's address. But Verity could have got it from Dr Lanbury. That had been her purpose, to not only get Freestone's address but also access to his cottage to search it for information connected with Phorcys. The same for her relationship with Lanbury, and when Lanbury had finally unearthed something relevant, Verity had ensured he was eliminated. Perhaps Bradshott had been the killer and, having taken out both Freestone and Lanbury, he had become expendable. Bradshott should also have killed him but had failed.

It was clear to Marvik that Freestone had known all about Phorcys but, instead of contacting him, he had laid a complicated trail to the truth, which Marvik might never have found if he hadn't looked inside the fishing rod and remembered that Freestone had told him he hated fishing. So why the subterfuge? Was it because Freestone had enjoyed setting those kinds of puzzles, or because he had needed to make sure that the path was so heavily disguised that no one else followed the trail and closed it before Marvik could get to the truth?

Marvik's thoughts had carried him to his boat, where he winched the tender on board. He took a long, cold drink and made a sandwich. He was exhausted, both mentally and physically. It had now been twenty-four hours since he had slept and then only for a few hours with Caroline. He could still smell her perfume on board. It made him feel uneasy. What part did she play in all this? Was she a killer? Not of Davington or his parents, but maybe she had Sarah's blood, not to mention Freestone's, Lanbury's and Colmead's on her hands. And now also Bradshott's.

As he ate, he again considered if Caroline's purpose had been to prevent him from taking that call from Lanbury in order to give the killer enough time to take him out. But as before, he came up with the same problem: how could she have known Lanbury would call him? There was one way though, and swiftly he considered it. Professor Galt had admitted that Lanbury had called her and mentioned the name Fenella, but unless Galt had contacted Caroline when Caroline had been with him, which she hadn't, then she couldn't have told her what she knew. Except . . .

He groaned. While in the bistro, Caroline had excused herself to go to the ladies. Had that coincided with a call from Galt? Convenient timing if it had. But Caroline could have called Galt, who had instructed her to keep him occupied for the night and make sure he didn't answer his phone.

Marvik tensed at the thought, which was quickly followed by anger at his stupidity for letting himself be sidetracked by sex. Galt had told him Verity Taylor would use whatever means she could, including sex, to advance her career and Galt had asked Caroline to employ the same tactics.

Was Professor Letitia Galt a killer? No, he just couldn't believe it. Why should she kill his parents and a former colleague, not to mention Sarah Redburn and Hugh Freestone?

But the small voice in the back of Marvik's mind told him it was possible. Sarah could have told Galt about the computer disk when she had worked with her. And Galt would have known that Colmead had Freestone's address, and neither Freestone nor Lanbury would have seen Galt as a killer. Both, like Sarah, would have been fooled, until it had been too late.

His thoughts returned to Hillingdon as he heard the deep throb of a boat's engine spring to life. He was certain it was Hillingdon heading out of the marina. Why had Hillingdon been left alive with such deadly knowledge? Why mention *Fenella* to him in the first instance? Why put that memorial of Frederick Davington on the sappers website and draw attention to his friendship with Davington? Perhaps that had been a simple act of comradeship. Perhaps mentioning *Fenella* had been a slip of the tongue. Or perhaps Hillingdon *had* been testing Marvik to see if he was from British Intelligence sent to silence him. How did he know that Hillingdon was telling the truth about Carl Woolmer's death? He didn't and he doubted he would be able to access any information from the Ministry of Defence to verify the story.

Thoughts of the Ministry of Defence brought him back to Freestone, who had worked for them. Julie Pembroke had confirmed that, and Marvik had seen from the bank statements in the cottage that Freestone's pension had been a generous one, indicating he had retired at a very senior rank. In 1976 though he would still have been trying to make his mark and as such perhaps had been the junior civil servant in charge of commissioning, or overseeing, Phorcys. If that was so, why the dual identity of Culverham? Or was Culverham someone completely different who had also been involved in Phorcys? Was Hillingdon's purpose to reveal enough to see what Marvik did next? Or was Hillingdon the man behind all this, and the frightened appearance and manner an act? If so, it was a damn good one.

Marvik was too tired to think straight. He needed sleep and he needed to get away from the marina. He disabled the tracking device, wondering which of them had planted it

— Hillingdon, Caroline or Verity — and cast off. He made for the relative peace and solitude of Osborne Bay, where he had come before with Verity Taylor on board. There, he dropped anchor. He would hear anyone approaching his boat and sense any movement on deck but just to be sure he rigged up a couple of sensors on deck that Strathen had previously supplied him with and connected them to his mobile phone.

He lay on his bunk and let his weary brain return to Phorcys and the puzzle Freestone had set out for him. Marvik recalled from his brief time spent living with Freestone that he had enjoyed word puzzles and crosswords, like the one he had been completing before being lured into the garden and killed. He hadn't got very far, just a few words filled in and the clues ticked off as he'd completed them. Marvik's photographic memory conjured it up. In the column to the left in black ink he recalled the letters with spaces in-between, U — I — A, and A — G — L, eighteen across and eighteen down because they were circled.

Something nagged at his tired brain, but he couldn't grasp it. His head was throbbing with fatigue. His scars were itching. His leg and shoulder wounds ached as though to remind him his days of peak fitness were over. He glanced at his watch for what seemed the hundredth time. It was almost 4 a.m. He felt he was wasting valuable time by sleeping. But he needed sleep to clear his mind. Without it he wouldn't be able to function let alone think and act rationally.

He tried to shut down all thoughts of the last few days but around his head spun all that had happened like an endless video loop. There was something he was missing, something important. He felt there were only a few critical hours left between life and death. His? Maybe. Four hours' sleep would do but the way he was going, he thought he'd be lucky to get one.

CHAPTER TWENTY-THREE

Wednesday

He woke with a start and a sense of urgency burning in his gut. He'd been shaken from sleep by a noise, which, with a sense of relief, he saw was his phone and not an intruder. It was 8.15 a.m. His caller was Verity Taylor. He had expected her to be in touch, he just hadn't been sure when. He knew she couldn't leave it too long — she'd have been eaten up with curiosity, desperate to know what he was doing and if he had discovered more.

'I'm worried about Stuart,' she said as soon as he answered. 'He's still not replying to my text and emails.'

He won't. 'Why tell me?' Marvik said, rising and crossing to the galley.

'Because people seem to be dropping like flies and it's connected to what you're looking for,' she declared.

'And what you're after.'

'We can't talk on the phone. Where are you? Can we meet?'

And that had been the purpose of her call. She needed to see him and certainly not for his good looks, he thought wryly. 'I'm on my boat at Shamrock Quay,' he lied.

'I can be there in an hour.'

He rang off and flicked on the kettle. Who was Verity really working for? Herself? The killer? Again, he wondered if she had sent Stuart Bradshott last night to try and eliminate him and was now wondering why he wasn't replying to her. Or had she shot Stuart?

He shovelled a spoonful of coffee granules into a mug — he couldn't be bothered to make coffee in the machine. The thought conjured up Professor Galt and her sludge of coffee. From there his mind leaped to Caroline who had told him how Galt had lied to him. But it wasn't that which lay at the back of his mind, it was something else, something elusive that had come to him during sleep and then vanished in the morning light. Maybe caffeine would provoke it into the open, that and breakfast.

Breakfast! Suddenly he had it. Last night, just before sleep, he'd been thinking of Freestone and his crossword puzzle. His mind flashed to the picture of Freestone's kitchen — the coffee cup on the island unit with dregs of coffee in it, the plate with bacon and a small piece of toast left on it, and beside that, the *Daily Telegraph* with some of the crossword completed. Puzzles. Freestone couldn't tell him outright what he knew because he had suspected that his phone might be tapped and, if anything happened to him, his house would be searched for evidence that could betray his part in the Phorcys experiment. So he'd set him a puzzle.

Eager to check out his theory, Marvik abandoned breakfast and switched on his laptop. The newspaper had been dated Saturday 30 April, the letters to the clues of eighteen across and eighteen down, U — I — A and A — G — L—

He logged on to the *Daily Telegraph* crossword answers for 30 April and eagerly scanned eighteen down and eighteen across. None of the letters matched what Freestone had entered in the boxes. Either Freestone had completely misjudged the cryptic clues, or he'd written in those letters for a reason. Why not complete them all though? But Marvik had the answer almost immediately, it was because he was cautious and he knew someone was coming for him, perhaps by the river. Freestone had caught the sound of a small boat's engine, a RIB maybe. Or the soft, even flow of oars through the water. Or maybe his killer had arranged to meet him by the boathouse and Freestone had known his days were numbered. What's more, he didn't care if he was killed, not if that letter from the hospital was anything to go by. Freestone knew he was dying anyway.

What letters could fill the spaces between U, I and A? Marvik played around with various combinations, inserting a P and a T, UPITA, then a T and an N, UTINA. That was a possibility. It sounded like a woman's name. Could there be a woman involved in this? Or was it the name of another boat? The *Fenella* had disappeared in 1976. What had occurred in 1976 that might have a bearing on A — G — L —?

Hillingdon's words came back to him. *We had the Cold War . . . the Sahara War, that madman Pol Pot in Kampuchea and his killing fields rule . . . the Angolan Civil War, the Lebanese Civil War, Argentina's Dirty War.* Marvik had it. In an instant he filled in the gaps with an N, O and A. ANGOLA. The Angolan Civil War.

He looked it up on the internet, not that he needed to — he knew its bloody history. His pulse was racing as he quickly devoured what he read on screen. Then with a grim smile he filled in the letters between U, I and A. UNITA. Not a variation on a woman's name, not the name of another vessel that had gone down at sea, not even a code name, but the name of a political party in Angola, the National Union for the Total Independence of Angola, the second-largest political party in Angola. UNITA had fought alongside the Popular Movement for the Liberation of Angola, the MPLA, in the Angolan War for Independence between 1961 and 1974, and then against the MPLA in the ensuing civil war from 1975 to 2002. The war had taken place during the Cold War period with UNITA receiving military aid from the United States and South Africa, while the MPLA had received support from the Soviet Union and its allies. What it had to do with Phorcys, Marvik didn't know, except that a deadly bacteria or parasite had been developed at Porton Down by Zueker and Greyman, who had then been killed in a maritime accident.

Or had they? Had the *Fenella* met with an accident or had it been deliberately sabotaged by a marine explosives' expert — Hillingdon. Or someone like him — Davington, who had then been despatched with his parents in 1991 to locate it? Or had the *Fenella*, its passengers and its bacteria ended up elsewhere? In Angola?

He still had a few minutes before he needed to cross the Solent for his meeting with Verity. He keyed Stuart Bradshott's name into the search engine and came up with several references to him. They made intriguing reading, and from the photographs, Marvik was a hundred per cent certain he was looking at the same man who last night had been shot dead on his boat.

He closed down and scrolled through his phone until he found the text that Dr Hilda Eklund had sent over yesterday and the contact details for Orion Wellby's sister. He called her, apologized for disturbing her so early and, after passing on his condolences for Wellby, asked if there had been a phone, computer or any mention of the name Marvik in her late brother's belongings. The answer was exactly as he had expected, negative on all accounts.

He took a quick shower, then made for Shamrock Quay in the blustery, dull morning. Hillingdon's large motor cruiser had gone. Perhaps Hillingdon had told Verity Taylor about their meeting last night and she had been despatched to lure him to an isolated spot where he could be eliminated, this time for certain.

Marvik moored up and then made for the car park, where he found an area out of sight of arriving vehicles. There were still thirteen minutes before Verity was scheduled to arrive, but he saw her car pull in. No one followed in behind her and no car stopped across the road that led to Saxon Wharf. Before she could alight, he hastened to his boat and waited. It was a good ten minutes before she showed. Maybe she simply wanted to be punctual but Marvik was convinced she had called or sent a text to someone. That didn't mean it was anyone connected with this mission, but he wasn't going to take bets on that. Perhaps she was getting last minute instructions. Not from Bradshott, obviously, but from Hillingdon, Dewell or Galt. Or, dare he think it, Caroline Shaldon.

Verity was striding towards the boat. Her dark, sleek hair was flying around her face in the gusting wind whistling through the masts and gently rocking the boats in the shelter of the marina. With a gesture of annoyance she pushed it from her eyes. She was wearing black trousers, flat shoes and a red jacket over a T-shirt, but it was the small black leather rucksack she had over her shoulder that drew his attention. He wondered if it contained something more deadly than the usual day-to-day items.

'Stuart's still not answering his phone. I'm worried,' she announced without any form of greeting as she climbed on board.

'He's dead.'

'You've killed him!' she cried, freezing. Her brown eyes widened, and her hands twitched nervously on the strap of her rucksack.

'No, but he was shot last night while he was with me, and I was almost killed.' She looked at him disbelievingly. Roughly, he said, 'Cut it out, Verity, you know exactly what's going on.'

'I have no idea what you mean, all I know is that a great many people seem to be dying around you,' she barked.

'And you don't seem at all concerned to be fraternizing with a potential killer. And I'll tell you why, because you know for a fact that I am not one.'

She made to reply, then closed her mouth.

He turned into the main cabin. She followed him.

'Sit down,' he commanded.

She hesitated, then did so, sliding along the U-shaped seat with the table in front of her. Marvik took the seat opposite.

'Stuart Craven, or to give him his real name, Stuart Bradshott, was an environmentalist,' he began. 'According to his social media and web profile, he was an extreme marine activist and not a marine biologist as you told me. And he wouldn't know the Arctic if it hit him with an iceberg and gave him frostbite. He's been involved in corporate sabotage and has been arrested and convicted of causing criminal damage to pipelines and other marine structures, which he and his ilk see as harming the planet.'

'There's no need to sneer. It's a reality.'

'But that's not your motivation in all this,' Marvik retorted. 'No doubt you told Stuart that you were deeply concerned for the Planet Earth, and maybe you are, but you are also very clever and very ambitious.'

'Nothing wrong with that,' she declared.

'There is when people are prepared to murder for it. Especially if they don't get the credit or kudos they think they deserve.'

'I've killed no one.'

'Your boyfriend has.'

'How many times do I have to tell you, Stuart is not my boyfriend,' she hissed.

'Fine, but he's still a killer.'

'Environmentalists don't kill.'

Marvik raised his eyebrows. 'Are you really that naive, Verity?'

Her face flushed.

'Like all fanatics, he'd kill if he thought the means justified the ends. And if he had access to information so powerful it would make governments sit up and listen, then he'd use it.' Marvik could see that she well knew this. 'His friend and former colleague at Southampton University, where he once worked as a computer technician before leaving — probably sacked for hacking — told Stuart that he had just such information in his possession,' he continued. 'Orion Wellby, while working in the Vasa Museum in Sweden in early January, along with a marine archaeologist called

Sarah Redburn, came across a computer disk containing information that could ignite an international political and environmental scandal and open up a worldwide debate on the harmful chemicals dumped in our oceans. He claimed as much to Stuart in that email you told me he received from a cybercafé in Sweden.'

She looked as though she wished she hadn't mentioned that now.

'Orion said that the information he possessed was worth a great deal of money to certain organizations, and to the media, both of whom would pay handsomely for it. Not going too fast for you, am I?'

She scowled at him.

'But before they could sell the information to the highest bidder, Orion Wellby died in a so-called motor accident in mid-February. He skidded off the road and hit a tree, and the car burst into flames, leaving Bradshott with no idea where the computer floppy disk was, which contained this information. Orion's computer and mobile phone weren't listed in his belongings, not because they had been frazzled in the fire, as was believed by his colleagues and his sister, but because someone had already taken possession of them: his killer. Orion had also confided to someone other than Bradshott. Did you know that?'

She shook her head.

Marvik wasn't certain he believed her. 'Stuart knew Orion had confided to someone else because that person approached him and enlisted his help. Stuart thought he'd play the game both ways — foolish of him but he didn't set much store by you obtaining the information and being able to pay him the generous amount the other party promised him.'

The deep throb of a motorboat engine vibrated through the air.

Marvik continued. 'From Orion's phone and computer the killer discovered that it wasn't Wellby who had unearthed the computer disk but Sarah Redburn, who had asked him to open it. Orion told Sarah the data on it was corrupt and handed it back to her, but he lied, and before he handed it back, he wiped it clean.'

Marvik recalled what Galt had told him about not trusting computers in 1997 and that any researcher with an ounce of brain would also have written notes. Marvik guessed that the floppy disk told where both the hard-copy and online backups were held. He believed it had originally been written in that little hardback navy-blue notebook that had contained the disk, but his father had realized that to have the two together was inviting danger and so had torn out the pages and sent them to Michael Colmead in a sealed envelope for safekeeping, not to be opened at any cost. Not unless he came to retrieve them. He never did.

Marvik wasn't certain what had happened to that envelope. It should have been placed in his parents' archived files and perhaps it had been until Colmead had retrieved it, or it could have got pushed in with other papers. But Marvik believed it was these notes that had been burned in Colmead's fireplace. Possibly by Colmead himself when he realized he'd been duped. And before he'd been abducted by his killer.

The computer disk, and perhaps even the written notes, had given the password and the location of the online backup. Orion could have accessed the latter and, if he had, he could have used a computer in the same cybercafé where he had emailed Stuart Bradshott so as not to leave a trace on his own devices for anyone to find. Orion, after reading the full story, had approached someone named in Dan Coulter's report, whom he believed would pay a fortune to suppress it. Instead, he paid with his life. But the killer had made a mistake. He had killed Wellby before finding that password and the online provider.

To Verity, Marvik said, 'Orion's killer didn't know that the floppy disk was blank, not until it was stolen from my safe deposit box a week ago. And neither did Bradshott know, not until the killer approached him that same day.'

'How did this killer know Stuart was involved?' Verity said, sceptically.

'He'd found references to Stuart on Orion's phone and computer, and did the same as I did — he looked him up on the internet and discovered that Stuart had not only worked with Orion but was a marine activist and a computer hacker. The killer hoped he wouldn't have to enlist anyone else's help but Stuart could help him locate this vital information. Stuart was easily persuaded to join forces with the killer to try and find the online provider and password to the account that Orion had set up, or the one my father had used.'

She shifted uneasily. It was evident she was rapidly trying to make sense of this. 'Do you think Stuart told this killer about me?' she said.

'Of course.'

She pushed a hand through her hair, looking troubled and a little sour.

'Stuart was asked to play it both ways. Either you'd get to the truth or he would.'

She didn't much care for that.

'Stuart told the killer that he had approached you after Orion's death, not in April as you told me at a phoney conference, but in March, and directly because it occurred to Stuart that you might be able to help him. He remembered you from his days at Southampton University, a clever scientist, an expert on ocean turbulence and currents, the Arctic and the Barents Sea, and with particular knowledge about the works of Professor Dan Coulter, the author of the information on that computer disk. Bradshott contacted you and from what he told you, you immediately recognized the power of that research and how it would make you even more revered in your circle, and world famous. You contacted Professor Galt to see how much she knew about those missing years of research and was satisfied that she knew little and that she was also suffering from the early stages of dementia, so you didn't waste any more time on her. Then you approached Dr Lanbury. You didn't ask Galt to pass on your details as you told me because you didn't need to. You and Lanbury were both working in the same field of expertise.'

'All right, so you worked that out,' she sniffed.

'You soon realized that Lanbury was a better bet than you had hoped. Perhaps he even hinted at having some knowledge, or that he had something from my father written down somewhere that might lead you and Bradshott to the password. You persuaded Lanbury that he should pull together all his old papers and letters and turn them into his memoirs and you'd be delighted to assist. And what man could resist an attractive woman like you turning on the charm, although I've seen little of it.'

Her eyes narrowed but she said nothing.

'You steered the conversation towards my parents and their research and Lanbury told you about my guardian, Hugh Freestone. Freestone wasn't difficult to find. You visited him but you got fobbed off. You and Stuart decided to return to search his house. It just happened to be the very day and time I was there.'

'Yes, OK,' she said at last. 'But we had no idea who you were. I had never seen any photographs of you.'

And she wouldn't have done. Marvik's career in the Marines had made certain of that.

'I suspect it was Stuart's idea to head for Freestone's cottage that day.' Judging by her expression, Marvik was correct. 'Because it was the day after the disk taken from my safe was found to be blank, and Bradshott knew that Freestone wouldn't be there because he'd already killed him.'

'That's ridiculous.' But she was now doubting that. 'All right, so Freestone was dead, but I didn't know that. Stuart never said. And he told me Orion's death was an accident.'

'Sarah Redburn being strangled wasn't an accident.'

'The police said that it could have been a boyfriend.'

Marvik shook his head a little sadly. 'You're very good at selecting what information you want to believe.'

She shifted and her hands went to the bag on the seat beside her.

'Let's talk about Dr Lanbury,' Marvik continued. 'When he telephoned you in the early hours of Tuesday morning to tell you he'd discovered something about my parents' expedition, someone was listening in.' But Marvik paused for a moment. He saw Verity's keen eyes on him and in them, he saw that he was wrong. Yes, Lanbury's phone had been tapped but the message to Verity hadn't come from Lanbury, as she had claimed, but from the person listening in, who had got there ahead of both him and Verity and had taken from Lanbury what the poor man had found and had then shot him. The listener knew that he, Marvik, was on his way. It would be a tight thing, and it was. Verity was intended to find the body and possibly him with it.

'I'm wrong. Stuart Bradshott called you.'

Her surprised expression told him he was right.

'Stuart had probably asked you to tap Lanbury's phone on one of the occasions you were at his house in case Lanbury decided to call a colleague, or Professor Galt, with anything he discovered. Stuart called you after he had killed Lanbury and after he had taken from Lanbury what he had discovered — the password perhaps to that backed-up disk, or the location of the missing research papers. Lanbury died before you could get there and I only just managed it. Lanbury did say 'Edinburgh' in his dying breath and you were only too keen to run with the HMS *Edinburgh* story when you realized I didn't have a clue as to what my parents had really been doing. You thought you could still get hold of Stuart and find out what he had learned from Lanbury before he shot him.'

'I didn't intend anyone to get killed. That wasn't the deal.'

'Deals get broken,' Marvik said dryly. 'Stuart should have stuck with you, but he was naive and greedy enough to be persuaded to go in with the killer. Last night he was killed by a cold-blooded assassin.'

She looked worried and Marvik thought this time it was genuine.

'Do you know who that is?' he asked.

She shook her head.

He was wasting time here. He had to ditch her. And perhaps she'd be glad to be ditched. But before he could speak, she said, 'Where is Stuart's body?'

'He could be anywhere in the Solent by now. I don't care. I've finished with it all.'

'But you can't leave it there.'

'Why not? I no longer care what happened in 1997. Now if you don't mind, I'd like to get under way.'

'But where are you going?' She quickly sidled out of the seat as he turned to the helm.

He started the engine and, heading out into the cockpit, tossed over his shoulder, 'Too many people have died, Verity, because of my parents' last exploration. I don't intend to be the next victim.'

'You're giving up?' she cried, following him.

'Yes.'

'I don't believe you.'

'That's your privilege.'

'We can join forces. Together we can find that research, we can discover what your parents were doing and why they were killed,' she said fervently.

'Bit late for that, Verity. You should have hitched yourself to this bandwagon before, and besides, everyone you link up with seems to end up dead. I don't like the odds.'

'Don't you want to know what your parents were doing?'

'I already know.'

She started with shock, then eyed him disbelievingly. 'Fine,' she said. 'Duck out. Run away.'

He climbed off the boat and loosened the stern line. She glared at him, then alighted. He watched her march away before letting off the for'ard line and jumping back on board. He eased the boat from its berth and headed out into the Solent. He felt the adrenaline surging through him, not just because of the danger that lay ahead but because the long journey that had begun for him in 1991 when he'd been sent away to school was finally coming to an end. He didn't have all the answers, but he had enough to make one phone call, which he did on deck when he was far out to sea. All he had to do now was wait for the killer to arrive.

CHAPTER TWENTY-FOUR

Marvik caught the distant deep throb of a powerful RIB motoring up the river. From where he was standing he couldn't see it. She was half an hour early. That didn't surprise him. For their rendezvous he'd chosen the quayside of an abandoned brickworks on the western bank of the River Medina on the Isle of Wight. There were no boats in sight, and nothing had passed him since he'd moored up. Neither had he seen any boats in the trots once he'd passed Island Harbour Marina to the east. Fields now stretched out across the river to the east. To the south were more fields before giving way to the business estates and houses of the capital of the Island, Newport. To his left and north were further fields and patches of scrubland and a thicket before giving on to industrial buildings and the houses of West Cowes, which he had passed earlier. The shores both opposite and to his right were deserted. The road behind him lay cracked, uneven and weed strewn just like the derelict quayside where he was standing. The scattering of buildings around him had been abandoned years ago. Behind him was a solid red-bricked structure, minus its windows, with another smaller building to its right, which boasted a tall, thin chimney. He'd searched them and had found them empty save for some pieces of rusting machinery, chains, rope, cracked bricks and brick dust. The heavy cloud that heralded rain made it gloomy. The wind had risen and was driving through the reeds and long grass. He felt a few spits of temperamental rain.

In order to lure his prey here he'd told her he knew what his parents had been doing during those missing years from 1991 to 1997. It was the truth, at least. The lie was in the statement that he had discovered documented evidence of it. He wasn't sure whether or not she believed him but that didn't worry him. He knew she had to come.

The RIB came into view and swung towards the quayside. On board and alone was the bony, grey-haired figure of Professor Letitia Galt. Expertly, she tied off, silenced the engine and climbed off, giving him a critical gaze.

'Shall we go on board?' He gestured to his boat. The rain was getting heavier.

She gave a curt nod and followed him. Her eyes swept the salon and the helm. 'We're alone,' he said. 'But if you want to make sure, go ahead.' He gestured an arm.

'No need.'

'Do you want to sit?'

'No. I prefer to stand. Well, Marvik, what have you got?' she said brusquely, folding her arms against a thin chest enveloped by a large sailing jacket.

'Something you might not like to hear,' he answered.

'You think I'll be upset over learning the truth behind Eerika's death? It was a long time ago.'

'Dr Lanbury's wasn't and neither was Hugh Freestone's or Sarah Redburn's.'

'Tragic, but I can hardly mourn for people I wasn't close to.'

'I don't think you'd mourn for anyone,' he said coldly. 'I don't even think you mourned for my mother. In fact, I think you were glad she was dead.'

Her lips drew in a tight line. 'If this is about closure, Marvik, then I can't give it to you.'

'Oh, but I think you can. Because you killed Eerika and Dan.'

'Tosh!' she dismissed lightly, but her eyes were hard and calculating. 'I was nowhere near the Straits of Malacca, and why would I want to kill my closest friend?'

'Professional jealousy is one reason, because my parents were commissioned to undertake some high-profile major explorations that you would have given your eyeteeth to undertake, including their mission in 1991 with a vessel that had all the latest state-of-the-art equipment. You originally believed they had been detailed to look for HMS *Edinburgh*'s missing gold.'

'I had absolutely no need to be jealous. And I didn't kill them.'

'Not directly. You didn't plant that underwater explosive, but you know who did, and it's a secret you've kept for twenty years, and that you've been allowed to keep whereas others have been killed because of it. Before her death, Eerika told you what she and Dan had discovered on the wreck of the *Fenella*.'

'Eerika told me nothing. Why do you think I asked Colmead where the research papers were for those years?'

'You didn't, or if you did, it was only for show. A bluff because you already knew what that research was and have done all these years, only you didn't bargain for one rogue notebook belonging to my father to turn up with a floppy computer disk attached to it. James Dewell, or whatever his real name is, was despatched to the solicitor's archive storage company to go through the files to make sure there was nothing in them to hint at your involvement or betray your knowledge.'

'I don't know what you're talking about.'

He ignored her. 'The killings should have stopped, Galt, with my parents' deaths and Davington's. There was no need for the others to die.'

He caught the faint rustle of movement outside.

'You think I killed them all!' she cried. 'You're mad. I wouldn't even know which way to point a gun, let alone strangle someone, and I wouldn't have the strength to beat anyone over the head.'

'Then you know how Hugh Freestone was killed.'

She glared at him, realizing she had betrayed herself.

Evenly, he said, 'I'd say you'd have considerable strength to pick up a heavy object and bring it full force down on a man's skull, especially that of a man who trusted you and who had his back to you, crouching down perhaps to tie up your RIB or to retrieve something in it when you visited him at his cottage outside Arundel.'

'Fiction.'

'And when Lanbury phoned you just after calling me that night, he said more than the word "Fenella". He told you he knew what Eerika and Dan had been doing between 1991 and 1997. He'd found some written evidence of it, probably stuffed away inside one of his books or files. He said that he'd called me but had to leave a message. I bet you wet your knickers with delight over that. It gave you time to reach him, retrieve what he had and then shoot him in the back as he went out to investigate someone moving about in the garden. Maybe he even thought it was me arriving.'

She sniffed and said nothing.

'But let's go back a stage, to February,' he went on. 'Orion Wellby contacted you after he had managed to open the computer disk that he and Sarah had found buried in the archives in the Vasa Museum in Sweden.'

She remained silent but from her expression he knew he was correct.

'Orion recognized your name in the information the disk contained. He'd know all about you, him being in the same line of work. Your paths might even have crossed on a marine heritage project, possibly on his work with the *Mary Rose*.' Marvik had clearly hit the mark. 'He thought he'd found a lucrative source of blackmail. You flew out to Sweden to meet him and made sure he met with a car accident and was killed.'

'So now I'm supposed to be a mechanic,' she scoffed.

He ignored her. 'But you made a mistake because, although you had taken his phone and computer, you could find no information of where he had backed up the data online. And no computer disk in his belongings. However, you discovered that he had been working with Sarah Redburn when the notebook and floppy disk were found, and it was a fair assumption that Orion might have given it to Sarah to bring back to the UK. You also discovered that Orion had been in touch with a man called Stuart Bradshott, but we'll come to him later.' Again, Marvik caught the sound of a faint rustle. He didn't think it was the wind.

'You called Sarah from a pay-as-you-go phone, which you later ditched, and asked her to meet you on the beach at Ballard Point in Dorset. There you learned little more except that Orion Wellby had told Sarah the data was corrupt and he couldn't get anything from it except that my parents could have used an online backup and he was searching for that. She didn't know he was dead. You knew that she had met me earlier that day. You didn't have to kill her but you didn't want her around to testify to your interest if it all went tits up. You easily obtained from her where her possessions were kept but learned I had got there first and taken something from Sarah's belongings before the house was set alight.'

'Now I'm an arsonist, quite versatile,' she quipped.

'Versatile, yes, but not an arsonist or a mechanic. For those skills, and for strangling Sarah, you needed specialist help.'

For the first time during their conversation she looked troubled.

'Do we really need to persist with this fairy tale?' she bluffed. 'Who else am I supposed to have killed?'

Marvik eyed her coldly as a sudden squall of rain drummed on the deck and the wind whipped through the grass and shrubs. 'Michael Colmead.'

'The solicitor!' She raised her thin eyebrows.

'You approached Colmead, who told you that I had been asking around about the research for those missing years and that I had a safe deposit box in a bank in London. After that you had help threatening him into giving your accomplice access to my safe deposit box, only to find that the disk was blank. Orion Wellby was dead and you had no idea if the data on the disk had been corrupt, or if it had been backed up somewhere, and that's when you remembered Orion had been a friend and associate of Stuart Bradshott, the man you knew Orion had communicated with. By then Bradshott had enlisted the services of Verity Taylor. But you knew he was easily persuaded and naıve when it came to women, no matter what their age. He was also very keen to make a name for himself in the environmental political circle, not to mention eager to get his hands on a large sum of money. You promised him both if he could locate where Orion had backed up the information. Did he find it? Is that why you gave him an explosive device to plant on my boat and then shot him?'

She gave a hollow laugh. 'You've been watching too many thrillers.' She unfolded her arms and walked around the salon to stand by the helm.

'I've been living in one for the last two months. Do you want me to tell you how it ends?'

'If you must,' she said dismissively.

His body tensed as he felt the soft lift and fall of his boat. 'But then we don't know the ending yet. And I'd prefer it not be a bullet in the back of my head like Stuart Bradshott.' And with that he reached out, grasped her arm, twisted her round and rammed her arm high up her back. He thrust her in front of him, at the same time placing his forearm against her throat, forcing her head back. She gave a strangled cry. Her eyes bulged as the large, bearded, grey-haired figure of Guy Kranton appeared in the doorway. In his hand was a gun.

'If you want to shoot me,' Marvik said, 'then you'll have to do so through her.'

'I could aim for your head. You are slightly taller than Letitia.'

'You could but it would make it trickier and messy,' Marvik said casually, but he knew that Kranton was right and that he was also a crack shot. Because, despite what he'd said to Galt about her killing Bradshott, he knew she hadn't. She'd sent her man to do her dirty work, just as she had for Orion Wellby, Sarah Redburn, Hugh Freestone, Dr Lanbury and Michael Colmead, but she had lured each one of them to their deaths. If Kranton chose to shoot him, he wouldn't miss.

'And I wouldn't need to worry about cleaning up,' Kranton added.

'Like you've been doing for most of your life.'

Kranton smiled. 'I could make your death look like suicide. Distraught over not being able to discover why Sarah Redburn was strangled, and why your parents were killed, you shot yourself. Or maybe it was because you were suffering from depression or post-traumatic stress after leaving the Marines. That would fit well with your medical and service records.'

'What was on the computer disk, Kranton?'

'Nothing.'

Marvik had been correct. 'Which was why you needed Stuart Bradshott's assistance to locate where Orion Wellby had backed it up online. Did you find it? You must have done to have shot him after you told him to place that explosive device on the hull of my boat, when the first one in my cottage was unsuccessful. It was you in the RIB.' Marvik had been sure of that the moment he had heard Galt motoring up the River Medina. It was the same RIB he'd vaguely seen and heard leaving Newtown Harbour after Bradshott's shooting. And when Galt had slowed down on the approach here, he knew she had been dropping off Kranton, who had worked his way along the shore on foot.

Marvik stared at the big man in front of him with anger in his heart. But the depth of his fury was directed at the woman he had in his grip.

'Doesn't feel too nice being strangled, does it?' he hissed at her, tightening his hold.

Kranton stepped forward and raised the gun.

'Go ahead, shoot me. I can break her neck before you pull that trigger.' And he could. Kranton knew it. He lowered the pistol. Marvik knew that Letitia Galt was the one person Kranton wouldn't kill because it was the opposite of what Caroline Shaldon had told him. She'd said that Galt was besotted with Kranton but it was Kranton who worshipped Galt. And the tale that Kranton had spun Caroline about Galt possibly having early onset of dementia was just that, a lie designed for her to tell him so that he couldn't possibly believe her capable of murder. How far was Caroline involved? Had Kranton or Galt given Caroline instructions to find him, discover the progress of his investigation and prevent him from meeting Lanbury until it was too late? He didn't like to think so but he couldn't be sure.

Marvik eased his pressure. Galt coughed. 'Water,' she choked.

Kranton made to move forward, but again Marvik tightened his grip. 'Don't move or I'll snap her head off. No water. Neither of you showed any mercy to Sarah.' Tautly, Marvik addressed Kranton. 'You set fire to the house on Eel Pie Island and you sabotaged Orion Wellby's car.'

Galt tried to clear her throat. She was looking grey. Marvik continued.

'You threatened Colmead into telling what he knew, which was where my safe deposit was located and the code to it. You forced him to give James Dewell, not his real name and a man who was working for you, the identity of a dead client, a letter of authorization to access the safe deposit box and the archived files. Then you killed Colmead. Where is his body?'

'In the depths of the New Forest.'

'A hose from the exhaust into the car, made to look like suicide,' Marvik snarled, as he had anticipated.

Kranton didn't reply.

Marvik continued. 'And James Dewell is the body that was fished up on the shore at Milford-on-Sea. You killed him because, like the others, he had served his purpose. I guess he was knocked unconscious or drugged and thrown overboard from the boat when no one except you and her were on board. You also killed Freestone. She lured him to the end of the garden by the boathouse and you struck him from behind, then pushed him in the river.'

'We did him a favour. A quick death instead of a long, lingering one full of false hope and gradually going mad. It was a brain tumour.'

'Then, taking his keys, you searched the house for any information about Project Phorcys because it was something that you were deeply involved in.'

'Let Letitia go, and I'll tell you.'

'You must be joking. Besides, you don't need to tell me. I know.'

'That Freestone ordered the killing of your parents?'

Marvik stiffened. He glared at Kranton. Was this another of his lies? But no, Marvik knew it wasn't. He had begun to suspect it because it made sense of so much that previously hadn't added up.

Kranton said, 'Freestone gave your parents the mission of locating the *Fenella*, which they did, and they reported directly back to him. If they had just left it there, they and the others might still be alive today. Freestone has, or had, a lot of blood on his conscience. And if you hadn't decided to nose around and stir up the past, Bradshott, Colmead and Dr Lanbury wouldn't be dead.'

That didn't wash with Marvik. 'So none of this is your fault,' he scoffed while his mind raced to put all the final pieces together. His parents had discovered the truth about the *Fenella* and had told the one man they trusted, the man who had given them the exploration and who had arranged for *Vasa II* to be their vessel, Hugh Freestone. Twenty years later Marvik had come along asking questions of Colmead and Bell. Colmead had told Freestone, because that was what he had been instructed to do. But Colmead had no idea of Freestone's involvement in Dan and Eerika's death. Freestone knew his time was up, and not just because he had cancer. Maybe he had finally developed a conscience and had wanted Marvik to learn the truth.

Marvik steeled himself not to betray his emotions at the lies and treachery. He felt sick inside but didn't have time to examine or indulge his feelings.

Kranton said, 'What your parents didn't know was that Freestone had been in charge of Project Phorcys and was detailed to get rid of it when the experiment went wrong, which he did using the *Fenella*.'

That fitted with what Hillingdon had told him. 'And he saw a way of making money out of it. He looked for a market to sell the bacteria and came up with Angola.'

Kranton's brow knitted. 'How do you know that?' he asked sharply.

'I know a lot more.' Galt was weakening under Marvik's grasp. He removed his arm from her neck but still held her tightly in an arm hold.

She coughed. Kranton stepped forward.

'Stay where you are or I'll—' Marvik made to return his arm to her throat.

Kranton held up his hands and froze.

Marvik continued. 'It was 1976 and the Angolan War.' He saw no need to tell Kranton about the crossword, which he had overlooked when searching the house after Freestone's murder, even though it would have given Marvik some satisfaction to see Kranton annoyed that he had missed it. 'Angola has an Atlantic coastline with major ports including Luanda, Lobito, and Namibe, all very important strategically. It was this coastline and its ports that the Soviet-backed government, the MPLA, held so no exports were possible. Freestone thought the Western-backed UNITA would be delighted to get their hands on a seaborne bacteria that could be used to penetrate the MPLA's hold of the coastline by destroying the fishing industry and creating panic in the food chains and more famine, hoping to starve the rebels into submission.

'Instead of making sure that the canister was on the *Fenella* with Zueker and Greyman, Freestone gave it to you, an experienced bosun who had worked unofficially with Freestone on various Intelligence missions. You were given the position on RV *Acionna* despatched to the Skeleton Coast off Namibia and Angola in 1976, so called because of all the wrecks there, many lying on the sands like rotted beached whales. It's a treacherous, fogbound coastline. You were ostensibly searching for the *Vento Do Mar*, a sixteenth-century Portuguese ship.' As Caroline had told him. 'But in reality, the *Acionna* was a spy ship used to assist UNITA if they needed it. In order to make it look authentic the research party needed divers and marine archaeologists. Galt, a young marine archaeologist, aged twenty four, was on board.'

She spoke, but Marvik noted her voice was slower than usual and not so crisp. 'You need hardly go on. You know it all.'

Marvik addressed Kranton. 'Your job for Freestone was to sell the bacteria to a contact of his in Angola, after all, Freestone worked for British Intelligence, another name for the Ministry of Defence. Who did you sell it to, Kranton? Which faction — the MPLA or UNITA? Or perhaps it was both. In exchange for what?'

'You tell me,' Kranton said cockily while Marvik knew his brain was searching for a way to destroy him and save Galt.

He stepped back a little and continued. 'I'd say it was diamonds. A common currency in that country, especially for illegal goods, and easy to hide and transform into money later, which you and Freestone split because this was a very unofficial mission. Freestone was giving the orders and had made certain that the *Fenella* would be lost in the Barents Sea, and if anyone queried it, he could say that Zueker had been taken out because he was selling out to the Soviets.'

'Project Phorcys was not the Intelligence Services' or Porton Down's finest hour. Let Letitia go.'

Marvik ignored him. 'When my parents finally located the wreck of the *Fenella*, they discovered that the canister was not on board but Davington already knew that. He was

Freestone's man on the inside. Freestone had no choice but to send a team to explore for the *Fenella* when the harp seals off the Norwegian coast were found dead in 1990 from a mysterious bacteria that no one could identify. The Intelligence Services had to be certain the canister wasn't leaking. The government was scared the Norwegians or Russians would find it. Every environmental marine tragedy in that region after 1976 would have been put down to it, no matter that it had nothing to do with the canister or the bacteria. Foreign governments would have demanded compensation; the Russians would claim it had been developed and was being used to attack them and their fishing rights. It had been Freestone's project, and he made sure he was chosen to oversee the expedition.

'Dan and Eerika found that the wreck had been sabotaged and the canister was not there. They told Freestone, who, as you so rightly said, was the wrong man. He said he would report back and that was the end of it. But nothing came of it. Freestone told them they were bound by the Official Secrets Act and that they could be in danger if they ever spoke of, hinted at, or wrote up the expedition. But my parents began to sniff around and ask questions and my mother came to you, Galt,' he said with disgust. His grip tightened.

She cried out. Kranton stepped forward.

'Stay,' Marvik commanded.

'She's in distress. She's ill.'

'Tough,' Marvik hissed.

Kranton's hand gripped the gun.

'Don't even think of it, Kranton. Kill me, and I'll kill her first. You told lover boy,' Marvik hissed in Galt's ear through gritted teeth, and yet his eyes remained hard on Kranton. 'And you, Kranton, told Freestone. He used the same tactic he had used in 1976. He despatched a research vessel, yours, with you and a small Filipino crew you recruited. You planted an explosive device on an underwater structure timed to go off when they were diving in the Straits of Malacca, where they'd been enticed by Freestone on another exploration. It was far enough away to prevent too many questions, and it gave you and Davington time to remove any material, including their computers, disks and notes from their boat, which might incriminate you and Freestone.

'You set that underwater explosive, you killed them, boarded *Vasa II* and, with Davington's assistance, made sure to clean up on board. Davington knew he couldn't say anything, but maybe he developed a conscience. He became a liability, so you killed him by putting a lethal dose in his inhaler. And Freestone became my guardian because he told his Intelligence bosses that he had to make sure I had received no correspondence from my parents about Project Phorcys and that I knew nothing about it. I didn't, and everyone was relieved when I appeared to show no interest and went off to join the Royal Marines as soon as I could. Problem solved for another twenty years.'

Despite Marvik's intentions to control himself, he felt sick and angry inside. Everything he had believed about Freestone was a lie. Freestone was a lie. There was Freestone's dual personality and the fact there was nothing in his parents' papers or their will naming Freestone either as a friend, colleague or guardian. Far from being a quiet, unassuming man and old friend of his parents, he was ruthless, corrupt, greedy and their killer. He was also a man under orders from the government, orders that he had carried out as far as the *Fenella* was concerned with one exception: *he* had stolen the bacteria and given it to Kranton to sell for diamonds. What had become of that money? Perhaps some of it had ended up in that account Freestone had opened in 1991 in the name of Culverham — one of his cover names — and in Marvik's name as part of the deal with his parents. It was done to reassure Dan and Eerika their son would be well looked after financially if anything happened to them. A generous regular sum had been paid into it while they had worked for the British government in their search for the *Fenella.* Then Freestone had given Kranton orders to kill Marvik's parents and Frederick Davington and that, he thought, was the end of it until February, when Sarah discovered the computer disk and Orion Wellby contacted Professor Galt, who in turn told Kranton and Kranton told Freestone. OK, so Freestone had left Marvik a trail to follow to get to the truth but that didn't make anything better. Marvik thought it had been more in devilment than because Freestone really wanted him to discover the truth.

Kranton's eyes flicked to Galt. Marvik felt her body sag in his grip then suddenly go limp. Her eyes rolled and closed, and it was all Marvik could to do to hold on to her. In a flash Kranton stepped forward, Galt was on the floor and the gun was at Marvik's forehead.

'Slowly,' Kranton said evenly.

Marvik rose. The hand that held the gun was steady. Then Galt groaned. Marvik thought her collapse had been feigned and Kranton must have believed the same, but it wasn't. In that instant Kranton was diverted by his concern for her, the gun moved and so too did Marvik.

With one powerful blow, he knocked the weapon from Kranton's hand, sending it clattering on to the deck, then balled his fist and rammed it hard into Kranton's face. Blood spurted from his nose. He reeled back and tried to make for the gun, but Marvik reached it first and had it cocked and pointed steadily at Kranton's head. In a cold, even voice he said, 'Stand very still or I shoot.'

Galt lay on the deck, grey and immobile.

'You won't pull the trigger,' Kranton said, while his eyes darted to the prone woman.

'I've killed before, and this time I don't give a shit if I get arrested. I'll happily hand myself in and tell the court everything.'

'Think they'll let you?' he scoffed.

Kranton meant the Intelligence Services. 'No, but I'll have had the satisfaction of killing you before they kill me. Move and don't try anything, because I'd just as soon shoot you in the back of the head as the forehead.'

'But . . .' His eyes dashed down to Letitia.

'Do I care if she's dead?' Marvik spat. 'Out.'

They stepped into the cockpit in the steadily falling rain. Marvik raised the gun and looked into the eyes of the man who had killed his parents. His fingers pressed on the trigger. It was a matter of seconds. He had only to squeeze, then Guy Kranton would no longer exist.

Marvik took a breath. A dull thud sounded. Kranton's grey eyes widened with shock, blood spouted from his nose and mouth and, just as had happened with Stuart Bradshott, he fell forward on to the deck.

Marvik remained where he was. He didn't even bother to take cover. He knew he wasn't the target.

His eyes scoured the opposite side of the river. Nothing. He put the gun in his pocket and reached for his phone.

CHAPTER TWENTY-FIVE

'Who killed Kranton?' Marvik addressed the dark-haired solemn man in front of him.

Crowder's serious face remained impassive. They were in the salon on Marvik's boat. Galt's body had been airlifted to the mortuary. She'd suffered a fatal stroke. He felt no guilt that his action might have prompted it. Kranton's body had also been removed. Marvik didn't ask where they had taken it. He doubted he'd be told anyway, or if he was whether it would be the truth. There would be no police report, no scene-of-crime officers, no investigation. Marvik had done his job and that was to provoke a killer into the open, not to eliminate him — that had been the role of another party. Someone, he thought, who might have been despatched by Verity Taylor, unless it was she who was the crack shot, and that was still possible.

Or perhaps it was someone Kranton had made an enemy of during his long and dubious career. Perhaps one of them had finally caught up with him, and Marvik wondered if one of the last acts of Hugh Freestone had been to shop Kranton to someone from his past. If he had then whoever had got the tip-off had timed it to perfection, which brought Marvik back to Verity, because she had placed another tracking device on his boat. The first he had disabled but this one he had left. He'd found it when he was out to sea on the way to the Island and the rendezvous with Galt. It was what he had expected when she had called and asked to see him, and which he had seen her place when her hands had gone down to her ruck-sack. Perhaps she knew, like him, that the end to this quest was in sight. Perhaps she had guessed, or worked out, that the killer was Galt's skipper and lifelong lover, Guy Kranton. Or perhaps her bosses had always known that Kranton had been involved in the sale of Zueker's bacteria and the deaths of Dr Eerika Marvik and Professor Dan Coulter and had wanted their son to flush Kranton and Galt out into the open.

'Is it important?' Crowder asked, answering Marvik's question about the identity of Kranton's killer, his deep-brown eyes fixed steadily on Marvik.

Was it? For the last half an hour Marvik had been examining his emotions. Did he feel cheated?

As though reading his thoughts, Crowder said, 'Would you have squeezed that trigger?'

'Killing him would have made me the same as him. Corrupt, evil, without emotion. A cold-blooded, ruthless killer.' And the same as Letitia Galt, who, in his opinion was equally as evil as Kranton, perhaps even more so as she had given that address at his parents' memorial. 'Did you know Kranton killed my parents?'

'No.'

'Or that Freestone had given the orders for him to do so?'

'No.'

Marvik believed that was the truth. He caught the sound of an outboard engine heading towards them and said, 'The moment you told me that Sarah Redburn's murder was connected with my parents' deaths it became a mission for your unit. Our unit,' he corrected, 'the National Intelligence Marine Squad.'

'Are you sure that was when you were engaged on this mission?'

Marvik's mind spun.

'When the National Intelligence Marine Squad was formed early this year and I was appointed to head it up to investigate crimes that had occurred at sea or that have, or had, a marine connection, your parents' file was passed to me, along with your service record.'

Marvik raised his eyebrows. 'Did Strathen know this when he asked me to help him investigate the missing computer scientist in connection with Esther Shannon's murder?'

'No. But I knew that you and he worked efficiently together. Strathen was chosen for the Squad for his unique intelligence-gathering and analytical skills and for his cyber expertise, which he has put to good use on the missions.'

'Including this one,' Marvik said, as the boat rocked and Strathen appeared. 'Your timing is perfect, Shaun. Have you been eavesdropping?' He knew Strathen's ability to tap into conversations.

Strathen grinned. 'No, but I have found what Orion Wellby backed up.'

'It's all there?' Marvik asked keenly.

Strathen nodded solemnly.

Marvik turned and opened the fridge and reached for a bottle of water. By the time he turned back his emotions were once again under control. 'There was no client call or meeting. Or rather there was — it was Crowder.'

'Yes, with instructions not to tell you. Sorry, Art.'

Marvik shrugged and smiled to show there were no hard feelings. He understood the reason why, and he trusted Strathen implicitly.

Crowder continued. 'There were a lot of questions surrounding the deaths of Professor Dan Coulter and Dr Eerika Marvik. No one knew why they were in the Straits of Malacca or what they had been doing in the years before that from 1991, but it was on file that one or both of them could have been a security risk.'

Marvik's hand froze as he raised the bottled water to his lips. He frowned. 'Freestone's work.'

'Probably.'

'Backed up by Davington, who was scared he'd be next on the list if he didn't play ball, which he was. Why was I allowed to enlist in the Marines if my parents were suspected of being politically active and foreign agents?'

'Because not only were you deemed to be too young to have had any knowledge of their activities but the powers that be were only too pleased when you enlisted. You were safely engaged elsewhere with no time, energy or inclination to ask questions about your parents' deaths. And you never did until primed to do so after Sarah Redburn's murder.'

'By you.'

'And you've proved yourself loyal to the Crown several times over.'

'I see you've been thorough,' Marvik said acidly.

'It's no more than you'd expect.'

He was right. Marvik was beginning to wonder if Freestone had put the idea into his head about joining the Marines. He couldn't recall any conversation about it but perhaps the suggestion had been more subtle than that. Freestone had been a clever, manipulative man. Marvik wondered if he had sensed something wrong about Freestone even at the tender age of seventeen. He'd thought his grief and anger had distanced him from the man who had become his guardian for two months, but perhaps he had never trusted Freestone. Marvik had been only too keen to get away from him and to never have contact with the man again. Why such strong feelings? Was there something he'd seen, heard or just sensed that had made him feel that way?

He put his mind back to what Crowder was saying.

'No one from your parents' past, as far as your file indicates, has made any attempt to contact you over the years.'

'No, because I gave Colmead instructions that I didn't want to see, speak or hear from anyone connected with my parents. I played right into Freestone's hands regarding that request.' Marvik wondered again if Freestone had planted the idea in his young mind that it was best to cut all ties and move on.

'Your parents had a wide circle of friends and colleagues, some of whom were very politically active in the Cold War period, which came to an end in 1991 when the Soviet Union collapsed and you were sent away to school.'

'Which puts paid to the theory they were spying for the Russians because they'd have been targeted long before 1997.'

'The file stated there was the possibility that they were working for both sides and by 1997 working for others.'

So Freestone had still been spinning his lies even after their deaths and when Marvik had been living under his roof. But when information, disinformation and lies were part of your life, how could you stop?

Crowder said, 'The file claimed that *Vasa II* was a spy ship sent to the Barents Sea to gather intelligence on the Russians' expanding submarine fleet. Twenty new submarines had entered the service since the Soviet collapse and their strategic importance was growing, not to mention the fact that some of those submarines carried ballistic missiles.'

Marvik's experience of spy ships while serving in the Special Boat Services was that they came in varying shapes and sizes, sometimes naval vessels, sometimes trawlers controlled and operated by Special Boat Services Officers like him and Strathen and others from the Security Services. Freestone had used that cover story to despatch Kranton, not only to the Skeleton Coast to trade the bacteria but to the Straits of Malacca to kill his parents, and no one had thought to question it or the seizure of their documentation and computers because of what the file said. A file fabricated by an arch manipulator.

'Your parents could have been detailed to gather intelligence by means of sophisticated electronic eavesdropping equipment,' Crowder said, 'although no recordings or evidence were found on the vessel after their death.'

'Because it was never there in the first instance.'

'Quite. But it was also flagged up they had a strong connection with Professor Lawrence Ansler, an expert in underwater robotics and sonar equipment.'

'They would have. It was equipment used by my parents in their fields of interest and by that, I mean maritime archaeology and oceanography,' Marvik said pointedly.

'Which gave them reasons to travel across the world. The file also suggests the possibility of them being double agents feeding intelligence to the Russians via their stopovers in Norway and in their travels to the Baltic Sea and at Swedish ports.'

'And who came up with that bright idea?' Marvik said, as if he didn't know. Freestone. He swallowed some water and exchanged a brief glance with Strathen before putting his attention back on Crowder. 'Freestone fabricated that, while in reality they had been despatched to look for the *Fenella* because, although Freestone knew the canister containing the bacteria wasn't on board, he began to wonder if there had been more than one canister, and, of course, his masters didn't know he had taken and sold the bacteria to UNITA.'

'Correct. The government were worried that the mysterious deaths of the harp seals were caused by a chemical agent released by the Russians. The British offered to mount an expedition to try and establish whether this was the case when in reality Freestone's bosses were worried that it was our bacteria that had caused the deaths.'

'And Freestone not only needed to be certain that there were no other chemical canisters on board but also to cover up so that, if the *Fenella* was found, no one would discover it had been wrecked by an explosive device.'

'The mission was classified as highly secret because of the fear of causing panic in the fishing communities of Norway and their markets, thus creating an international incident. Professor Coulter and Dr Marvik were given *Vasa II* for the expedition, Coulter was chosen because of his expertise on ocean turbulence and the ocean seabed, particularly that of the Arctic, and Eerika Marvik because of her expertise on submerged structures and wrecks.'

'And Freestone falsely manufactured a story that Zueker and Greyman could have defected to the Soviet Union and were on their way to Murmansk when disaster struck.'

'What about Zueker's research?' asked Strathen. 'He must have documented it.'

'There was a fire in his laboratory two days after his disappearance.'

'Convenient,' said Strathen.

'My parents duly reported back to Freestone when they located the *Fenella*,' Marvik said, 'which probably took them some time, and again after exploring the wreck. Freestone probably told them he had to take it to a higher authority and that it would be thoroughly investigated. Maybe Freestone thought they would forget about it. Possibly he told them to return to the Barents Sea to search further for the canister, strengthening his lies that they were operating as a spy ship. Eventually my parents grew suspicious and documented their findings and fears.'

Strathen said, 'Yes, but they had no idea about Kranton or that the bacteria had been sold to Angola. But they did suspect Freestone.'

'My private conversation with Langton, the psychiatrist, after my head wound was given to the Intelligence Services. Someone got curious about my parents' deaths.'

'Yes. Your file, and that on your parents, were extracted. You had an exemplary career and all the qualities needed — tough, fit, courageous, intelligent and a past like a sore that itched, waiting to be scratched, and one we were very interested in putting to bed. You said you weren't. But out of the services and away from its protection perhaps you'd change your mind. No one foresaw Sarah Redburn's involvement or her death at that stage, because the computer disk hadn't come to light. If she hadn't died another way would have been found to prompt you to start asking questions.'

'What will happen about the murder investigations into Sarah's deaths and the others, Lanbury's and Bradshott's? I know that Freestone's will be put down to accidental death and Colmead's to suicide. There's also Kranton's death.'

'The sea is a dangerous place.'

Marvik knew what he meant. Strathen did too. Kranton's body would be lost at sea.

Crowder added, 'The files on Lanbury's murder and that of Sarah Redburn will stay open.'

'And Bradshott? His body is currently in the reeds close to my cottage.'

'Not any more it isn't.'

'And Verity Taylor, what will you or I tell her?' He eyed Crowder steadily.

'Nothing. She's been picked to work with a government-backed high-profile exploration to the Arctic and will be kept very busy.'

Marvik gave a wry smile. 'And Caroline Shaldon?'

'Working on a new and very prestigious contract in the Norwegian Sea.'

'All very neat,' Marvik said a little sourly, but he knew there was no alternative. 'How did you know that Sarah could have information connected with my parents' murder?'

'Stuart Bradshott was being monitored as an extreme marine activist. He'd already been involved in corporate sabotage and causing criminal damage.'

Which Marvik had read about on the internet as soon as he'd learned his real identity.

'The fact that Wellby had mentioned *Vasa II* in an email to Bradshott alerted us that Sarah's death was connected to your parents. I think you know it all now.' Crowder rose.

Marvik followed suit. 'What will happen to the information that Shaun's found, my parents' testimony about the *Fenella*?'

'What would you like to happen?'

Marvik didn't really need to consider this for long. 'Nothing — or rather something,' he quickly corrected. 'I'd like it destroyed.' He knew it would be anyway.

He followed Crowder on deck. Strathen stood beside Marvik as Crowder climbed aboard his RIB. Looking up at them both, he said, 'I've got a new mission for you. You'll be briefed later.'

As Crowder's RIB set off towards the sea, Marvik turned to Strathen. 'Do you know what it is?'

'No idea. Want to come back to my apartment?'

Did he? Marvik wasn't sure. 'Not for the moment.'

'Just turn up when you're ready, you usually do anyway.'

Marvik stayed on deck until the sound of Strathen and Crowder's RIBs faded and there was only silence. He examined his emotions. What were they? Emptiness, regret, sorrow, anger? A mixture of all of those.

Was there also peace now he knew the truth? No, there had been too many lies, too much treachery, too much corruption, murder and death for that. Maybe peace would come in time. But he did acknowledge that he no longer wanted to blot out the past. He had to face it. The slate wasn't wiped clean, because it had been soiled to begin with and would remain that way, but he could draw a line under it as he could his career in the Marines. What the future held he didn't know, and that suited him fine. The only thing he did know was that his work for the National Intelligence Marine Squad would continue and of that he was glad.

His phone rang, startling him. He'd forgotten he had switched it on. But he was pleased the outside world had once again intruded. For an instant he thought of Caroline Shaldon and her warm body and spicy perfume.

'What does a girl have to do to get a drink?' A voice he recognized so well echoed down the line, causing him instantly to smile. It felt good.

'Helen!'

'Oh, you remember my name,' she said. 'That's something at least. It's a bit much when a girl's got to ask a fellow for a drink. It's my shout. Gunwharf Quays, Portsmouth, half an hour. I'll meet you at the marina entrance.'

With her customary abruptness she rang off.

As he cast off and swung the boat round, he let out a long, slow breath that turned to a broad smile and a silent 'thank you' to two — no, to three loyal friends: Philip Crowder for making sure Helen was close by; Shaun Strathen for calling her, and Helen Shannon for being Helen.

THE END

THE JOFFE BOOKS STORY

We began in 2014 when Jasper agreed to publish his mum's much-rejected romance novel and it became a bestseller.

Since then we've grown into the largest independent publisher in the UK. We're extremely proud to publish some of the very best writers in the world, including Joy Ellis, Faith Martin, Caro Ramsay, Helen Forrester, Simon Brett and Robert Goddard. Everyone at Joffe Books loves reading and we never forget that it all begins with the magic of an author telling a story.

We are proud to publish talented first-time authors, as well as established writers whose books we love introducing to a new generation of readers.

We have been shortlisted for Independent Publisher of the Year at the British Book Awards three times, in 2020, 2021 and 2022, and for the Diversity and Inclusivity Award at the Independent Publishing Awards in 2022.

We built this company with your help, and we love to hear from you, so please email us about absolutely anything bookish at: feedback@joffebooks.com.

If you want to receive free books every Friday and hear about all our new releases, join our mailing list: www.joffebooks.com/contact

And when you tell your friends about us, just remember: it's pronounced Joffe as in coffee or toffee!

ALSO BY PAULINE ROWSON

THE ART MARVIK MYSTERIES

Book 1: DEADLY WAVES
Book 2: DANGEROUS CARGO
Book 3: LOST VOYAGE
Book 4: FATAL DEPTHS

THE SOLENT MURDER MYSTERIES

Book 1: THE PORTSMOUTH MURDERS
Book 2: THE LANGSTONE HARBOUR MURDERS
Book 3: THE HORSEA MARINA MURDERS
Book 4: THE ROYAL HOTEL MURDERS
Book 5: THE ISLE OF WIGHT MURDERS
Book 6: THE PORTCHESTER CASTLE MURDERS
Book 7: THE CHALE BAY MURDERS
Book 8: THE FARLINGTON MARSH MURDERS
Book 9: THE OYSTER QUAYS MURDERS
Book 10: THE COWES WEEK MURDERS
Book 11: THE BOATHOUSE MURDERS
Book 12: THE THORNEY ISLAND MURDERS
Book 13: THE GUERNSEY FERRY MURDERS
Book 14: THE RAT ISLAND MURDERS
Book 15: THE LUCCOMBE BAY MURDERS
Book 16: THE SOUTH BINNESS MURDERS

Manufactured by Amazon.ca
Bolton, ON

54029296R00152